John Ingham is an award-winning environment journalist. He has had a lifelong interest in the Vikings and has visited many of their sites across Britain and Scandinavia. He has a PhD in History from Durham University and also studied at universities in America and Canada. His interests include football, food, birdwatching, beer and travel.

To Christine

Copyright © John Ingham 2022

The right of John Ingham to be identified as author of this work has been asserted by the author in accordance with sections 77 and 78 of the Copyright, Designs and Patents Act 1988.

All rights reserved. No part of this publication may be reproduced, stored in a retrieval system, or transmitted in any form or by any means, electronic, mechanical, photocopying, recording, or otherwise, without the prior permission of the publishers.

Any person who commits any unauthorised act in relation to this publication may be liable to criminal prosecution and civil claims for damages.

This is a work of fiction. Names, characters, businesses, places, events, locales, and incidents are either the products of the author's imagination or used in a fictitious manner. Any resemblance to actual persons, living or dead, or actual events is purely coincidental.

A CIP catalogue record for this title is available from the British Library.

ISBN 9781398410442 (Paperback)
ISBN 9781398410459 (ePub e-book)

www.austinmacauley.com

First Published 2022
Austin Macauley Publishers Ltd®
1 Canada Square
Canary Wharf
London
E14 5AA

John Ingham

Blood-Eagle Saga

Austin Macauley Publishers
London * Cambridge * New York

Many thanks are due to Max Bacon, Philip Gomm and Rob Douglas, a fellow Viking fan, who were the first to read my saga and provided vital encouragement. I'd also like to thank Ed Poynter, who shares my interest in saga-age literature, for his advice. There are also special thanks to Southern Railway. I wrote this while commuting. If they'd run even a half-decent service, I'd never have finished.

Chapter 1

Light there was none the night Snorri told his tale.
Well, he always did like to exaggerate.
It was the shortest day
And the longest night,
The snow was rime-frost crispened.
No moon, no stars, no sky glow,
All smothered by racing storm clouds.
Inside the sword-rich long house,
Smoke floated free from the spitting fire,
Clinging like glue to hair and clothes.
But why would the killers care?
They who had flagons of mead-ale
Served on demand with a smile
By flaxen-haired slave girls,
Booty and beauty looted from Frisia
And rings of gold and silver aplenty,
Given with gratitude by Sven Ravenfeeder
Scourge of monks, plunderer of monasteries,
Son of Erik Beartooth, battle-king.
Sven sat, double-headed axe by his side,
On an oak bench with Kristin on his arm
And Wersil, his sole blood heir, to his right.
No mention was ever made, ever,
On pain of being bitten by Sven's axe
Of his true blood heir, his elder son,
Wulf, banished with slavers,
Ten bitter winters past,
Ten raiding summers since.

Wulf, as all know, is dead
But not in his birthright, Valhalla,
Bloodslaker in his battle hand,
But whip fodder on a slaver's longship,
Doomed to roam the north seas forever,
Doomed to freeze forgotten in icy storms
Doomed to face an outlaw's fate,
To be flayed on sight on his return.
Wulf betrayed his Beartooth name
In his first youthful taste of the shieldwall.

He and Wersil were sent to outflank
The "oot" shouting Saxons—
Sven craved glory for his heirs
Or death in the bloodletting.
What bloody use is a son
Who cravenly shirks battle?
But the Saxons stood fast,
Wersil fought, Wulf ran.
Wersil limped back
Sword blood on his face
While Wulf was unscarred,
His sword unsated,
Wersil told how Wulf, his elder,
Had quailed like a girl
While he, Wersil, parried lance
And clashed his sword
And clad his shield in arrows.
Wulf did not move to deny
His unmanning shame.
As Sven and his swordmen
Sailed back from the Fenland,
They crunched ashore on Orkney.
There, Sven did what a warlord must.
He sold his son to Valdar the slaver,
His parting, smarting words

A spell of total contempt:
"Work him hard,
"Whip him hard,
"Kill him at will.
"He is no son of mine."
The scar-faced Wersil
Saw all and smiled.
Wulf, head held high,
Turned his broad back
And stared out to sea,
Unflinching as Valdar's
Leather lash fanged his cheek
Much as a Saxon sword had Wersil's,
One scar a battle badge of honour,
One scar a battle badge of shame.
But of this blood scandal
Not a word was said.
None was needed.
All knew the pitiless past;
All could predict the future.
Soon Sven's famous sword
Would rest and go to rust.
Soon he would raid no more,
Leaving Wersil to take the blood axe
On the war road as trade for jewels
Waiting, glittering, across the sea.
Sven was feared and loved.
He fought like a rabid bear
And rained rings on his men.
Wersil could also raid and fight—
His Saxon cheek scar proved it.
But to him, sadly, ring-giving
Did not come naturally.

Faces lit by the flickering flames
Warriors and wenches,

Warlord and women
(Sven always had many.
No complaints from Kristin.)
Dug in for a midwinter feast
While the beasts lowed and grunted
From the longhouse's fetid byre.
Then, a shout from outside.
Hreidar's sword scraped its scabbard.
Sven nodded. Ronald and Stigg rose,
Sword-girded, dagger-ready and
Shouldered the shield door into the snow.
Hreidar's sword was soon back abed.
Before him, in fur whiter than the snow,
Stood a tall man, sword unsheathed,
Long white hair, a face lined and dark
But young yet for all the cracks.
"I am Snorri the Skald,
"Come alone, no band with me.
"I seek shelter from the frost
"And will repay your hospitality
"With a salt-saga from my home,
"The fiery whale hills of Iceland.
"Tales you'll never have heard before
"Of dark ale and white wine,
"Of glorious war and lusty wenches,
"And bravery and black betrayal."
In the snow gloom, Ronald
Looked Snorri in the eyes.
He scowled then nodded to the door,
Leading Snorri into the firelight
Of dancing spirit shadows,
Up to Sven and Wersil's table.
The humid hall fell silent
Even the tankards stood still,
And the dogs stopped their begging
As all eyes strained in the smoke-light

To study the stranger in white fur.
Ronald stepped up. "This here is Snorri
"The Skald, from Iceland,
"With tales to tell
"To pay his way."

Sven stroked his veteran's beard,
Kristin whispered in his ear.
Wersil's rock-like features
Were inscrutable to all.
Sven spoke, his deep voice
A purr rolling from the Rus:
"Snorri, you say's your name?
"We would never turn a man away
"In a freeze as frost-fierce as this.
"Tell us your tale, freely,
"We've got time enough.
"No-one is rushing off
"On a wolf night like this."
Snorri smiled, bowed his head,
Unfurled his long white cloak,
Unbuckled his black sword,
Propped it up against the table,
Then climbed aboard
The wooden platform from where
Sven surveyed all
Like a falcon on high.

But Sven was not finished.
Sven would find his sport
Even in midwinter's tedium.
"Do you enjoy a wager?"
He quizzed the skald,
Voice tender now,
Slavering at the bet.
"Let's make your storytelling

"A touch more interesting.
"You sing for your supper,
"But sing also for your life."
A growl blew through the hall
Like a breeze through a bear's fur
As the wolves woke to pleasure.
"Let's see how good a skald
"You really are, Icelander.
"Amuse us, entertain us,
"Hold my men's attention,
"And you can have the pick
"Of the war raid prizes: wenches,
"Riches, rings, gold, silver.
"But bore us, make us yawn,
"And you must amuse us
"And entertain us without words.
"Did you spot the stout oak
"With the big bough, out back?
"Disappoint us, bore us,
"And there you will dance,
"To the silken caress of
"The horse-hair collar.
"What do you say, skald?
"Are you confident of your skills?
"Will you stick your neck
"Where your young mouth is?"

Snorri's smile never relaxed,
The only dark clouds racing
Remained outside over the oak.
"If you so desire, lord," he said,
His voice clear and falter-free.
"Then let it be. I will win
"This bet, this Hel-wager,
"And you will all remember
"Snorri's Blood-Eagle Saga

"As long as you all shall breathe."

The warriors roared and gloated
As a bison-bearded throat-slitter
Slipped a noose, long-knotted,
Round Snorri's slender neck.
But the skald lived yet and
Was still a longhouse guest,
So, a slavegirl served him a horn of ale.
Snorri sipped, wiped away beard foam,
And studied his death-lusting audience.
"Thanks to you a thousand times,
"Sven Ravenfeeder, of heroic fame.
"I hail from Iceland and rest easy -
"From the northernmost fjords
"To the remotest farmsteads,
"Even on the seal floes of Greenland,
"All know the name of Sven Ravenfeeder.
"All fear Sven's bloodletting band
"All toast his raids on the men in skirts,
"And all young men seek his glory."

Warriors growled approval.
Rudi the Rough stood up,
Turban-headed, an eastern trophy,
And downed a flagon in one
Before spraying an ale-fuelled chant
Of "Ravenfeeder, Ravenfeeder, Ravenfeeder"
Over his bearded brothers.
The battle-blooded rose as one,
Spilling beer, spreading brawn
And joined in Rudi's anthem.
Sven let the hall fill and
Echo to the shieldwall song,
A chorus of menace and stamping
Before signalling his men to sit down.

One wave of his hand
Was all it took
To control the killers.

Chapter 2

Snorri stroked his frosted beard,
Licked ale from his moustache,
Cleared his throat and commenced:
Come with me to where the sun
Never sets, where the sea
Is pale as ice, where blue
Flaunts a thousand colours, and
The cod are so common
A warrior can walk on water.
We will go beyond where yellow men
Hunt white whales with narwhal tusks
To where red men, near naked,
But for the plant paint smeared
On their chests and faces,
Stalk troll-sized cattle
With manes like the lions
Helgi the Bold
Battled in Barbary.
We will sail to a green land
Where many a warrior
Will sup from Odin's salver
Snorri paused. His watching eyes
Studied the tattooed warmen,
Veterans of deadly shieldwalls
From Dyflin to the Don.
Will you come with me?
He cried; eyes fixed
On the front ranks,

Or do you fear the fable?
A defiant roar arose as
The sword-skilled swore
And vied, devil against devil,
To brandish their bravery.

Snorri grinned. He had them now.
Words were his weapon,
Men's minds his dagger.

So, climb aboard the dragonship
Meet the great Asgeir, our hero,
And taste the salt spray
Greeting Grim the Greedy's
Seasteed, Waverider.
But before we set sail,
Let me just ask you this,
And listen well, all of you:
When is man not a man
But still a man?
When is a man a man
But not a man?
Don't know? None of you?
You soon will. He smiled,
I think you'll like it.

As bafflement filled the crowd,
He continued, with a grin:
Grim's name was hard won.
His oarsmen were mainly slaves
Beaten mercilessly by day,
Lashed ruthlessly by night,
And if they faltered
Dumped in the deep
For the fish to eat.
Only the tough survived.

Grim's warriors were tougher still.
With Waverider they raided
Far and wide, east and west,
Till the slaves struggled to row
So heavily laden was the gold.
Happy the warrior whose
Warship is loaded with loot,
Gleaming gold, silver
And bejewelled books.
Asgeir and Hrolf and Ketil
Had fought hard for
Fantastic riches and renown
But Grim's name was hard won.
No ring-giver he. No -
He ruled by the lash,
Flogged freely, with ease,
Through his one-eyed slaveleader
Aethelfrith the Vile,
A barrel of a brute
With runes lining his arms
And a flame-flaring dragon
Inked crudely on his forehead.
Even when the North wind
Blew blizzards over the deck
Aethelfrith never needed a shirt
(The cur was captured on
Cold, grey, Northumbria's coast
And traded to Grim on the Tyne).
He guarded the gold
For Grim's paltry payment.
Food and foaming ale,
And the occasional wench
Were his sole reward.
But that was not enough
For the loot-winning warriors.
Asgeir had gold-hunger

Like all true sea-raiders.
He wanted his blood share
And sought how to unshackle it.

A plaited beard stood up
Sword in his left hand
Broad arm ring-bulging
Before the fire flames.
"With this," he growled,
"Widowmaker speaks for me."
Sven beamed at his berserker.
Wersil's eyes barely widened.
None could read his mind.
None ever could,
None ever would.

Snorri regained his thread,
Like the fate-spinning Norns.
Now Asgeir was special,
He continued, bold in battle
But bright as a Bible.
Not for nothing was
He known as The Fox.
Listen and learn, shipmates;
Skippers and commanders
Must beware young warriors
Who go to war for no reward.
The raiding season was closing,
Swallows were flying South,
Black-bellied geese replacing them.
Asgeir and his battle mates
Were dreaming of humping
Plump young slave girls
In winter's warming fire-glow,
Dreaming too of fine food,
Fresh fish from the fjords,

War tales instead of war fighting.
But Grim wanted one more raid,
Even as the salt sea turned grey
And Aethelfrith the Vile donned
A fur helm for first time in months.
Grim told his men:
"The monks of black Whitby
"Have had it easy for too long.
"Time to let Thor and Odin
"Put their God to the test.
"The old gods always win
"But the skirtmen never learn.
"There'll be gold galore
"To console us all through
"The long days of darkness."

Asgeir the Fox, tall as a young fir
And just as spring supple,
Never shirked bloodletting,
Loot or skald-fame
But he and his blood brothers
Felt little better or valued
Than Grim's sea slaves.
Their miserly master would
Always promise rings, rubies
And rich, glittering, rewards
But he alone had his own
Farmstead, cattle and steeds.
Grim was drunk on more
Than mere mead and ale.
With Aethelfrith as his Fenrir
He was fiercely fixated on power.
Never did he mix with his men.
It was his mortal loss.
He only knew of Asgeir
The axe-wielding gut-slitter.

He knew less than nothing of his
Other skills, of his fox fame.
Lazy leaders always pay
In the end, always it is
The blood price of the aloof.

With Grim on Waverider
Were three raid-won wenches,
A redhead from Ireland,
A ravenhair from Frankia,
And a blonde from Frisia,
The redhead, Mary, was Grim's,
The other maids were warrior loot,
And Aethelfrith's if he was lucky.
So is loyalty earned.
Aethelfrith slavered to Grim
As this wolfhound slavers to Sven.
Here Snorri nodded to
The greying long hair
Nestled at Sven's feet.
It flickered an eyelid,
Sniffed, licked its balls,
Then slipped back to slobbering,
Dreaming of bucks and bitches.

Aethelfrith was true and trusting.
But slaves desire more than dogs.
Aethelfrith the Vile stood over
Waverider's wave-taming slaves
And he saw what Grim had
And he liked what he saw.
Asgeir saw all, said nothing
But wisely stored all away.
He, too, liked Mary. True,
Her red hair was matted
Her lush lips salt spray split,

But her eyes gleamed green
And looked as knowing as a cat's
And they spoke, snarled, defiance.
Norse, she had learned,
A little, in her thraldom,
A devil's tool of survival.
But her eyes said so much more
And had so often kissed Asgeir
From afar, unseen, unrequited,
But Asgeir had sensed her warmth.
He knew, and that was enough.

Whitby's cliffs came into view
Hovering over low autumn cloud.
As light faded, Waverider landed,
Crunching up the shingle.
In dusk's twilight the warriors
Flexed to feed their swords.
Aethelfrith was left to guard
Ship, spoils and slaves.
But softly from the wench end
Asgeir the Fox witch-whispered
In Mary's worldly, velvet, voice.
"Aethelfrith, Aethelfrith, Oh Aethelfrith."
Aethelfrith needed no more.
Grim had already splashed ashore
So now was Aethelfrith's chance.
Already half-naked
The bald brute shed the rest
And readied to feed his sword as
Asgeir slipped over the side
And told Grim a slave was loose.
Fuming, Grim climbed back aboard,
Blood-axe firmly in hand,
Ready to feed the fishes.
And in his fury, he found

His righthand man
Ready to ravish
His right-hand woman.
With one flash of the axe
Aethelfrith the Vile became
Aethelfrith the headless
And Grim the Greedy became
Grim the Unguarded.

Chapter 3

His huge head rolled
Along the sea-slick deck,
A hot scarlet fountain
Soaking the screaming wenches.
Grim barked at his rollocks-slaves
Who lifted Aethelfrith,
Once feared, now flabby,
Over the side to slump
Onto the grey sea gravel.
But the bloody hacked head,
Eyes wide awake in shock,
Grim kept in its blood pool
As a commander's reminder.
The wails of the women
Had woken the monks
But Grim could not care.
Bald men in black frocks
Were no martial match
For Waverider's wild mob
Of snarling blade slashers.
As the slave women wept
Asgeir, Hrolf and Ketil
Stormed uphill and slaughtered.
For shields the holy men used
Only their arms. Some did less,
As if they welcomed oblivion.
Grim's men obliged them.
Some monks foreswore manliness

To sink meekly to their knees
And entreat, eyes tightly closed,
The lone god who always failed them.
A pleasure it was to lop off their heads.

Here Ravenfeeder's dogs
Drooled their approval.
Blood was their livelihood,
Battle was their pleasure.

In the monk's cloisters
Hearth embers flared happily
As the bodies built up
So swift was the fighting
From first swordthrust
To last death rattle.
One monk alone held out
Guarding a golden chest.
A light axe to his belly
Soon flayed his fears.
Grim, blood-soaked beard
Dripping death in the firelight,
Clattered the lock open
With one blow of his blade.
But in it were bones.
A whole skeleton.
A whole mangy skeleton.
Grim smashed the chest
To cheapest cook's kindling and
Scattered the skeleton
Across the flagstone floor.
In all these god cells,
Gold there was none,
Just silver candlesticks,
A lousy, tawdry haul
For such a blood slaughter.

But Asgeir grasped the value
Of all the monks' magic.
As Grim raged, Asgeir
Grabbed the skeleton's skull.
He smiled – payday was close.
Light-handed the war-dealers
Slid down Whitby's blood-slimed slopes
To Waverider where Aethelfrith
Had blackened the beach
With his coagulating blood.
The slaves saw the Vikings
Carrying only reddened swords
And knew this long night
Could only get darker.

But as Grim led his men
A moan from the Underworld
Jolted the raiders' jet night
And ushered in winter's chill
A full month too soon.
"Master, help me,
"Help your helper,"
Pleaded the unbodied.
Grim span around,
Monk-fed sword
Moving for more.
"Master, why, why did you
"Slay me, your loyal thrall,
"Without a moment's thought?"
Keened the headless slave.
But Aethelfrith was silent.
It was Asgeir the Fox
Who often times amused
Warrior and wench
With his many imitations.
But Grim would never mix

With his shieldwall men and
Knew nothing of this magic.
To him the sing-song voice
Was one man's
And one man's alone.
"What is this?" roared Grim
Though his voice was ebbing
Like the black tide below.
He wheeled round and round
As his band began to scatter
Back to Waverider's wealth.
As Grim floundered
Asgeir prospered.
Swiftly back on deck he
Silenced the fearful
With one finger to his lips,
Hurled Aethelfrith's head
To float in the foam where,
Unseen, it bobbed and sank,
And on the bloody deck
He placed the holy skull
Maggot-cleaned, flesh free.
With a light leap Asgeir
Looped down behind Grim
And followed him to his hell.
Grim, cursing, climbed aboard
To see, tar torch-lit,
Aethelfrith's skull
Lying raven-ready
In his blood pool.
The light guttered
As Grim's guts shuddered.
He searched for support
But his team of killers,
Their strong arms ringless,
Circled stony-eyed

Like wolves around
A wounded elk.
Asgeir stepped boldly forward
While Grim's piggy eyes widened
And whitened in the torchlight.
Asgeir grabbed his chance.
"It's over, Grim the Greedy.
"Now you do as we say
"Or you die and die slowly,"
Said Asgeir, his voice laden
With a warlord's weight.
"If you resist
"You will surely lose
"And face the blood-eagle,
"Staked out in this salt mud,
"Choking in the cold sea,
"Entreating the high tide
"To end your agony."

Sven gave a bleak smile,
Wersil's eyes narrowed.
In the hall goblets
And a chant took flight,
Soft at first, growing louder
To stamping and table thumping:
"Blood-eagle! Blood-eagle! Blood-eagle!"
Warriors all love sport
And no sport more than
The blood-eagle.
Sven let his men revel
In memories of Saxons
And Slavs slain slowly
As a lesson for the living.
Then a flick of a finger
Calmed the cruelty cravers
In a flurry of backslaps and beer.

Grim knew the long agonies of
The blood-eagle well.
With Aethelfrith slain
Hope had forsaken him.
So, he handed his sword,
His ship, his safety, his spoils
Over to Asgeir, the upstart.

Chapter 4

Minutes earlier, Grim
Was more than a match
For any seafaring man.
Now, swordless, shipless
And stripped as a skipper,
He was broken like
The skeleton cask
In Whitby's looted Abbey.
As the holy house burned
He was bound in chains
To the cheers of his chattels.
But Asgeir was not done.
Warriors fight as freemen,
So, he freed Waverider.
"You are slaves no longer,"
He told the whip-lashed.
"Leave now if you like
"But don't linger long here.
"Better to stay with me
"And split the wealth
"Which we earned
"With your rowing.
"Only one slave remains,
"Grim the Greedy.
"Stay and sail with me and
"Make him pay dearly
"For every flogging,
"For every cruelty."

A warlord has to be hard,
Willing to sacrifice a warrior
Even if he be a friend.
To win in war
A warlord must kill
To enforce his iron will
But must always reward
Loyalty as the fuel
Of his fighters' fire.
But Grim the Greedy
Had forgotten the first rule
Of every wise warlord.
His battleplan relied
Only on cruelty and fear.

The slaves were overjoyed.
Until this undreamt-of day
Every dawn they had seen
Had been a priceless bonus
Until Aethelfrith's whip awoke
To re-flay their ribs and backs
While sea salt cracked their cuts.
Some spoke little or no Norse,
But Mary translated their liberation
And relayed all to Asgeir.
When you've lived as a slave
You're grateful for anyone
Willing to talk for you.
"We will all stay,"
She said in accented Norse,
"But at next landfall many
"Will seek their loot share,
"Sink roots on solid land,
"And leave hell behind them.
"But I will not be leaving.
"You, lord, freed me from

"Two foul-breathed brutes.
"With you I will stay
"Wherever you will sail."

Asgeir nodded. He would
Have taken her anyway,
But better a willing woman
Than a whining prisoner.
But he knew that she knew
Much more than other women.
Magic sparkled in her eyes.

Up above, flame-lit,
Whitby was stirring,
Clifftop battle calls
Rolled down the slope
As Waverider readied
To return to her home.
Asgeir gave his orders
And shieldwall warriors
Worked with one-time slaves
To leave carnage trailing
In Waverider's silver wake.
As her broad sail unfurled
And the wind filled her belly
Grim could see, moonlit,
His ship's battle badge
Swelling in the west wind,
A blood-red eagle,
Wings flying in warning
Like a captive's lungs
Ripped through slashed ribs
And plastered over his spine
For the pleasure of the victors.

Chapter 5

For three days and three nights
Waverider sailed northwards
Not for Norway and
Fjords and family
But for sea-fenced Orkney,
Great crossroads of the Vikings.
Former slaves, now freedmen,
Rowed proudly alongside warriors
But soon a strong south-easterly
Took the strain of cutting
Through teeth-curled white caps.
Plenty of time, then, to
Give Grim a good lashing
Under the wind-plump eagle.
Grim, to his great credit, never
Cowered, complained or cried out.
He took it all with
Rueful resignation.
Only when Asgeir spoke
Of splitting the spoils -
His bloody spoils, mind -
Did Grim grow restless
But a thundercrack of leather
Soon cast him back to
His new lowly station.

Up past Gannet Rock
Rode Waverider though

Diving sea geese were scarce now.
And after moonlit studies
Of the lone North Star,
Clouds low on the horizon
And boiling, howling seas
Heralded islands ahead.
A pale sunrise next morning
And slowly, like ghosts in the mists,
The tall cliffs of Orkney emerged.
Waverider worked the shallows
And pulled gently into Stromness
Alongside many a dragonship.
But her dragon was skull-crowned -
Aethelfrith's, or so Grim thought,
But Asgeir alone knew this talisman
Was the long-lost skull
Of some Christian holy man.

On Stromness's ship-rich beach
Asgeir made good his promise
And set free the ship slaves
Well, all save one.
Grim, steel-shackled,
Shuffled ashore to be
Sold to Thorfinn the Bald,
A sly fur-clad shipmaster from
The ice mists of the north.
Grim betrayed no emotion -
But for the briefest flicker which
All-seeing Asgeir missed.
Even a fox must blink his eyes.
As Thorfinn dragged Grim to hell
Asgeir gave his slaves their freedom
With words they had never hoped to hear.
"You are as free as birds, sea slaves,"
He said amid the hemp rigging.

"You can go home to your families.
"See them run as the ghost returns
"And savour their pleasure when
"Spectre becomes brother,
"And terror turns to tenderness.
"Or you can stay and sail with us,
"Commit to our pack of wolves
"And fight for the blood-eagle."

"Tomorrow, early, you will get
"Your well-earned war gold
"And we will hear your wishes:
"A life of war and skirtmen's wealth
"Or a life of peace and pasture.
"But put that to one side now.
"Now we have important business
"With beer and mead, bread and meat."
With a familiar battle-rallying roar
Asgeir led his loyalists,
Leaving two sulking swordsmen
And the flaying holy skull
To guard a summer's gold.

Chapter 6

No Vikings ever came closer
To sampling Valhalla's beer pleasures
Than Asgeir and his band.
After months of wind hammer
Wave batter, sun burning
And bloodletting from
The lower Seine to the Skerries,
Asgeir, Hrolf, Ketil and the throng
Had a sailor's thirst so great
That it took several barrels to
Slake their wassailing.
The slaves were thirstier still
For the barley taste of liberty,
And soon firelit shambling shadows
Began to stumble and stagger.
Beer and mead and wine and beer
Never taste better than when
Well-earned and long desired.

Wassailing is what warriors do best
When they willingly lay down their
Widowmakers and weave tales
To thrill even Odin and Thor.
Fight hard, drink hard,
Should be every warrior's watchword.
But wassailing can never be free.
As leather tankards turned to flagons
And beer dripped from beards,

An icy draft invaded the beerhall,
Svalbard cold, like a Christian
Walking into Odin's warrior feast.
In the blink of a bear's eye
All, even the bladdered, were sober.
One of Waverider's guards,
Oddo the Hairy, clutched
A blood-soaked sword arm
Streaks of red matting his beard.
"Hurry," he groaned. "Grim is free
"And retaking Waverider with
"All our war-won wealth."

Beer-fog lifted as
Fast as Oddo's blood flowed.
Warrior and slave alike
Shook off the brain blanket,
Embraced cold reality
And grabbed sword, axe and shield,
Bow and arrow and prickling spear,
Cast flagon and tankard aside
And raced for Stromness shore.
In shaky torchlight Waverider,
Blood-Eagle fed by the breeze,
Was making for the cliffs of Hoy
And the wide-open ocean beyond.
Wind and wave-roar drowned
Asgeir's blood-curdling rage
But carried on the light gale
Came a jeering, leering howl
Of victory and vengeance
To haunt the treasure-losers
Over the endless depths
Of black winter nights.
All that was left of their hoard
Was a flaking, grinning skull,

Gurning in the shingle.
Some loot is not valued
Even by Grim the Greedy.

Ale fumes filled the air
Sour as Asgeir's bile.
A slave puked on the pebbles,
Pleasure remnant swallowed
By wind and white-topped wave.

Asgeir, fist aloft, swore to the gods:
"Run and hide, Grim the Greedy,
"But no sea is big enough
"To gift you sanctuary.
"I will seek you and find you
"And take my battle-loot
"And then splay your lungs
"Where they always belonged -
"Over your goat-grizzled back."

Sometimes a wise man
Should show discretion.
But one man could not
Resist the spectacle
Of Asgeir's curse-rich ruin.
Learn from his vanity,
All who want a long life.
In the shoreline's shadows
Asgeir lit on a movement,
A gleam in the moonlight
And grabbed his double-headed axe
From its sentry stance in the sand.
Without a word he struck.
One swing was all it took
And sly Thorfinn the Bald
Was more legless

Than all the wassailers.
As he writhed, retched and bled,
Asgeir held Doublefang's teeth
Against his pulsing, throbbing neck.
"How did Grim the Greedy escape?
"Speak now if you value your other leg."
Thorfinn knew he had only one hope
Of hunting narwhal and ice bear again.
Through gritted teeth and bloodfoam
He grunted: "Grim the Greedy did not escape.
"He gained his freedom through friendship.
"We are old raid-riders, fyrd-fighters,
"I bought him to redeem a debt.
"He saved me from ten Tartars.
"We swordsmen know such a debt
"Can only be paid in kind or blood."
Asgeir nodded his cold assent.
"You speak sense but now you owe me."
With one clinical blade swipe
He cured Thorfinn's Baldness.
The Northman paid his new debt
In blood not kind. Narwhal and ice bear
Became a little safer as the
Sea supped at Thorfinn's claret.

Asgeir placed Thorfinn's sword
In his still twitching hand.
"He helped Grim rob us,
"Helped him make his escape,"
He snarled, spittle-flecked,
"But for sound, warrior's reasons.
"We should not hinder
"His journey to Valhalla."

With that he crunched over the beach
Past sleeping ranks of longships
Til he came to an oak beast
With the bared teeth of an ice-bear
Where others displayed dragonheads.
Its guards, unalert, beer-befuddled,
Were soon nursing eternal hangovers.
Red sword aloft, arms gore-crowned,
Asgeir roared his triumph and anger:
"Thorfinn's Stormmaster is ours.
"It is what he would have wanted."
He turned to his band: "You are free
"To stay or go. But if I have to sail alone
"I am going to get Grim the Greedy
"And reclaim our blood-soaked war booty.
"If you wish to stay, stay with my thanks
"For your welcome summer solidarity.
"Wassail well on Orkney.
"But if you want what is yours
"We have a greedy bastard to gut."
Hrolf Hardheart and Ketil Killfast
And the other battle-stalwarts
Stepped forward as one,
War weapons brandished aloft,
And chanted through beer-beards
"Asgeir, Asgeir, Asgeir."
Ten freed slaves climbed aboard too,
And seized the stacked spears
Of Thorfinn's ship-switching crew
To climb aboard the warrior ranks.
No swords for them, no chainmail,
But freedom feeds the righteous.
Only the three wenches wavered.
Raven-hair studied her toes,
Blondie cast a longing glance
At the flickering lights of Stromness.

To the redhead they turned,
Whispering their wishes in secret,
With one eye each on Asgeir.
Mary, flame-haired, swept soot
From her cheeks and faced
Stormmaster's new leader.
"Ghisele and Jena beg leave, lord,
"To swop sea for sanctuary,
"'Storms for shelter, raids for respite.
"For their freedom they thank you
"But they have seen enough slaughter
"And suffered sea-hell long enough."
So do women always think.
War is best left to warriors.
Let women stay home to weave
Cloaks, blankets and wisdom.
Asgeir nodded, silenced the last
Groans of one of Thorfinn's guards
And quizzed: "But what of you, maid?"
Mary, supple as a willow, red mane
Like a banner in the breeze,
Gave a grim, vengeful smile.
"You saved me from a monster.
"And I have scores to settle with Grim.
"You and I both seek the same thing.
"And I can help. I know more than Norse."
She lifted a cheap leather necklace
Over her head, a bone its only ornament,
Threw it up and let it land in the seafoam
Which flung it out to the northwest.
"Grim is going to Iceland,"
She said, replacing her necklace
Over her wild copper curls.
"He dares not return to Norway,
"And risk fighting your kin.
"But Iceland is filling with fortune-hunters

"And Grim has gold enough
"To fund a king's family
"In the frozen heart of the fire lands."

Chapter 7

Three days out on this act of faith
With no sign of Waverider,
Crude curses began to rain
On Mary's lonely crown from
Warriors and freedmen alike.
Acid grumbles spilled when tired men
Took a palm-blistered oar-break,
Or retired from rigging the Ice Bear sail
Or rested from the sea's chillest chore,
Foot and hand-numbing bilge-bailing.
Four days out and the doubt growls
Grew stronger and wilder as the gods
Whipped up wind and wave and
Dared Stormmaster to live up to her name.
One minute sky and sea were autumn green.
The next sky and sea were night-time black
Save for mare's manes white against the jet.
No Viking has seen sea-wrath so wild,
Well, no Viking has seen such and lived.
Waves mast-top high, mountainous peaks,
Plunging, maw-like troughs, spray-flayed,
So fierce, such sail-ripping wind-driven hail.
For two days and nights –
Though day was night throughout –
Stormmaster flirted with Hel,
Tossed like wind-borne thistle down.
Stormmaster was alone on the maelstrom
Even the oil-snorting sea skimmers

Had stopped scything the sea,
Opting to desert the deep.
For two days and nights –
Though day was night throughout –
Asgeir commanded his gut-heaving men
Til there was nothing left to heave.
Even the battle-hardened begged for mercy.
But on the third day's dawn a patch of blue
Flared far to the cold northwest,
Sun rays filtered through smouldering cloud,
Mare's manes yielded to pale grey wavelets
And Thor's roar became a mere whisper.
But in his hasty pursuit of Grim
Asgeir had sailed Stormmaster food-empty.
Water barrels, too, had long since floated off,
Prised away by relentless sea fingers.
So when it rained men leaned, heads back,
And stuck out tongues to catch the damp
While Asgeir turned ice-bear sail
Into life-saving water barrel.

Blind despair is for spear carriers,
Not for commanders,
Who must always lead
Or let another warlord
Supplant their rule.
Yet for the first time Asgeir
Tasted true fear –
Of failure, of the future –
But hid it from all around.
As he held lodestone aloft
To find Iceland's lost way,
Mary, hair long and lank
After the rain and salt lashing,
Cast her necklace up and read
As it rolled on the gleaming deck.

"Go south," she said, "Sail south,
"For a day, and we will live."
Asgeir frowned, raiders swore.
"Iceland is away to the Northwest,"
Raged Ketil Killfast, "that way."
Asgeir looked into Mary's green eyes
And saw sea wisdom as well as beauty.
"Rig the ice-bear," he snarled.
"We sail south." With ill grace,
His scowling crew stood to,
And turned Stormmaster away from
Food, water and safety, life itself.
Mutinous rumblings stirred that
Asgeir had surrendered Stormmaster
To a woman – a slave wench.
"We were better off with Grim,"
Griped Ketil Killfast, lips salt-sore.
"Tight-fisted bastard he was,
"But he was master of the seas."
The spreading blue patch beckoned
But was spurned by battered Stormmaster
Which battled gamely against
A braking breeze from the south.

Every hour took them from sanctuary,
From Waverider, wealth and Grim.
Every hour the sea was as bare as
The sand deserts Helgi the Bold
Had braved in bone-dry Barbary.
Rebellion crackled in the air, but
Hrolf Hardheart stood by his master.
Few were willing to dispute with
The tattooed hero of mortal combat,
Before battle, before the shieldwalls
In Wessex, Wales and Wallonia.

In the last hours of light Mary,
Eyes closed, looked westwards.
"There," she claimed, "there is
"Where salvation lies."
Stormmaster tacked to the leeward
And the lazing sea began to boil.
Gannets were diving headlong,
Like arrows unleashed by a bow,
Exploding in a splash of white,
Rising with bills full before wheeling,
Swallowing and returning to the salt-fray.
Across the green-blue expanse
Cod were gathering in a feeding frenzy
Rivalled only by Asgeir and his pirates,
Scooping sustenance from the sea
In bailing buckets – life-savers twice over.
Even a water barrel bobbed up,
Bounced back to its steed by the sea.
And in the raw-fish feast that evening
The Vikings forgot their fears and fury,
And confessed – to themselves, quietly –
That on this rough raid they had found
Two fine Stormmasters –
Ship and skipper together.

Fish-fed, lodestone-led,
The loot-men carved a course
For little Norseland and
Soon the slumbering
Snow mounts of Iceland
Loomed on the horizon,
Like sleeping sea monsters,
Piebald, humpbacked, blue-capped,
Threatening to breathe fire
Whenever they awoke.

And still, despite the storm,
The grinning holy skull reigned
On the sea-soaked dragon head.

Chapter 8

Driftwood floated past,
The skeletons of dragonships
Smashed by the tempest,
As Stormmaster crept into
Vestervik's shallow bay and
Inched up its shingle slope.
Mary's leather necklace
Had led them here,
Only this time Asgeir met
No mutinous warrior moans.
The cod haul had shown
Mary's life-saving skills
And landfall anywhere
Was gift enough for the sea-mauled.
But a bigger haul lay in store
As Asgeir, Ketil Killfast and Hrolf Hardheart
Scaled a lacerating lava ridge and
Looked down to the next bay along.
There, shingled ashore, dragonhead broken,
Was a raid veteran the warriors
Knew well. Flapping loose in
The breeze was final proof:
Grim's Blood Eagle was in reach.

But the bay sheltered another gem.
Shackled to a sheep hurdle,
Shirt ripped, back white,
Was one of their own,

Oddo the Hairy's sentry-mate
Broddi the Bloody who
Was now well-named.
On Orkney he was Waverider's guard;
On Iceland he was Waverider's prisoner.

Now he had two guards
Hooded and heartless
Like the lustful ravens
Wheeling lazily overhead,
Longing to peck out his eyes
While Grim and his leather-lashed crew
Strolled into the warm glow
Leaking from a beer hovel
Tucked among the tussocks.
As moon replaced sun
And dew started to settle
Asgeir made his move.
"Never," he told his men,
"Will I leave a man to his fate.
"We work with the Norns,
"Not against, but the Norns know
"When a man has hope.
"Once you are in my crew,
"You are ever in my crew."
But how to rescue Broddi the Bloody
Without risking the rest of the crew?
As Asgeir stared through the gloom
And watched Broddi battling
With the binding leather thongs
Grip-tightening at every wriggle,
A grey old crone ghosted through
The thin, rolling, masking, sea mist.
Bent double, she shuffled to Broddi
And stroked his blood-matted mane.
A guard growled for form's sake

But the other barely glanced
At the frail, wild-haired fret-walker.
What man looks at wart-faced women?
The guards returned to narwhal dice
Unheeding as the bundle of rags
Whispered briefly in Broddi's ears and
Shuffled off, melting into the night.
Asgeir frowned. Broddi stopped fighting,
Surrendering, yielding to his fate.
The guards were dice slaves,
Seduced by fortune's fancies,
And in enough time to whet a sword,
Mary returned to the lava ridge,
Shape-shifted, lissom, once more
Stormmaster's flame-haired seer.
"Master," she said to Asgeir,
"Broddi will battle again.
"Bloody by shield-badge,
"Bloody by beatings,
"He is to die when the east lightens,
"As a pirate, a robber of Waverider.
"Grim has got us outlawed
"To be slaughtered on sight
"Like sheep-worrying wolves
"For the same sea stealing sin.
"We all live and flirt with death
"But Broddi's is but hours away.
"Grim has twenty men
"And ten more islanders
"Able to slash and stab.
"But let me lead two men
"And Broddi can live in victory."

Asgeir smiled, his teeth white
In the silver moonshine
As Mary outlined her plan.

He addressed his raiders:
"The odds and the gods
"Are finding in our favour.
"Grim is so fucking confident
"He's now supping and shagging,
"Dumping just two bored men from
"An untested crew as sentries.
"Only he knows what we look like.
"Cursed as outlaws we may be,
"But his men must catch us first
"And a blind hound sees no fox.
"Broddi will bring Grim to us
"And Waverider will be ours
"War booty, blood-eagle and all."

A brief huddle on high, a few quick ayes,
And below Broddi counted his breaths
Knowing each took him closer
To an outlaw's screaming torture
With sword and Valhalla out of reach.
In the dark he heard a velvet voice
And there, barely wearing a bear's fur,
Hair tumbling down, ripe for picking,
Was Mary, purring in the moonlight,
Whispering promises of another heaven
Through full, moist, inviting lips.
The guards dropped dice
And seized their swords
But soon opted for another
Display of swordsmanship.
"You go," leered one, "but be quick.
"My turn next, so get on with it."
His partner untied his sword belt
And slipped lustily into the night
To make moans of pleasure so deep
He might have been in mortal pain.

"So it should be," slavered his mate,
Already steeled for his turn.
Minutes later he got his wish when
His cowled comrade staggered back.
The shagseeker forsook talking
In his rush to sample the fleshfeast
And soon he was moaning and panting too,
Not from his swordplay but from Hrolf's,
Stuck deep down his throat
Until it scraped his scrawny ribs
And he drowned in his own blood.
Soon a hooded Hrolf Hardheart
Was standing guard with Ketil Killfast
And telling Broddi the swordpath to
Life, loot, legend and vengeance.

Chapter 9

Blood seeped into the sky
Like a rising tide from Stavanger.
The door of the ale shed
Creaked open in a death shriek.
Broddi lifted his head, spat,
And prepared to die like a Viking.
He knew his shipmates were primed
And together these pirates had survived
Many a scrape with sword and spear.

But still his hands were tied, his back bare,
And forty bearded axe-wielders,
Shoulders hunched like battle crows,
Were crunching out his death march,
With Grim the gore-grinner at their head.

Cowled Ketil snarled and kicked Broddi,
While Hrolf, head down, sneered
In the half light which was slowly
Turning to pale autumn blue.
Grim and a massive Icelander
Known throughout the northlands
For his finesse with a knife,
Finnvid the Back-Flayer,
Towered above Broddi on
His wicker torture table.
And so began the slow death rite
Of denunciation and humiliation,

Almost as painful as the first slice
Of Finnvid's easy, icy blades.
Grim delivered the shame taunts
While Finnvid ambled behind Broddi
As if on a gentle morning stroll.
So, it went on, Broddi the bugger,
Broddi the sheepshagger,
Broddi the whining woman,
And never could Broddi know
When the Flayer's first exquisite
Slicing would begin.
But he heard all too well
When Finnvid started
Whetting his butcher blades
On a stone right behind him,
Heard Finnvid joking and boasting
And taking bets on just how long
He could make Broddi squeal.
And then there was silence,
More ominous than a drum beat.
Grim grabbed Broddi by his matted hair,
Twisted and jerked his head up
And jeered on beer breath:
"So, you thought you'd blood-eagle me?
"You and that snake in the boat, Asgeir?
"You reckoned you could beat me?
"Goat-shagging scum, shieldwall fodder.
"Now you will fly like an eagle and
"Feel the ravens, skuas and gulls
"Eat you alive and peck your lungs
"As you breathe through boiling blood."
Broddi spat once more, his last stand.
Through his filthy fringe he saw Grim nod
And behind him Finnvid salivated,
Held up the knives with a devil's grin
And gloated: "Prepare to die, arsehole,

"But, Hel, we'll go easy on you, sonny.
"We'll keep you screaming 'til sunset."
He traced a line down Broddi's back
And a trickle of blood followed the blade.
The showman scanned his audience
And shouted: "Now the fun begins."
But as the taunt left his mouth,
Finnvid's death fun was over.
A fleet arrow of Saxon ash,
Best Jorvik steel and
White fjord feather
Whistled amid the murk
And skewered his muscular neck,
Showering Grim, Broddi, Hrolf and Ketil
In a steaming, pulsing red river
Like a mud-spewing geyser in the
Brooding mountains above.
As Finnvid dropped his knife,
His hands palsied in a death dance
Of arrow shaft, blood and sweat,
His eyes wild, his mouth drowning.
Hrolf caught the knife handle and
With one sharp swipe slashed
Broddi free, throwing him the blade.
He had time enough to straighten up,
So stunned were Waverider's warriors
And their unworldly Icelander allies,
While Ketil hacked down all around,
Slashing and stabbing, punching and jabbing,
As frantic foes fumbled for shield and sword.
While the shingle brightened from brown to red
More arrows rained death on
This remote vik's torture-worshippers
And from behind sea-wet rocks
Asgeir, Oddo and the freedmen
Roared into the slaughter.

Heads rolled, arms flew, legs dropped
Never to walk again but instead
To fuel raven flight for weeks.
But Grim was well named.
No stranger to ambush,
He knew when to fight.
He knew when to flee.
As Icelanders defended their bay
He bellowed his order of retreat
And led a headlong rush to Waverider,
Leaping aboard as his crew hauled
Their haven into surging sea with strength
Only death's cold breath can give
Before all scrambled aboard and
Rowed with the frenzy of the Furies
Far out into the grey-green as
Gore-greedy birds cawed and circled
Waiting to be left in peace
To savour the spoils of war.

Icelanders are as Norse as the Norse
And fought as all Norsemen should,
Spear-shafting two of Stormmasters'
Newly liberated oar-pullers, mere boys,
Before Asgeir's ambush fed the islanders
To the cruel bite of arrow, sword and axe.
As he surveyed the blood-red battle scene,
Asgeir laughed: "Now we really are outlaws."
By then an easterly breeze had filled
The Blood-Eagle which was flying
Into the western wastewaters of the deep.
The race was on again but first Asgeir
Seized beer barrels and herring pickle,
Fuel for this winter fox hunt,
Pausing to torch the beer shacks.

Up over the ridge to rush back down to
Stormmaster raced the vengeance-seekers,
The loot-lusters and the blood-hungry
And soon Stormmaster was heading west again
Leaving a pall of smoke and a pile of bodies
As the blood price of their outlawry.

Chapter 10

Not for the first time Stormmaster rode
Into the grey-green unknown,
Into the jaws of an ice-wind,
Winter's harbinger, a warning that
The race had to be won without delay.
The Ice Bear swelled, pregnant with wind,
And the holy skull grinned westwards
To where Grim and his greed
Were seeking sanctuary in lands
Stalked by man-eating giants and trolls.
Stormmaster ploughed the sea furrows
Flying to who knew what or where!
Well, they were all free warriors,
Even the former oar slaves.
They knew their destiny well -
To battle, bravery and skald-boasts,
To warm wassailing winter hearths
Or join Valhalla's heroes in the trying.

Grim had a head start
And fear fed his oar team
Every time the wind waned.
But Grim was no ring-giver
And Grim's crew were not his.
To a man, to their sword tips
They were Thorfinn the Bald's.
And where Thorfinn shunned the lash
Where Thorfinn shared gold and glory,

Grim wielded the whip,
And hoarded, worshipped, his wealth.
Worse, Grim had led them to Hel
Leaving five crewmen bleeding,
Abandoned on the fire-land shore,
Without giving a backward glance
And, worse still, was now taking them
On a winter voyage to a land
Where only white bears thrive.
Fear drives men on, on, on,
But warrior doubts destroy
The terror of endless threats and
Expose worthless warlords.

Mary's necklace was Asgeir's guide,
Leading Stormmaster in Grim's
Invisible, long vanished wake.
After three days the wind dropped
Just as Oddo shouted the news
Every man wanted to share.
Waverider was ahead, Blood-Eagle
Hanging limply from the mast.
Loot-love and vengeance-lust
Are far stronger than fear
So before long Stormmaster
Was homing in on Waverider,
A summer's spoils and Grim's hide.

But a windrush stirred the ship,
Chilling all, as ocean light changed
From pale blue to bronze,
Turning the sea's azure into gold.
Spices filled the air and sea serpents,
Fins rippling above the waves,
Snake-tails flicking, fangs drool-dripping,
Wailed warnings to all around.

A fleet of dragonships glided
Silently into view, sails part full,
Oars sleeping behind weathered shields.
Warriors of our world beheld
Warriors of the next world,
The spectral ships of Viking lords
Sent to sail the seas for ever more,
Swords in hand, keys to Valhalla,
Gold and silver and jewel-studded hilts
Proof of their power in life and in death.
How many Saxons had fed Swiftslaughter,
Scumslicer, Headsplitter and Brainshaver?
The fraying banners of the dragonships
Announced their passing tenants,
Here the double-axe of Yngvar the Slayer,
There the snarling wolf of Norri Knifemaster,
Here the towering troll of Helli Sigvaldison,
There the tufted lynx of Starkad the Strong.
Asgeir had no need to order his men
To drop oars. Open-mouthed they stood
As the otherworldly parade passed by.
No-one sought to seize the
Jewel-laden sea graves surging past
Even though each one held a king's ransom,
Rich payment to the gods for a smooth
Passage into Odin's beer palace and
The wench-heaven of Valhalla.
No-one save Grim the Greedy.
For Grim had worked hard to earn his name.
Asgeir, Hrolf Hardheart, Ketil Killfast, Broddi the Bloody,
Oddo the Hairy, Mary and the rest of the crew
Stared in horror as, in the ghost-light,
Grim steered Waverider across the
Smouldering fire-flame of Egil the Skinny,
Son of Magnus Rognarson, hero of
Battles across the Baltic and beyond,

Prince of the Kopings, King of the South Swedes,
And clambered aboard to plunder the dead hero
Of his eternal, priceless, warrior wealth.
Grim dropped sack after laden sack
Onto Waverider, laughing with lust
As the jewels glittered in the golden rays.
And then, most depraved of all, he leapt
Down to his dragonship brandishing
Egil's hallowed sword Shieldsplitter,
Ripped from the hero's gnarled hand,
Slamming the sacred, heavy oaken doors
Of Valhalla for ever in his face.
And as the spirit-fleet drifted past,
Well before Asgeir could react,
Grim gave the order to row and raise sails,
With his ghost-booty battened in the hold.

A roar filled the beer hall.
Sven's bloodhounds had all
Witnessed war's vile horrors,
Even inflicted a few,
As have all worthy warriors,
Gore and waste enough to give
Women a lifetime's weeping.
But Grim had looted
Where no man should.
He had mocked the gods and
Condemned a great man
To a lost eternity as a nomad
Instead of his blood-won glory.
Sven, eyes like helmet slits,
Scowled through the smoke fug
And with an unsmiling nod
Restored order to his mob.

Snorri drank deep of
Sven's winter ale.
A pause was welcome.
Now was a wise time
To break the skald spell.
Warriors, bellies beer-full,
Went outside as one
To turn snow into steam
And curse the godless Grim,
All while wenches refilled
Beery wooden tankards
With mind-soothing balm -
Or battle-stoking bile
Depending on the drinker.

In the time Snorri had been talking
Sven's men had drunk without break
But for now, their war rage was aimed
At one man only: Grim the desecrator.
Soon the bearskins and sheepfleeces
Grunted back into the fire glow,
Shaking off the cold like Sven's wolfhound.
And though the noose pricked his neck,
Snorri knew he had passed a vital test.

Another sip, another cough, another chapter.
With shield-shakers sitting and waiting,
Snorri led them to the westbound longship
And span for his life as the Norns spin for us all.

For every crime against the gods,
Snorri continued, seducing
The wolf-eyed with words,
There is a price to pay.
But Odin's justice is fickle.
The gods do not always play fair,

And for pure, petty devilment
May compel the wrong man
To redeem their blood bounty.
As the Blood-Eagle slunk away,
A sea serpent, by name of Haki,
Sought to avenge Egil the Skinny,
In the only way she knew how.
Haki reeked of fish, stale fish,
And from sharp snout to spear-tipped tail
Was three times longer than Stormmaster
And more than five times as heavy.
Giant kelp hung from her scaly head
And flames roared from her belly,
Surging up her long swan neck,
To belch death from her foul mouth.
And if fire failed, her forest of fangs,
Each longer than a shieldwall spear,
Would finish the job with strength to spare.
But Haki was short-sighted and stupid,
A dullard even for a sea serpent,
And in her blurred world one dragonship
Looked much like any other dragonship.
So it was that as Waverider
Vanished over the horizon,
Brazen with the god-stolen gold,
And the ghoulish ghost fleet
Floated past in its eternal golden glow,
Haki dived down and rose up,
In a spray of salted sea spume,
Bloodied jaws open, battle cry roaring,
Right in front of Asgeir as he stood cursing
Below the skull atop his stolen sea stallion.

No time to think,
No time to breathe.
It is often the best way.

A true warrior fights by instinct,
Nature leads his sword arm and
Battle memory fuels each stroke,
Each parry, each lunge,
That decides who lives or dies.
So it was with Asgeir,
Golden hair blown back by
The sour serpent roar from
Deep in Haki's fetid belly.
Asgeir did not hesitate.
A bark to Ketil Killfast
Who hurled Deathbringer
Through the ghostly light.
Asgeir grasped the well-worn hilt
And plunged headlong into
Haki's chosen icy battlefield.
Ketil and the crew knew
Their lives hung on the thread
Of this uneven combat between
Viking and vicious sea monster.
For two days and two nights
The deep boiled white with foam.
Oddo the Hairy's arrows bounced
Off Haki's steel scales like pine cones
Unleashed on a Saxon shorefort.
Asgeir drew blood, shading the sea scarlet,
But Haki had plenty, gallons to shed.
A gaping gash cut in her
Was like a nick in a man.
And her fangs made Asgeir's leg
Weep long tears of life's juice,
The sea salt stinging it clean
So the sea sword could fight on.
For two days and two nights
Monster battled man,
Yellow fangs and fire

Against sword and shield,
Brute force against brutal speed,
Might against mind,
Crowing against cunning.
Then Haki surged skywards,
Unwisely exposing her belly
And filling the reddening sky with
A roar from the underworld which
Rolled across the sea swell.
Asgeir readied Deathbringer for
The gut-spilling death lunge,
But Haki held back and
Slowly lowered her lissom neck
To Asgeir in graceful submission.

Stormmaster rocked with roaring
As Ketil Killfast and Broddi the Bloody
Hauled Asgeir and Deathbringer aboard.
Mary brought balm to his wounds,
Blending magic and herbs
To heal the miraculous hero.
Haki slipped below the waves
But a trail of bubbles led
Off towards the ghost fleet
And its slimy, cold-eyed guards.
"From now on," said Ketil Killfast,
To nods, smiles and laughter,
"You shall always be Asgeir Dragontamer
"And your saga fame will spread
"From the frozen fjords of Greenland
"To the searing deserts of the Saracens."
Asgeir grinned through blood-cracked lips:
"I will wear the name like a gold ring
"Given by Thor or Odin themselves,
"But first we have to find the thief,
"The fiend lower than a sea serpent,

"Grim the Greedy, Grim the Despoiler.
"No Grim, no loot, no Norway,
"And my Dragontamer fame
"Will be Stormmaster's eternal secret.
"Mary: Read the runes, let the bones speak,
"Let you and the holy skull lead us to Grim."

Chapter 11

For days Stormmaster bucked and strained
In the Atlantic's bitter wind and spray,
The grinning, weather-beaten skull
Of the skirt-Men's holy relic gazing
Hollow-eyed towards the west.
And ever westwards they went,
Tacking in the counter wind which made
Even the bulging white bear banner shiver.
Asgeir's sole guide was Mary and
Her magical, mystical necklace,
That and his gut, animal instinct.
Norway was no haven for Grim,
Iceland would be on the lookout
Long after the sea washed away
The blood of his last rapine visit.
Erik the Red's great joke, Greenland,
Was no refuge for a raider in autumn
When ice floes whip the seas to stone
And stores built up over summer months
Decide between life and freezing death.
England beckoned, with its green fields,
Great loot and growing, wealthy towns
But its kingdoms were getting far too crowded
And Grim was known to far too many.
No, Grim had to shrug off Asgeir,
So, he had to go into the unknown.
And where Grim sailed, Asgeir followed.

Stormmaster, chomping at the wind-bit,
Reared up and galloped like a race horse,
Snorting past vast snow-capped mountains,
Coasting islands as big and black as Norway,
Cresting cod-shoals so thick Broddi plucked them
From the sea in his hard shovel hands
And hung them to mast-dry in the salt-breeze.
Westwards was no longer an option,
As a new land blocked their way,
So southwards they turned,
Sailing in sight of rocky shores,
Coasts barren of trees and man,
Moving one day ahead of the snow
Which muffled this empty land in silence.

By now Grim had been gone a week,
And the faith of Stormmaster's gold-cravers
Was under the same groaning strain
As a sea stallion in a winter storm.
As the warband's mood began to creak
Like Stormmaster's oak skeleton in the teeth
Of a west wind-whisked ship-slayer,
Asgeir waited 'til a moonless night
To tip beer, precious fighting fuel,
Over the side to sate the sea.
He looked up to the cloud-racing sky
And mouthed a silent prayer to Thor.
Even the greatest leaders feel lonely,
Even the toughest warlords sense
The wolves snarling at their heels
And know that courage alone is not enough:
Luck, the fate-spinning Norns and the gods
Must ever be with them, always.
So, over the side went some beer.
Better to have Thor in your shield wall

Fighting your foes than challenging you,
Flaunting your enemy's war banner.

The next day, as a wan sun limped to its peak,
Thor passed his verdict. And Asgeir cursed
That he had sacrificed in secret.
Happy the leader whose men know
That Thor is smiling on his side.
As Stormmaster bucked round a headland
A tiny speck could be seen on the horizon,
Once more, hugging the coast westwards.
Warriors who minutes earlier were sulking
Stiffened once more, men who for days
Had grumbled and mithered and feuded,
Grinned and mastered sail and spear,
Scenting the long yearned for reckoning
On the bleak noon's snow-filled air,
Glad despite the menacing sky
That Grim was once again
Within their oar-hard grasp.

So began a mission to outshine all the sagas,
To mock monastery raids on Saxon shores,
To belittle ice-breaking and bear-fighting
Around Greenland's blue, wailing glaciers,
And to beat Hakon the Sly's Rusland ride
Into the spice and silk markets of Araby.
Every minute that passed led Stormmaster into
Lands unknown to the most nomadic of Vikings.
Stormmaster tracked Grim from afar for days
Like a wolf pack stalking a wounded bear.
Time was on their side. When the moment came to strike
They would know and Grim would be at their mercy.

Forests thickened, the sea narrowed,
Shaggy-furred wolves drank from the shore

As another riverbank rose to the south.
And on both sides their advance
Was greeted by the natives' anthem,
A drumbeat that rolled relentlessly,
Ominously, chillingly, ahead of them,
An alarm call for hunters and hunted.
Hugging the middle of the great river
Stormmaster sped past villages of tents
Like caves, but made of skins and bark,
Woodsmoke rising sleepily from the top,
And the aroma of roasting meat
Wafting over the waves like a taunt.
Occasionally war canoes launched,
Near naked warriors, heedless of the cold,
Paddled in flimsy boats dragonship-dwarfed.
War whoops filled the frost air
As beardless braves,
As brown as Arabs,
Feathers in their hair,
Faces brightly painted,
Bayed for blood and
Brandished slashing axes
Or sun-glinting blades and
Loosed off flint-head arrows.
But Asgeir had flaxen sails and
Ocean-taming oarsmen,
Who easily outpaced
The wild and war-painted.

So the Norse stuck to the centre
Of the slow, sea-like river
Just like lonely Waverider
In the land's silver distance.

And as they sailed on unshaken,
Their round shields soaked up arrows

'Til Stormmaster's oaken hull
Prickled like a huge sea hedgehog.
On they went, hauling their sea steed
Past frothing rapids, along trails
Well-worn by warlike natives,
And crossing a chill inland sea.
For days they could hear a bear's roar
That never once paused for breath
But moaned ever more loudly
With every passing, sapping minute,
Until one misty morning a mountain of
Foaming water plunged before them,
A white wall of steam and spray
Pouring in troll-torrents from the sky,
Buffeting and battering Stormmaster,
Forcing it to bob and bounce in
A beard-freezing ice-steam
And making warriors face a foe
No sword or spear could tame.

But Vikings never flinch from fight, foe or fury.
For three days they heaved and hauled
Up fjord-steep slopes, shouldering Waverider
Well beyond the thunder shower and
The frantic flood that fed the beast.
Finally, on a sandy shore fringed by firs,
They floated their steed to safety,
On a flat calm, wide, water racecourse,
Unfurled the Ice Bear and once more
Resumed their pursuit of Grim the Greedy.
But all the time they felt an invisible horde
Of eyes needling into them like winter hail
From the eternal night of the forest bank.

Grim, they knew, was not their only foe.
Before long they faced a reckoning

With the wild killers of the woods.
A true Viking goes where Thor takes him
And mocks death as a herald of glory,
Leaving whingeing and whining at fear
To wailing women and bawling bairns,
But even Asgeir, Hrolf Hardheart, Ketil Killfast
And their battle-hardened, sea-toughened crew
Would soon taste terrors never known
By Norsemen, Danes, Geats or Icelanders.
As they picked off winter plump deer
With arrows fletched in bustling Jorvik,
Plucked blue berries from prickle bushes
And slaked their thirst with iced water,
This land of plenty was preparing
To bite the hands it so easily fed.

The Blood-Eagle banner gulped down the east wind
And the Ice Bear gorged on the same brew
A respectful distance behind, safe on
A lake with endless blurred horizons.
But as night fell so did the wind-drinkers
And oar-hard hands sought shelter on shores
Of scented spruce, fir and towering pine,
Of peeling birch and witch-gnarled oak,
On forest floors silenced by centuries of needles.
Around glowing, spitting kindling fires
They slept and snored, swords by their sides,
Taking turns to guard dragonship and crew,
Squinting into an unending blackness
Broken only by pairs of yellow eyes
Flitting through trees, as elusive as
A woman's glance through a veil.

Sentries found every night nerve-shredding,
A fight against mind-flaying exhaustion
And the unfamiliar calls and cries of a

Foreign forest packed with wolves and
Creatures unseen and, worse still, unknown.
And so, the Vikings' descent into Hel began.

Padraic, one of the freedmen, was first to fall
But only after hair-whitening horrors beyond
Even the terrors of Torshavn's baby-eating trolls.
Stocky as a beer barrel, strong as a stallion,
His luck began to ebb as the sentries
Picked fateful straws for their night posts.
His fellow freedman, wild-haired Eoin,
Taller, wirier, sprightlier than Padraic,
Was to guard Waverider by the water,
Moonshadow-dappled on the sandy shore.
But Padraic was ordered deeper inland,
Thirty cold paces from the camp's edge
Where moon and sun were strangers.
Padraic was no sapling but a mature oak,
Captured by Sigrid Olafson on Bandalough,
Traded in Dyflin's sweat-foul slave markets.
His wife was by now a burnished Saracen jewel
But fate flung the Bandaman northwards,
Powering dragonships when the wind slept.
Now, face long scarred by Grim's cruel leather,
He found himself, sword held two-handed high,
Blinking into the eternal, frozen night of
A forest full of wolves and jet-haired devils.

Every sound presaged death,
Every single breeze whisper,
Every quavering owl hoot,
Every sudden snow tumble
From unseen swaying boughs.
The hooting began to fill the forest,
To the left, to the right, and head on.
The only silence was lakeside, save for

The snoring of oar-exhausted axemen.
As the first weak rays of a snow-morn
Turned grey to green, white to dazzle,
A sudden movement to the left
Made Padraic spin to face a foe
Only for a rough hand to cup his mouth
And a hand axe to cut through his neck.
Hooting turned to whooping,
A gloating dirge of death
At the axe-wielder's pleasure.
Bleary Vikings battle-scrambled,
Grabbing shields, swords and helmets,
Axes, knives and spears,
Arrows, bows and quivers,
And swiftly shield-shaped
A shuffling, cursing circle
Which clawed slowly, warily,
Back to Eoin and lake-safety,
Swallowing him much like
A salmon might a mayfly -
But this salmon let him live.
As arrows whistled into shields
Asgeir shouted out his orders:
"No yielding, shields tight,
"Straight back to Stormmaster,
"Make Thor proud. Sell yourself dearly."
In the half-light howling trolls charged up
To the shieldwall, so close Asgeir
Could smell their stale breath and
See their painted, manic faces,
Wilder than animals, white-feather crowns
Standing proud like a dragon's crest.
Some wore a full wolf pelt,
Snarling head worn as a hood,
Others antlers or long quills
In their unkempt, uncombed, raven hair,

Which hung in top knots from shaved heads.
Whoops heralded a charge by a wolfman
Then a rutting stag, then a black bear,
Claws and teeth hanging round an ochre neck.
Then, running past, in an ever-slowing circle,
A fountain of blood steaming skywards
Was the Vikings' lost guard of the woods,
His head clean off, but his sword
Locked firmly in his death grip,
Still slashing, stabbing and slicing,
Scattering wild arms and legs,
Painting the pure snow crimson,
Turning whoops to wails,
Before his wounds won out.
Staggering and stumbling,
Padraic slumped to his knees
And surrendered to death's
Icy, merciless, embrace.
Once a slave from the peat bogs,
Padraic was now a Viking for ever.
As wolf warrior and bear battler
Danced and whooped around
The spear-bristling Viking circle
Grim broke from the forest glades
To lob a bloodied rock into the war-ring
Where it was caught by Eoin
Who screamed only one word:
"Padraic." For the rock had reddened eyes
Haunted by a horror only the dead know
And where once a shaggy black mane
Blew when the Ice Bear filled with power,
Now there was only a bloody, weeping sore
Exposing bone as white as last week's snow.
And if Asgeir and his warband wanted to know
Where lay the fate of Padraic's prized pelt,
All they had to do was look across at

A leering wolfman licking a blood-dripping scalp
In a battle taunt more potent than words.
A warrior wearing just a loin cloth
Protected from the cold only
By black and red body paint
Brandished a big stick from which
Other scalps swayed with each sweep.
Black, grey, black, black, grey, black, black,
Twitching in the clearing like horse's tails,
And, surely not, thought Asgeir, blinking,
Squinting through sweat-stained hair,
But yes, it was true, yes, a blonde mane.
Grim was in league with these savages.
Had he sacrificed one of his own
To buy a black-hair army to save his gold?

These jarring thoughts flashed through
Asgeir's mind in the time it took
A painted arrow to splinter his shield.
A wolverine warrior, teeth bared,
Raced up to the shieldwall and
Prepared to hatchet his way through.
But the shieldwall was now a living beast
Fighting without words, without thought,
Fighting on animal instinct, fighting for survival,
Powered by muscle memory of battles
With Saxons, Britons, Franks, Scots and Irish.
The wall parted to offer a two-fingered gap
And Broddi the Bloody jabbed his spear through
To harpoon the wolverine in the belly
As if landing a whale off the Faroes.
One twist and steaming guts stained the snow,
Leaving Wolverine to flap like a codfish,
To writhe and scream, foam and falter,
The latest in a long line of Broddi's victims,
Littering lands from the rivers of the Rus to

The shores of this hostile, friendless new world.
Asgeir and his men were at Stormmaster now
But a rain of arrows bit into ship and shield,
Bouncing off steel helmets like April hail,
But sending Valmar the Vain to sup with the gods.
So close, but to board meant to break ranks
And that meant death at the hands
Of howling half-men half-beasts
So, the circle stood its ground,
Begging Thor to unleash his hammer
And scatter the growling scalp-cravers.
In the heart of the huddle was Mary.
For days now a freeloader, a passenger,
Eating deer, trout and fruit for free.
Now it was time for her to pay her passage.
Mary rubbed the bone that never left her sight,
Chanted a cryptic charm in Gaelic and crushed
Leaves as dry as the skirtmen's skull
As Broddi the Bloody fed his spear
On a native prickling with long quills,
Leaving him howling like a snared wolf
Gnawing through its red-raw leg.
Flaming arrows seared the air,
Fizzing into Stormmaster in dazzling arcs
But the dragonship bucked in the breeze
And spurned the sparks, still soaked
By weeks of sea spray and river rinse.
Its stubbornness seemed to stun the
Painted pack of rabid predators
And the arrow blizzard began to slow
To a drizzle of spiteful devilry.

Limbs, heads and guts lay silent
In the trampled blood-red snow
Like a human harvest of pine needles.
The shield circle held firm,

Braced for a new onslaught,
When the fire-arrows sang again
In a frenzy of warrior whooping,
Icy enough to chill Thor's furnace.
But these arrows from invisible avengers
Saved Asgeir and his Viking brothers
And bit into the tribe of Wolfman,
Stag warrior, Snakeskin and the rest,
With flying teeth of flint and bone
Reddened with every rushing flight.
"Ready yourself," grunted Asgeir,
"Nobody falters. The fight is still on,
"Hotter than an Iceland geyser."
The shieldwall, backs to Stormmaster,
Watched in grim, hilt-tightening wonder
As another wild tribe of man-beasts
Charged, whooping from the woods,
Hacking and hatcheting at Asgeir's foes,
Splitting skulls and bludgeoning heads
With sharp blades and rock-like cudgels,
All powered by iron-muscled arms.
As Wolfman and his startled pack
Clawed for cover, crawled to
A safety that could never come,
Blades flashed; death screams cut
Across the lake like rabbits
Squealing in the fangs of a fox,
And dripping scalps were yanked free
In a jubilation of howling and hooting.
"Now," growled Asgeir, "Now,
"Break apart and get aboard,
"Get Stormmaster back out to sea
"As far from shore as possible."
The shields parted, the shaggy-bearded
Turned as one to heave her waterwards
But found themselves facing

A firing squad of feathered arrows
Formed on Stormmaster by as many
Painted scalpers as were squeezing the
Life out of Wolfman and his cowering band
In the brightening, bloody clearing below.

Chapter 12

Too late to close the shield wall,
Too late to run and, anyway,
There was nowhere to run.
Stormmaster was their sole salvation
But the sea stallion had new riders
Who could end this Norse adventure
In as little time as it took to unleash
The flint-tipped falcons in their bows.

Asgeir the Dragontamer and his men
Steeled themselves for the agonies ahead.
They had witnessed what the painted packs
Did to their own. Odin alone knew
What they would do to men whose
Skins were as pale as theirs were brown.
Death beckoned, screaming, merciless death.
Slowly Asgeir and his men removed
Their battle helmets, a last luxury,
To let their sweat-soaked manes
Dry once more in winter's warming sun.
But taut-armed archers suddenly switched
From fletch-twitching, ready to rain death,
To trembling, open-mouthed, white-eyed,
Jabbering, pointing, fingers for arrows.
Some fell to their knees, flattening
Themselves on the deck, barely
Daring to look down on the vanquished.
Only one of the natives kept his nerve,

A tall war-lover, as tall as Asgeir and
Of the same muscled vintage,
Face painted red, black and yellow
Around a line of four deep scars
All down his hollow right cheek.
Sitting proudly on top of his long
Jet hair like a home-made crown
Was a headdress of white feathers,
Fuller than any of the other savages.
He uttered a few words, gutturally,
Calmly, quietly, but it was enough.
His warband recovered, still very wary,
Raised bows, primed death flights once more,
And the fleeting chance to flee had fled
Just as the groans from the needle floor
Reminded Asgeir and Stormmaster's rowers
Of the terrible fate that lay in store,
A hell of unknown, exquisite agony.
But then Scarface said one word more,
Calmly, quietly, but with eyes firmly on Asgeir,
And it, too, was more than enough: "Vikings".

Death hovered still over Stormmaster's crew.
But as they walked, arrow-point prodded,
Past the scalp-shorn,
Past Padraic the Headless,
Past the axe-hacked legs,
Pushed down well-trodden snow trails
Deeper into the darkening forest
The malice had flown, the mood
Replaced with armed reverence.
Hours later, blind hunger stabbing
Like Padraic's ghostly blade,
The sweet tang of woodsmoke
Filtered through the forest
And Scarface's cup-handed hoots

Were hailed by echoing howls.
Slowly, hatchet-handed warriors
Melted from nowhere, out of the firs,
To a frenzy of air-frosted whooping.
The steady beat of a drum,
Always those drums, always beating,
The barking of half-fed curs
And the shrill keening of women
Grew ever, ever louder as
The pines, birch and maples
Parted to reveal a vast longhouse
In a clearing of snow-covered stumps.
Women and children ran out to welcome
Their scalp-wielding, prisoner-rich warriors
And cry relief at their safe return.
But joy rapidly turned to jibbering
When beardless warriors revealed
Their latest precious battle-loot.
The welcoming party dropped
Onto bended deerskinned knees,
All eyes on helmetless Asgeir,
Hrolf Hardheart and Ketil Killfast.
Unnoticed, a young cub scurried
Off to the bark-clad longhouse,
His excited shouts breaking the silence.
Now it was the turn of the tribe to shock,
For Asgeir and his gold-seekers
To gawp, open-mouthed, in awe.
Emerging from his long house,
Unhurried, steadily, coldly,
Was a huge warrior, brown face
Burnished red, black and yellow,
Brown bear skin on his back,
Arms and claws clinging to his chest,
Crowned with a feathered headdress
Far bigger than Scarface's,

And beneath it was a mane
That burned like a beacon
Beside his raven-haired race,
A mane of blond, fair hair and
An even blonder, paler beard.
The tribe swept open like a
Field of barley before a horseman
To let their chief stride through.
He stood tall, toe to toe with Asgeir,
And, with blue summer-sea eyes,
Looked him long in the face.
"Viking men," he said, unsmiling,
But in deep, slow, faltering Norse,
"We have waited a long time for you."

In Sven's steaming hall,
A low murmur arose
Slurred by winter ale.
Asvald Spearking, Ingimar Bjornson and Gills Bonebreaker
Had made widows of Berbers, Tartars and Ungars,
Turned brawn into blood,
Blunted axe and sword on the
Skulls of the worthless,
Spilled guts as thoughtlessly
As they now poured their pleasure-ale,
Fighting in snow and ice, rain and sun,
Dark forest and dazzling desert.
But the West is a wilderness
Of dragons, trolls, and giants.
And here stood a Skald
Telling them of devils,
Half-men, half beasts,
In forests of icy mists
A whole summer's sail
From Norway's black fjords.
But the fame-fond always

Lust for saga glory.
Sven scowled at the slaves
And bellowed for more ale.
Snorri, supping swiftly,
Noose tickling his neck,
Got the nod from Sven
To take his men to
Wherever Asgeir might wander.

Chapter 13

The dazzling snow sun soon faded
To the seclusion of a chilled night
Lit only by the thinnest moon sliver.
The chief's tribe-full long house,
Was glow-lit by a spitting pine fire.
Far from being penned in,
Prisoners packed in a dirt corner
In stark fear for their scalps,
Asgeir and his sea-strivers sat
Beside the fair-haired savage, Scarface,
And three other feathered hard men,
In the heart of the fug-house whose
Bark and fur-lined walls shielded against
The biting frost crisping the forest beyond.
All around sat warriors, some with feathers,
Some without, but all with blood-slakers
Belt-hanging, battle-itching, at their sides,
Sharp-bladed hatchets, dagger point behind,
Rounded clubs, knives of bared, jagged teeth,
And, nearby, bows and their soulmates, flying death.
Unarmed, Asgeir and his men felt naked before them.

For some time, the warlords gabbled
In a tongue as alien as any Arab's.
Mary rubbed her necklace, listened,
Nodded her head to the native rhythm,
Eyes narrow-closed as she soaked up
Sounds as mind-menacing as the barks

And howls of the alien wilderness without.
Soon she whispered to Asgeir: "All is well."
Asgeir frowned, seeking more with a glance
Than words could find under Scarface's gaze.

The Blond barked and ten young bucks
Promptly obeyed, padding outside in
Silent shoes of softest deerskin.
The Blond produced a long pipe,
Bears painted along its length,
A blackened cup at its end.
From an ornate pouch he plucked
Sweet-smelling, aromatic, moist leaves
And stuffed a thumb's worth into the fire-cup.
With a firebrand he lit the foliage,
Sucking deeply, sublimely, on the pipe,
Till the leaves glowed ruby-red,
And then lazily, drowsily, exhaled,
Scented smoke fleeing his hawk-like nose,
Like Egil the Skinny's dragon.
He passed the pipe to Asgeir
And glanced sternly at the rest
Of the battle-tested, the war-wise.
They watched wide-eyed as
The Dragontamer discovered
How men can breathe fire like Haki.
He copied the chief, held the cup
And, like a true Viking, did his best,
Inhaling deep down into his chest
And exploding in a fit of coughing
As black smoke and soot poured from
His nose and mouth much like
The scaly cave dwellers of Svalbard.
For the first time the tribe-leaders
Lowered their unsmiling guard and
Shook with laughter and shouts.

But mock the Vikings they did not.
They taught them, softly, kindly, instead.
The chief guided Asgeir in the ways
Of the warriors' fuming fire pipe.
Just a gentle puff was all he needed.
So proud Asgeir had another go,
And though his swirling head swam,
His eyes watered and his toes tingled
His lungs forsook rebellion and he passed
The pipe to Ketil Killfast, saying,
Smoke clouds pouring from his mouth,
Words few Viking warlords ever say:
"Gently is best, slowly, just go easy."
As the tribe-pipe was passed around
Asgeir's spluttering spear-braves,
The bearskin door opened,
Blowing icy breath into the hall,
And the band of bucks returned,
Bearing swords, axes, shields and spears.
A nod from the Blond and the
Bearded were handed their battle brothers.
As they embraced their sacred friends,
Weighing weapons in hardened hands
They all failed to spot a spectral beauty
Who floated across the earthen floor.
Oddo the Hairy, his bald pate
Sweat-shining in the flickering firelight,
Saw it first, and nudged Hrolf Hardheart,
Who elbowed Ketil Killfast who nudged…
Well, the message spread through the warband
Like a salmon swimming across a lake.
There, in native dress of beaded deerskin,
Arms as brown as Scarface's body,
But locks as blonde as a snow pony's tail
Was a tall blue-eyed tribe girl
Hair held in place by a leather headband.

The war leader spoke in stumbling Norse:
"I am Seenaho. I lead the Sushone
"Like my father and my forefathers
"Long, long before me.
"He," he looked to Scarface, "is Hackasu,
"Brave bear fighter in woods.
"And she," he glanced at the girl,
"Is my sister Charmadu. She
"Can say many more to you."
All the while the other natives
Watched respectfully, but clearly
Understood none of the words.

Charmadu stepped forward, fireglow
Lighting her beautiful face.
She looked around the hushed hall
And then held Asgeir's puzzled gaze.
"We have waited a long time for you,"
She said in a clear, flowing voice,
More confident than her brother's.
"My people were promised the yellow-haired
"White warriors would come again one winter
"In a wooden dragon boat fed by long sticks.
"And you would beat in battle our rivals,
"The Azarapo, and our forefathers were right."
All the while Seenaho translated for the tribe,
His deep bear voice contrasting sharply
With Charmadu's bird song tones.
Behind her warriors brandished
Sticks hung with reddened scalps taken
That very day in the battle of the clearing.
"You are welcome. You are our guests.
"But Vikings, please, answer one question:
"We have waited so long to welcome
"Your skull-clad dragon boat.
"Yet two have turned up at once.

"Who are these other yellow hairs?"

Asgeir, arms proudly bearing gold rings
Ripped from the arms of the sword-slashed,
Badges of saga-honour from bloodbaths,
Was beyond bemused, more shocked than when
The beast-clad savages shrieked their ambush.
A thousand questions pounded in his brain
But he also knew the fate of his men
Hung on him thinking on his feet.

He stood, coughed to clear his throat,
Nodded to Seenaho and his throng
And smiled warmly at Charmadu,
His best – possibly his only – chance of life.
"I am Asgeir," he declared, and regarded
The roomful of warriors. Time, he thought,
To impress, no time for the truth.
"I am the son of Thorvald the Brutal,
"Lord of Hangesund, punisher of the Picts,
"Whose ancestors battled Danes and dragons
"And fought wherever the great gods
"Chose in their wisdom to find them foes.
"I will answer your question
"As thanks for your kindness,
"But I have many questions too,
"To which, with your consent,
"I will return very soon.
"We have sailed for many weeks
"Across seas bigger and stormier
"Than the lake where Hackasu
"Rescued us from your foes,
"Who are now definitely our foes.
"We are hunting another Viking
"Who has stolen and run from us.
"That is why today two dragonships

"Have travelled to your land together.
"One carried Grim the Greedy,
"A vile man who murders his own.
"This Viking, Grim the Greedy,
"Has selected your enemy as his friend.
"We want Grim's blood much more than you.
"So, we are more than happy to help you
"Fight bravely against your foe
"So that we Vikings can fight ours."
He caressed his sword, held it aloft,
And proclaimed: "Let Deathbringer
"Work his magic." And as he spoke
His men rose as one, swords, axes,
And spears held high, chanting:
"Asgeir, Asgeir, Dragontamer, Dragontamer."

The warpainted nodded approval
Of this Nordic display of force, and
A murmur of unknown words
Raced round the long house.
But Asgeir was still standing.
"Now," he said to Charmadu,
"It is your turn to talk.
"How can you speak our tongue?
"Why have you waited so long
"For Vikings to sail back?"

Charmadu glanced at Seenaho
Who, stony-faced, nodded her on.
"I am Charmadu, daughter of
"Chief Sanoho and sister to Seenaho.
"He is victorious in every battle
"As his feathers and scalps prove.
"But our people tell that
"Many summers since, long before
"Our oldest elder was born,

"Yellow-haired water warriors came
"In a big canoe led by a dragon's head.
"They called themselves Vikings,
"Strong-armed, hard-fighting,
"And led by a worthy warrior,
"With a long yellow beard.
"He was Olaf Blodason
"From a land he called Nor-way.
"He came well armed like you
"With long sharp blades and hatchets
"With two heads on long handles and
"Spears that always thirsted for blood.
"Olaf was only truly happy feeding
"His weapons on the guts of Azarapo
"And flying their scalps from
"A tall pine pole by his house
"Which he built from logs and bark.
"They would sway in the breeze
"Telling all with eyes to see
"That Olaf Blodason was a warrior
"To rank with even our greatest braves.
"He came on a boat he called Sea Ruler
"From a land of white men and snow
"Many moons' sailing from here.
"Sea Ruler, like your boat,
"Was swift, magic-fuelled,
"Its Wolfhead wing drinking
"The wind to find its speed.
"Olaf and his yellow-beards
"Stayed and fought as Sushone
"For five happy summers and
"Savoured many victories.
"His men enjoyed our women
"Always with our chief's blessing
"And," here she flicked her hand
Through her own blonde mane,

"They made many babies.
"But one melting spring day
"As the lake came back to life,
"Leaving dead ice for live water,
"Olaf and his men set sail
"With newly sharpened knives.
"They kissed their women farewell and
"Told them all they were going Viking.
"They let the magic Wolfhead fill
"With wind, and we watched the lake
"Swallow their silver wake as they
"Sailed towards the golden land
"Of the setting sun and far off forests.
"They promised that by the time
"The pumpkins were fat once more
"And the maple leaves were blood-red
"They would be back, armed with scalps.
"But no more was ever seen of them,
"No more was ever heard of them,
"And we Sushone have waited
"And we have prayed ever since,
"Through countless cold winters
"For the homecoming of the Vikings."

Silence briefly followed. The longhouse
Filled with the aroma of roasting meat
As women boiled a brown stew
In a steaming blackened cauldron over
The flaring fire of long-dried logs.

Charmadu was still standing.
The floor of dirt and pine needles
Was still hers. All still looked to her.
"You ask how I speak like a yellow hair.
"Since the day Sea Ruler took
"Olaf Blodason to the land of bison

"The Sushone have chosen two
"From each new generation to keep
"The sacred Viking tongue alive.
"Seenaho and I, both yellow hairs,
"Are our generation's chosen ones.
"We were taught by our mother,
"Who was taught by hers
"Who was taught by hers.
"She was the true wife
"Of warlike Olaf Blodason.
"She blessed him with children,
"A strong son, a beautiful daughter,
"Both yellow hairs like us
"And over five winters with Olaf
"She learned the Viking language,
"Though he learned little of our words.
"I have said all this many times
"As have my forefathers,
"All alone in the forest,
"All alone picking fruit or
"All alone by the food fire,
"So I would ever be ready
"For the day the Vikings returned."

As Seenaho finished his translating
A fervour of approval filled the longhouse,
Warriors and women warmly chorusing
Their tribal, fraternal, otherworldly welcome.
But, always gut-listening, Asgeir well knew,
That these same new blood-friends could
Just as easily have revelled in
The Yellow Hairs' torment and torture.
Out there, too, were other tribes
Every bit as savage, brutes for whom
The sight of blond hair and beard
Would unleash war whoops and

A biting welcome of blazing arrows
And skull-splitting hatchets.
Asgeir needed these painted devils
To survive in this hostile wilderness.
But why, he wondered, did they need him?

This, though, was not the time to probe.
Imprudent is the guest who upsets
A benign host with ingratitude.
Beating drums, haunting singing
And shuffling dancing would in any case
Have suffocated any truth quest.
A feast that would last three days
Was about to begin and by the end
Asgeir's ringmen could scarce believe
That any more bucks were left in the forest.
But Asgeir had graver, blacker concerns
And, as Vikings and Sushone basked
In winter glut, as warm as summer,
Meat sweat fighting with fire sweat,
Though hoar frost deep froze
The Sushone's vast outdoor larder,
He sought assurance from Seenaho.
With Mary on his left, he mentioned
Stormmaster to Charmadu, on his right.

"We thank you for your kindness
"But a Viking missing a dragonship
"Is as naked as a warrior without an axe.
"We need it for war and without war
"We are nothing. We are no longer men."
Charmadu translated swiftly for Seenaho
Who was seated to her right, cross-legged,
On the pine needle floor. As snarling dogs
Battled over bloody deer bones, Seenaho
Turned to Asgeir and stared hard at him,

Straight in the eye, unflinching,
Like a peregrine fixing on its prey
Before stooping to kill in a feather flurry.
"You are correct," he said, "Quite correct.
"A Viking without a ship is like a stag without antlers,
"A wolf without teeth, a bear without claws.
"But my people know the dragonship
"Has magic powers which can help
"Or harm us. Yes, you can harness it for war
"Against our hated enemies, the Azarapo,
"But it can also carry you away from here
"Swifter than a swallow heading south.
"Sleep easy. Your ship is safe with us.
"Warriors guard it now and always will.
"But you will not use it until we are ready.
"The dragonship gave us Olaf Blodason
"But the dragonship also led him away.
"We have waited far too long for you,
"For you to drink the wind again so soon.
"Your arrival was long foretold.
"For us, Sushone, it is good news.
"For Azarapo it is bad, black news.
"But you will leave only when you
"Have completed the work begun by
"Our heroic ancestor, Olaf Blodason."

As the feast rolled on in a fog
Of smoke, sweat and stew steam,
Charmadu filled in the holes
In Seenaho's skeleton story.
"My brother," she told Asgeir softly,
"Is our best warrior. Just see his feathers.
"When he fights, he wins. Never,
"Never has he tasted defeat.
"But we Sushone are few, too few.
"The Azarapo are many, too many.

"We know you and your long knives
"Can do what Olaf Blodason did:
"Make our few the many
"So Seenaho can raid
"Whenever he wants
"And free him from being forced
"To pick his battles with care."

Like all the best Winter feasts,
These days of deer led to a thaw
In the cold tensions between
Captive guests and captor hosts.
In time, painted warriors and
The spear-band began to mingle
Like dogs sniffing a rival,
Ready to be friends,
But always ready to spring away
And snarl at the least threat.
One big native approached
Tubby old Oddo the Hairy
And touched his bald head,
All the while his brown eyes
Locked on the Viking's blue jewels.
He uttered a guttural question
And called for Charmadu to speak
Like a yellow hair once more,
"This," she relayed, "is Running Deer.
"He wants to know who scalped you."
Oddo felt his head and laughed.
"Tell him I've been scalped by
"Hard living and the ravages of old age.
"No man has taken my hair, only time."
Running Deer then stroked Oddo's
Silver arm rings and spoke in a
Voice deeper than a beer barrel
Before asking a question with his eyes.

Warriors understand warriors,
Without words passing between them.
Battle and bravery forge a bond
Beyond the sword-shy and women.
Oddo nodded and touched each ring in turn.
"This," he told Running Deer, "was for
"Slaughtering the Lapps, this for
"Saving my Lord, Sigi Singgison, from
"A great white bear on Svalbard,
"And this," he gap-toothed grinned,
Caressing a thick iron ring,
Marked with Thor's Hammer, Mjollnir,
"Was for being first over the walls
"Into the bastion of the Bulgars.
"Each ring was won with the blood
"Of the battle-hungry. They battled -
"But I was always hungrier."
As Charmadu's gentle tones
Told of far-flung heroics,
Oddo looked Running Deer in the eyes
And felt the white eagle feathers
Perching proudly on his raven hair.
Running Deer, his eyes fixed on Oddo,
Spoke through Charmadu, his voice
Like gravel under her mountain stream.
"This I won for a raid on the Azarapo
"Where I killed several warriors
"And captured many women who
"Gave us much sport for months.
"This feather I won in an ambush
"In a blizzard five winters back,
"And this for a walk in the woods
"With Hackasu when he killed
"A big black bear with claws
"As long as Viking knives and
"Teeth like the yellow fangs

"Of the dragons of Thunder Falls.
"Barely men, but we stood firm.
"Hackasu still bears the scars
"Across his face, proof he did not run.
"We killed the bear with tomahawks,"
Here he brandished his hatchet,
"Knives and animal strength,
"And brought back the biggest scalp
"We have ever claimed. It warms
"His tent still, a pelt of power."

But Running Deer still had questions,
Touching the tattoos on Oddo's face
And pointing to the soot-sketches
Decorating Viking arms and faces.
Oddo replied by pointing to the
Red, yellow and black paint
On the hairless faces of the Sushone,
Every man sporting a different pattern,
One brave with a blackened face,
One with rising red and black stripes
And another a black mask spotted red.
Yellow-Hair and Black-Hair alike
Were painted for battle and bore
The proof of past heroics and
Future valour for all to see.

But to Stormmaster's starving crew
Other longhouse dwellers held more appeal.
Six weeks at sea builds a man's appetite
And even the well fed would have lusted
After the pretty Black-Haired girls
Who kept casting cautious glances
At the newly arrived sword-strong.
Viking men take what they want
When they want it and women,

Foreign women, are theirs for the taking.
But Asgeir cracked his whip
To keep his wolf pack from biting.
Tactfully, far from Charmadu,
He told each man in turn:
"Leave the girls until Seenaho
"Unleashes you with gift-words.
"Seize a woman without permission
"And we will all perish for your lust.
"Flirting is fine. But there will be
"Women aplenty when we raid
"Grim and his Azarapo gang and
"Gain our freedom and our gold."

But weeks of ice spray and staring
Night and day at bearded brothers
Can feed a lust stronger than fear.
And as weeks of winter boredom
Tightened their relentless grip
Radnald Rogarsson soon did
What battle-Vikings do so well.
He grabbed a raven-haired vixen
As beguiling as a Valkyrie
Whose smiles promised warmth
After weeks of bone-numbing chill.
But Radnald never could read the runes
Never mind the wiles of women.
Put him in a shieldwall and
His spear skills were deadly.
Put him with a woman
And his spear skills were laggardly.
And so, the screams rang out from
A murky corner of the longhouse,
Breaking the brotherhood like an arrow
Shattering a stained-glass window
In a wealthy Saxon monastery.

Warriors with feathers or arm rings
Raced over and found Radnald's white arse
Pumping faster than a blacksmith's hammer,
Powered by the shrillness of the shrieks.
Radnald kept pumping even when
Scar-faced Hackasu dragged him
By the scruff of his hairy neck as if
He was a dog humping Sven's table leg.
Yellow-Hairs reached for swords and axes,
Black-Hairs for hatchets and knives.
Friends seconds earlier squared up
For war as quickly as the beer-filled
In a Trondelag shipside tavern.
Asgeir jumped between the blood-seekers
Unarmed but for bulging arm rings.
Calling for Charmadu, he shouted:
"We will deal with this dog."
But as women fussed and spat and
Radnald Rogarsson tried to fight
Hackasu and his boiling warband,
Leggings still round his ankles,
Seenaho too stepped in.
His bear growl needed no-one
To translate for the Norsemen.
Charmadu's birdsong could not
Soften this chief's verdict.
Radnald Rogarsson was the Sushone's
To punish as they pleased.
Learn from this, all you Vikings.
Defy your lord, defy his orders,
And one reward surely awaits: death.

Chapter 14

As one, Asgeir's warband looked to him
For the order to wield axe and sword
But the fearless were few
And the fearsome were many
And all knew Radnald Rogarsson
Had flouted the orders of Asgeir.
Asgeir shook his head in anger
And, as he sheathed Deathbringer,
So, the long-bearded cloaked their fangs.
While Charmadu plotted with Seenaho,
Asgeir huddled with his wolves.
"I warned you all to wait for women.
"This spearman may pay with his life
"For letting lust lead his loins.
"But Radnald is one of own and
"We will save him whatever the price.
"There's more than one way to
"Spring a spearman from a cesspit
"Of his own carnal creation."

As the sword-sheathed Vikings glowered in the gloom
White-feathered chief and followers strode over.
Seenaho growled through gritted teeth;
His sister hissed his hatred in Norse.
"This dog grabbed the first-born
"Of the brave who rescued you
"From the scalp-blades of the Azarapo.
"Hackasu wants his scalp and his liver

"To be fed to our dogs while he watches.
"But we have waited a long time for you.
"We also know only one of you
"Has mocked our tribe's great kindness.
"The rest of you remain our guests but,"
Seenaho paused to spit in the fire,
A fizzle of steam amid the smoke,
"This rape-rat must run the gauntlet
"Of our warriors as the women watch.
"The war braves are ready,
"Their hatchets are ready,
"Hackasu's daughter is ready,
"And if this rat lives or dies
"Is down to the spirits and his own speed."

Radnald Rogarrson was stripped naked
And two white-feathered warriors,
Tied his hands behind his back and
Dragged him out into the snow,
His bare feet sliding in the slush,
His fast breaths clouding the clearing
As he scanned in vain for an escape.
Before him bridled two vengeful rows
Of no less than thirty war-painted warriors
Wielding their weapons of death,
Faces warped with hatred and harm,
Ravening with animal blood lust.
Now Asgeir gave Mary a nod
And made his lonely way,
Head held high like a true Viking,
To Seenaho, death's dispenser,
Who had Charmadu by his side.
"We came here in peace, cast by
"The nine winds into your world,"
Said Asgeir, gravely, but calmly,
Speaking slowly so Charmadu

Could easily follow his plea.
"Our foe is a stranger to these forests.
"He has joined forces with your foe,
"Insinuating his influence like a serpent.
"That makes your enemy our enemy.
"We look forward to feasting with you
"On Azarapo scalps and slave girls.
"Our Radnald has done wrong, we know.
"He defied my command and must pay.
"But he remains one of us and
"We never forget our friends.
"So, remember: your foe is my foe
"But now Radnald is your foe.
"So, what will that make you?"

Seenaho's face was still as stone.
He stared deep into Asgeir's eyes,
As he raised a scalp stick and
Without a glance to the living dead
Cast it into the snow where it quivered
Like a spear in the back of a Saxon.
But like Grim before him
Seenaho had failed to see
That Asgeir was as wily as a fox.
All the while he had been talking
Mary had been working her magic,
Rubbing her necklace bone and
Whispering words of solace to the doomed.
"Radnald," she smiled, "stand tall,
"Die like a Viking and you will live on."
Radnald Rogarsson stiffened his sinews
And when the scalp stick speared the snow
His muscles bulged and he snapped
Free of the ropes around his wrist,
Raised his fists to the snow-grey sky
And roared as he ignored the path

Of death between the baying Black Hairs.
Like a battle berserker he foamed as
He battered the first in line with his fists
And grabbed his hatchet and club and
Smashed his skull into a scarlet torrent.
There were too many braves even for a berserker
And as the two lines circled in a worry of whoops
Mary caressed her charm and cast dust skywards.
Radnald had done his bit. Now she did hers.
The war-painted turned white with terror
As their victim transformed before their eyes
Into a snarling snow bear, all teeth and claws,
As tall as a witch hazel, malice on two legs.
Warriors who would charge without thought
Into the wounding arrows of the Azarapo
Were plunged into blind panic
By the shape-shifter,
By the big Arctic bear,
By claws like daggers,
By death-dripping teeth,
White fur as pristine as day-old snow,
And arms as powerful as Odin's oarsmen's.
One sweep of his left arm flung
Five wailers into a fir,
Burying them all in falling snow,
Another hurled a hatchetman
Bouncing into the boughs,
And the bear's roar of rage
Sent the rest fleeing into the forest.

Only Seenaho, Hackasu and Charmadu stood their ground
But even Seenaho's granite face began to crack
Before the power of the Yellow-Hairs' spells.
Asgeir chose his moment well and moved forward.
Quietly, calmly, he put them under his command.
"We can fight each other or fight together.

"Call off your men and I will call off
"The mighty snow bear of Svalbard.
"We will cure this mutt of his lust.
"And then we will slaughter the Azarapo
"And we will bring Grim to the destiny
"Decreed by the Norns of Norway –
"To the evil agonies of the Blood-Eagle."

Seenaho and Hackasu spoke without words
And a shout from the chief brought the bear
Back to earth. As Radnald slavered
And Mary handed him his trousers
Drums drew back the warriors,
White feathers wilting and hatchets
Held less tightly than when Radnald
Had seemed a lamb to the slaughter.
Asgeir gave Deathbringer life as
His men drew their own blood-letters.
"With you we have no quarrel,"
He breathed through his blood-sister,
"But remember: we are your brothers,
"We are not war's blood booty.
"We will lead your raid on the Azarapo
"But we will lead it our way.
"And first Radnald the rapist will
"Pay the price for his sins – our way."
Radnald, still panting hard, stepped forward.
Asgeir surveyed the silver rings
On the Spearman's arms, spoils
Of raids and rampages, loyalty rewards
Hard won from Ireland to Izmir,
And stripped him publicly of every one.
"These," declared Asgeir, "are to Vikings
"As priceless as your eagle's feathers,
"Hard-won and proudly worn honour badges.
"But defy me and all your daring

"Will vanish like the summer sun
"When the first snow falls.
"Radnald must now start again.
"He is worth no more to me in battle
"Than a woman with a whining baby
"Until he proves his name again.
"And all of you, learn this lesson:
"Let me down and all the white feathers
"From a sky full of eagles won't save you
"From my unforgiving pitiless wrath."

He let his words sink in for the Sushone
And then cracked his warlord's whip again.
"I tire of feasting, I frown on lazing
"Before the spitting fire. That is women's work.
"These are the last nights the Azarapo will know.
"Soon we will feed our fame.
"Steaming scalps will be your prize.
"Grim's greedy hide will be ours."
A murmur arose, as Black Hairs
Pointed to the woods' white cloak.
Asgeir laughed and spat into winter's fleece.
He said: "Snow makes slaves of man
"But Vikings make slaves of snow.
"Snow is the Sushone's captor
"But snow is the Vikings' wings."

Chapter 15

Buoyed by the prospect of booty
Stormmaster's axemen prepared for war.
Sushone watched them sharpen swords,
Shaft-check arrows and bend their bows,
Before Hrolf Hardheart and Ketil Killfast
Led Mary and a small band into the forest,
Returning much later laden with wood,
Pine it was, a welcome scent of home,
Plus, soothed by Mary's soft spells,
Ten snorting stags, a sound of home.
Each man knew just what to do
To wreak Viking vengeance on
The lodge-lazing, venison-bloated Azarapo
And Grim gloating over his gold.
Asgeir signalled Seenaho and Hackasu
To alert their war tribe. "We attack as
"The first sunrays rise over the Azarapo."
Unsmiling, Seenaho gestured westwards.
"They are two days distant," he said.
"Not to us," smiled the Dragontamer.
"You are snow's slave. We are snow's master."
He looked to the sky, to a white-headed eagle
Wheeling slowly over the spellbound.
Some Black Hairs pulled bowstrings taut,
Bracing arrows at badges of future glory.
Asgeir swiftly stayed them with a wave
And pointed to dust streaking the snow,
All that was left of the shape-shifter.

"Even now Mary is watching their warriors,"
He said. "We will know where they are
"Long before Hackasu hews his first scalp,
"Long before the wolfmen hear
"The howling of my wolf pack.
"Ready yourselves. We leave when
"The yellow moon lights the way to glory."

Black Hairs looked to the Yellow Hair
Who, face set firm, lit the fire
Of their first ever Viking raid
With one wave of his scalp stick.

Unnoticed, from the highest pine
Snow tumbled, a muffled fall,
Making way for two other watchers,
Two worldly-wise, jet-black ravens.

As the mid-winter sun waned
The sound of sawing filled the forest,
The scent of sawdust wafting over.
When moonshadows cast their stains
Hrolf Hardheart, Ketil Killfast and Broddi the Bloody
Emerged to gasps as they glided over the snow
Like snakes sliding after unsuspecting prey,
Their feet as long as they were tall
Thanks to supple skis bound by sinews.
But then Radnald Rogarsson made
Warriors whoop and drop to their knees
As he led out five dancing teams of stags
Each towing a long sleigh, crude, for sure,
But swift as a seal surging through the surf.
"Climb in," roared Asgeir, guiding Seenaho
And his headmen to the lead sleigh.
"Tonight, you will fly like an eagle
"And return white with its feathers."

As suspicious Sushone edged aboard,
Weapons jostling with warriors for space,
Asgeir gazed skywards to Mary wheeling above.
She swooped down to snow-laden tree tops to
Lead the way, pointing to paths through
Moonlit forests of shadow and murder.

Stags and skiers raced as one
Sliding trails through the snow,
Shrugging off icy showers
Brushed from branches on the way.
Silver plumes flew from noses and mouths.
And Sushone soon embraced the magic
As war-lust put awe to the sword.

By the frozen lake, in the torment of middle-night,
Stormmaster's guards also felt Mary's magic.
For weeks the sea stallion had been stabled
Beside the wind-flayed ice.
But tonight, like an old war-horse,
She bucked and bayed, tugged and tore,
Straining at the leather leashes
Lashing her to a larch tree mooring.
She sniffed battle, and as a breeze rose
She creaked and cracked, rocked and rolled
And broke free of her thongs, her ice bear lungs
Swelling like the belly of a tupped ewe.
She reared up in salute and rode the ice
As swiftly as Hrolf and Ketil skimmed the snow.
Black Hairs, eyes wide in witch-wonder,
Gripped longship-shields as she plunged them
Ever westwards past muffled, sleeping shores,
The blue ice cracking to reveal iron-grey water
Shielded from the sleeping sun for months.

As the birth of day heralded
The haunting death of men,
As the light hovered between
Half-moon and winter-weak sun,
The snow-fliers glided
To the fir-fringe of a clearing
Fashioned for killing by Odin
And the wilful woodland spirits
Worshipped blindly by Yellow
and warlike Black Hair alike.

War is men's work, whether in the
Viking world or among the savages.
But Mary, wheeling overhead, was not
The only woman with the war band.
Charmadu stood in the lead sleigh
With Asgeir and Seenaho either side,
A gentle bond between the brave.
In the near distance a dog cried
As another snaffled its bone
Unaware that it would soon
Drool at its best meal of winter,
Scraps from the raven's table.

Chapter 16

In the half-light Asgeir hurried
His loot-lovers into position,
Fanning them out around a village
Of huts beside a long central house.
But Seenaho and Hackasu and the
Rest of the Black Hairs held firm.
A mumble, light as a spring breeze,
And the bond between the brave
Whispered a warning into Asgeir's ear.
"We don't attack at night," proffered Charmadu
"It offends the forest spirits."
Asgeir blinked in disbelief.
"We're fucking Vikings seeking vengeance,"
He growled, battle foam flecking his beard,
"We attack when we want.
"To wait when our enemy sleeps
"Is how to offend our forest spirits.
"Tell your braves to block all paths
"So you trap the Azarapo here.
"We fight now. As soon as the sun rises
"You can follow and scalp what is left."

Then he melted into the frozen forest
To join his band of long beards
In what they did best: bloodletting.
It was as simple as monk-baiting
But with better booty before them.
The Azarapo slept, their guards slitted

As they snoozed, throat blood staining the snow,
Leaving the lakeside long house
And its feast-fillers at Asgeir's mercy.
Ketil Killfast, Hrolf Hardheart and Broddi the Bloody
Needed no orders from Asgeir.
They just did what they had done
So many, bloody, times before.

They barricaded the doors, grabbed
Blazing brands from the wolf-fire outside
And fed the straw roof with flames,
Making it hiss like a snake and
Sing like a skerry siren
And dance like one of Hel's berserkers.
The booty brothers waited to whet their weapons
When Azarapo and Viking could take
The searing, suffocating heat no more
And raced out into their razor embrace.
But as they salivated like circling wolves
The long house blazed and crumbled
In silence. No wails from women,
No coughing, no screams for mercy,
No outfleeing of the desperate,
Preferring the sword to the flame,
And, as the walls fell in with a crash,
No charred bodies littered the floor.
Nothing. Just the pyre-roar of the fire
Laughing at the scalp-collectors.

And then the drums began
Their beat of oblivion.
A choir of whoops revealed
The circlers were the encircled.
Stormmaster's oarsmen wheeled
To face a furious animal mob
Of wolfmen, deer devils, and worse still,

Bears with hatchets, battle frenzy wielded.
Asgeir, face streaked with smoke, barked
The only command left him: "Shieldwall, now."
And the Vikings became a human hedgehog,
Bristling spears and soaking up arrows
And spitting death to any war-painted
Warrior who carelessly got too close.
Over the whooping came a familiar
Malicious laugh, as Grim gloated
From the protected heart of the Azarapo.
He flaunted Shieldsplitter, the sword he stole
From Egil the Skinny's dragonship of death,
And taunted his old crew, his slaves and raiders,
His grizzled face lit by the blaze behind them.
"Can you hear the wolves?" he sneered.
"They're singing for their supper.
"Savour your last sorry breaths.
"Your scalps will soon be mine.
"Before the sun touches the treetops
"The starving long fangs will flock
"From the forest to fight
"Over your flesh-fat bones."

Asgeir glanced around, praying to the Norns
To release the sun from its icy slumber,
So Seenaho could charge with his gods' grace.
Stormmaster's oar-drivers edged ever backwards
Towards the shelving shore where
Grim's Waverider and hope waited.
A fizz, a thud, a groan, and Thorbjorn Borrason
Slumped bleeding onto the trampled snow
An eagle-feathered ash stinging his ankle.
He snapped the shaft and grabbed his spear
And limped back to his place in the shieldwall.
The wolfmen were circling ever closer
Drooling with delight as their prey huddled

In a last stand of hopeless, godless defiance.
And the drums beat out their alien menace.

But as the sun refused to rise
Mary mewed overhead, a wild cry
Of moors and fells missed by the Azarapo
In their battle mist complacency.
Wolfmen and stag-warriors, bear braves and
Dog soldiers were closing in for the kill
So why would they heed an eagle calling?
But a wise warrior always listens to the wild and,
To the surrounded, the eagle's shrill call
Was the Aesir's sweet song of salvation.
The wood-spirits speak through the birds
Or else why would Odin send Hugin and Munin,
His raven rovers, to spy for him every day?
And so, as Azarapo licked their lips,
And dreamed of new yellow scalps
They learned that a Viking longship
Is tied together by an eternal bond.

On the far fringe of the siege
A Black Hair head flew through the gloom.
His comrade turned in time to see
An axe slice through his knees
While another wolf-warrior slipped silently
As the log-axe split his skull.
On the opposite side of the copse
The snow was coloured claret as if a
Sack of Frankish red had burst.
Azarapo braves began to scream
At a transparent spectral Viking,
Right eye arrow-pierced,
Left leg arrow-raked,
Slashing through their thinning ranks,
And opposite a stocky see-through warrior

Wielding an axe like a berserker
In pre-battle shieldwall blood taunts.
This hellish warrior, too, was light as air
But packed a punch like a stallion kick
Even as Azarapo arrows sailed straight through him.
Worse, this death-dealing avenger had no head.
Asgeir's ship-host cheered and began chanting
"Padraic, Padraic, Padraic" while others
Hailed the half-return from the dead
Of Valmar the Vain and his sword, Victorious.
But the time for celebration would come later
So the Dragontamer marshalled his men
Just as the clearing shook with the roar
Of a sea-stallion crashing onto the
Sandy shore, sending shingle skywards.
Just then the first sunrays kissed Asgeir
And the sky began to rain arrows on the
Panicking Azarapo. Stormmaster had arrived.
She had scented battle and now unleashed
Her Sushone guards on their sworn enemies.
Lust for battle glory had overcome
Their ghoul terror of riding a ghost ship.
As carnage cries keened over the land
A shadowy soul scrambled through
The forest edge, flitting in and out
Of tree and snow, dark and light.
In the corner of Asgeir's eyes
A sudden bustling signalled trouble,
As Waverider's sails swelled to remind
Asgeir's loot followers why they were there.
The Blood-Eagle flapped its wings,
Embracing the ice-lake's breath,
Just as Grim was hauled aboard
By his Viking crew who had hidden
Like harlots from the fighting as if
Hedging their bets on who would win.

Now the dice had been thrown and
They were on the run again
Trusting wind and weight to let
Waverider break free from her frozen prison.
With a roar of shattering ice Waverider
Snorted clear and splintered westwards
Powered by sails billowing in the breeze –
Just as Seenaho and Hackasu whooped
Into the war, too little too late,
But they were happy – they appeared
In plenty of time for the pleasures of scalping.
Asgeir and his steadfast were no strangers
To the mercy-stripping horrors of battle rage,
The blind lust for blood,
The red mist of the murderous,
That makes men more savage than wolves,
But never had they seen such love of slaughter,
Not even in the byres before midwinter's feast.
Vikings, you may boast of your brutality
But the Sushone made you seem like monks.
Within minutes the clearing was a steaming mess
Of blood and bones, screams and laughter,
As Sushone took long-yearned revenge for years
Of raids and rape and taunts and torture.
But scalping the dead did not suffice.
Better, much better, to scalp the living
And let them live in skull-scraped agony,
To bald-bear for ever the shame-scar
Of loss, surrender and slavery.

At this stage, Sven's men got edgy
And Wersil, normally so stony-faced,
Flickered a grim smile, or did he?
Well, only Snorri noticed, but then
Only Snorri was remotely sober.
He was word-weaving his spell,

He and Sven's strong winter ale.
But then that is what skalds do.
Words' magic can only work so far.
Men must be in the mood to hear
And that night they wanted more,
More of everything: women, wine and,
Above all, Asgeir's blood-eagle.
Even the cattle lowed and the sheep bleated
From the back, in saga tension anticipation.

Snorri smiled and felt safe – for now.
The noose around his neck
No longer chafed his skin.
Eyes narrowed, he scanned his audience
And treated them to more tales from the woods.

Amid the blood fountains, Hrolf Hardheart
And the rest pressed Asgeir to pursue
Grim the Greedy before he escaped.
But Asgeir reined in the gore-thirsty.
"Grim cannot get far," he reasoned,
"And if we pursue him, we risk a fight
"On ice whose thickness we cannot trust.
"He is trapped with nowhere to go,
"No food, no friends, no local knowledge,
"And will leave a trail through the ice
"Even a blind beggar could follow.
"No, Hrolf, take some men and bring
"Stormmaster back to our hosts.
"Tonight, we will have prisoners,
"Pretty prisoners, ripe for plucking,
"Your well-earned reward for cheating Hel
"And routing Grim's painted protectors.
"Strangers should always be warned:
"Wherever that man wanders,
"He means misery to all who help him."

Hrolf led a small band to Stormmaster
And honoured it with its own badges of battle:
A dripping scalp hung from the
Top of the mast and painted Azarapo
Shields lined either side of the prow.
Other Vikings spread out, looking for loot,
Among them Radnald the Ringless.
His hopes of ring-redeeming valour
Had vanished in the huddle of the shieldwall
So now he scavenged for tawdry trophies or,
Better still, women to warm the winter day.
He passed Hackasu, kneeling, hand round
A shock of black hair, bloodied knife
Ready to slice it from its screaming skull.
But, even when badly beaten, Azarapo men
Remain worthy foes, glory-lusters all.
One wounded warrior had one last wish:
To take one more Sushone with him
To wherever his Valhalla lay.
Heaving himself onto an elbow,
He aimed his hatchet, right-handed,
Right at Hackasu's warlike head.
Radnald spotted the assassin and,
As the Azarapo drew his hand back
And Charmadu screamed a warning,
Radnald skewered him with his spear.
Hackasu, scalp in hand, bowed grimly
To the violator of his beloved daughter.
But Radnald then scalped his prey
And handed the trophy to Hackasu.
The word sorry was a stranger to Radnald,
In Norse or any tongue the Sushone favoured,
But sometimes actions say more, much more,
Than cheap and easy apologies.
Hackasu refused the Viking's scalp,
But then held out a red-gloved hand

To Radnald's own red-gloved hand
And streaked two bloody fingers across
The Viking's cheeks. Two men, two marks.
Warpaint is never stronger than when made
From the blood of beaten enemies.
And it is never better than when
Bestowed by a brother in battle.

Chapter 17

Curs barked a hero's welcome
As scalp-rich warriors swaggered
Through the yellowing light into the
Sushone village. Moccasined
Women whooped in triumph and terror
As they ran to greet their hatchet horde,
Scanning the line of braves to see
If their man had returned in glory
Or fallen in a Hel of Azarapo gore.
Some women crumpled liked dried leaves
On learning of their loss but recovered
On learning of courage to the end.
Pity any prisoner put in their hands.
But the Sushone had lost only a handful,
Far fewer than the waiting women had feared,
And the head-bowed harvest of Azarapo,
Hands tied behind their backs,
Many bleeding raw wounds where
Hours earlier had been their scalp,
Showed that the blood balance was
Firmly in Seenaho's favour, proof
Of a victory to warm many a winter night.
But warriors and Vikings alike
Had eyes on another prize,
One to warm this winter night -
Azarapo women, dragged from the woods
Where they had cowered in vain.
After weeks at sea, with only salt-spray

And the sweaty-bearded as company,
Asgeir's oar-gang salivated.
Well, every warrior knows that battle
Spawns a blood lust which in victory
Sires another more pleasurable lust.

Sven's wolves barked approval as one.
Veterans of blood-slaking from Cork to Kiev,
They knew well the power of battle lust,
The ultimate sealing of victory,
Beauty blessing bravery,
Booty crowning the victor,
Ravaging salving the savage,
All amid the elation of surviving
To wield valour-axe and sword again,
The Valkyries having flown away and
The fickle Norns still spinning on their side.

Snorri smiled, slyly, knowingly, cunningly.
He knew Sven's wolves better than Sven.
The old fox could lead his looters anywhere,
With roared orders, ring-gifts and rejection-dread.
In the face of such might Snorri was unarmed
Save for a mightier weapon; his word magic.
And so, he went on and wove his spell,
Leading the blood-lusting to heaven and Hel,
Heaven for them, Hel for the Azarapo.

Another sip, another cough, and Snorri continued.
Drums beat, fires crackled, warriors whooped
And the shadows of the flames showed
The ghost-mates of braves dancing around
The living dead huddled in the grave-cold snow,
The vanquished awaiting their own Valhalla.
But the defeated need not have feared the cold.
Sushone women were collecting kindling,

Large bundles of brambles, bone-dry bushes
And branches which broke like Saxon shins,
Piling them around posts sunk in the ground.
Azarapo, man-kindling, watched ghoul-eyed,
Lost in their own terminal trances,
Manifesting no fear of the fire ahead.
Hackasu grunted and his hatchet heroes
Grabbed the beaten by their arms and hair,
If they had any left to cloak their crowns,
And leather-strapped them, three
To each pole that towered above them
Like a giant rune stone of death.

There they stood, chafing at their thongs,
As their women were all handed over
To Stormmaster's sea-weary and
Vengeance-craving Sushone bucks –
And ravished right before them.

Another roar erupted from Sven's pack.
A burly redhead, lust for brains, shouted:
"I want to join the Sushone", and
His warband laughed and clapped,
Remembering those long hot nights
After taking the tower of Novgorod.

Snorri grinned, but declined to detail
The depravity, shocking even for a Viking.
He also knew he could not better
The fevered fantasies of Sven's raiders.
So, he let them savour the sordid,
Called for another ale, and watched
The saga-greedy fools lower their guard.

Asgeir and his men, said Snorri, were heroes,
And in front of the fire-fodder were given

Eagles' feathers, one for each Azarapo slain.
There were so many slaughtered that
The Sushone ran out of the flight wands
So they stole them from the fire fuel,
Stripping Azarapo of battle honours
Won on the back of Sushone blood.

The shrill, cruel jeers of Sushone wives,
Mothers, lovers and blade-waving children
Grew like a forest fire, feeding on itself,
And the dreadful beat of the death drums
Sped up, just like the heart beats of
The waiting Azarapo who would now reveal
Whether they merited the title of "braves".

Snorri paused and looked at the hypnotised
As the longhouse thrilled to the eager drumming.
You, he grimaced, are warriors of renown,
From Greenland to Gotland, from the
Sea-like steppes to the snows of Svalbard,
Wherever there are Vikings,
Wherever there is wine and ale,
We sing of your slaughters,
Your ring-rich raids,
Your bravery, your valour,
And your brutality in battle.
But I hesitate to tell even you of
The heart-ripping horrors, the liver-licking
Foe-flaying witnessed by Stormmaster's bravest.
At this Sven's men bayed for blood like
A pack of wolfhounds on Fenrir's trail.
But Snorri held up a hand and shook his head.
I could not tell you of the brave sliced
Ten-score times by Hackasu's victory knife
And who, as the sun rose over the clearing,
Still breathed though he could no longer

Tell night from day, moon from sun,
No, you would not thank me for that,
Or for the brave riddled with flint heads
From shoulder to shins, bows loosened
From just twenty paces but without delivering
The desperately yearned for death blow,
No, that would be too bloody even for
Veterans of the rape of Visby,
Or the brave debased by women
Who had lost their men and who
Made sure he was no longer a man either.
No, Snorri smiled, as the beer-swillers
Grinned and gurned and begged for gore,
It would be too grim, much too grim, for you.
Well, my warriors, this orgy of torture,
The battle price of defeat and
The battle prize of victory
Lasted two days and two nights
And never once did the Azarapo
Cry out or quail, dying warrior's deaths,
The price of a place in their Valhalla,
Much like Odin's demanding feasting fee.

The Sushone worked their way slowly
From prisoner to prisoner, taking their time,
Until they came to the unluckiest Azarapo,
The great chief they called Vee Ma Gog.
For this scourge of the Sushone
They had reserved a special torment
To be served up after making him watch
His men be cut to pieces one by one
And left hanging limply from the poles
Awaiting the release of the fire faggots.
Women ran white hot spear tips
Across his chest, arms and legs,
As sparks flirted with the kindling mound.

Vee Ma Gog, which means,
Simply, "Bear who Brings Death",
Bridled, teeth gritted, at his goaders.
A heart-stopping roar cut through the clearing
As Hackasu and his men prodded a bear,
As big as two men and much deadlier,
Not black or brown, but pale, sandy coloured,
Out of a cage littered with skeletons,
Controlling it with a wooden neck ring
And five long pine poles like a star.
A path opened through the tribe
And the bound and beaten
Bear who Brings Death
Stood face to face with
Another bound and beaten
Bear who brings death which
Drooled his blood hunger
At the dinner on a stick
Stretched out before him.
Poked and pulled, the shaggy tawny beast
Was in a spittle-spattered fang-frenzy,
Roaring with fury, clawing at the chief's face,
But was skilfully kept just out of reach,
So Vee Ma Gog felt the swish of every swipe.
Slowly Hackasu edged the bear in range
And with each claw slash he carved deep
Into the chief's chest, legs and face.
His brown skin held for some seconds
And then the white weals wept blood
Until his body was a sea of sticky red.
Vee Ma Gog knew a bear bite would be
Swifter than the suffocating agony
Of death by greenwood inferno
So, he spat defiance into the bear's face
And taunted Hackasu, whose cheeks
Carried the scars of his own bear battle.

Asgeir had no idea what he said but
Hackasu's bark was a clear command
Which saw his men let slip the bear
Which thrust its claws to the steel sky,
Tried to swipe away its star collar
And roared a fetid message of death
Full into Vee Ma Gog's stolid face.
He showed no fear, his barrel chest still,
And he stared back into the bear's eyes.
The two stood like warriors eyeballing eternity
Before the ordeal of single combat.
The watching death-lovers fell silent as
Vee Ma Gog whispered a few words
And the shaggy-coated blinked first,
Turned and rolled away on all fours,
Lush winter fur flowing with every step,
Star poles snapping as it crashed
And snarled through the snow forest.
Asgeir had seen enough. "Charmadu,"
He said, "I want him for my warband.
"His bravery has bought his freedom.
"It is my fee for this great victory.
"Tell him he can cheat the flames
"If he comes to join the Vikings."

Hackasu scowled hawk-like at such mercy,
Offered to his most reviled enemy,
A man with more longhouse scalps
Than even Seenaho had hanging
From his sacred scalp stick, well,
Until this day of gore and glory.
But Seenaho too had seen the grit
And warrior-worthy fortitude of his foe.
Vee Ma Gog had defied death,
Sneered at searing knife slashes
And even with his hands tied

Had seen off a blood-lusting bear,
A bear woken from winter's sleep.
Was it better to fry such a foe,
To put his toughness to the torch,
Or reward his warrior's death with his life,
Making him a Viking marauder but
Risking him returning for revenge?
But Seenaho knew well another truth:
Without Asgeir's men and their magic
The Sushone would be living for ever in fear.
Instead their formidable foe was now broken
And its braves were soon to be burned.
So, with a nod he harnessed his hatred
And agreed to pay Asgeir's blood price.
As Sushone watched in open horror
And half-dead Azarapo strained to see
A last drama before their deaths,
Seenaho marched up to his arch-enemy
And, as Asgeir learned later,
Told him coldly in halting Azarapo:
"You, Vee Ma Gog the bastard, have brought
"Death and destruction to my people
"For far too long, for too many winters.
"We can kill you now, as slowly as we wish,
"Until you scream for mercy like
"Our women mourning their sons scalped
"By your murdering tribe of dogs and bitches.
"You can die with your battle-dogs
"In the fury of the flames
"And feel your flesh melt into fat,
"Your body boil 'til it falls off your bones,
"And no man, no warrior, ever burns
"Without bawling like a new-born baby,
"So your last moments in this world
"Will see you crumble like a coward.
"But you have borne yourself as a brave should

"And our brothers, the bearded yellow hairs,
"Respect your resilience before our vengeance."

Chapter 18

"They want you to join their band.
"You'll be a warrior once more.
"But mark this: repay our mercy
"With revengeful, mindless murder
"And you will learn that fire
"Is your consoling, cooling friend
"Compared to your forest fire fate
"In our unforgiving, flaying hands."
Both men stared unblinking
Into the other's eyes, like dogs
Snarling before a fight in the dirt.
Without averting his gaze, Vee Ma Gog
Curled his lip to growl through the blood.
"And what of my loyal men?" he fumed.
Seenaho licked his lips. "Forget them,"
"They are dead already.
"They cannot come back.
"They fought. They lost.
"They knew the price.
"Now they must pay it.
"The fire will set them free."
Vee Ma Gog roared: "We fight together.
"We die together. Fire the flames.
"I fear no man. I fear no thing.
"And why would I want to join
"The Yellow Hair weasels? I hate them.
"I want to kill them not cling to them.
"Grim's men raped our women,

"Stole our winter food, slaughtered our deer.
"Another day and we would have
"Killed him and his cursed crew.
"But the other Yellow Hairs came
"And Grim and his axe-wielders
"Ran for their lives without a thought
"For their Black Hair blood brothers."
Feeble murmurs rose from the death poles,
The living dead vowing vengeance on
Grim the Greedy, even from the grave.
Seenaho grinned. Now he had him.
"Our Yellow Hair brothers share your hate.
"They have travelled for weeks over waters
"Which can swallow our lakes without
"Coming close to swamping the shore.
"You know they are worthy warriors.
"They have much more reason than you
"To want Grim the Greedy dead.
"They have sailed from another world,
"For one reason only," and his voice rose,
To rally all fighters in the forest,
Victors and vanquished,
"They are here to get Grim."

As one the Azarapo raised their heads
And began singing their death chants,
First one warrior, then another,
Weak at first, but the war losers
Swiftly forged a chorus of fury,
Strengthening with each gut-call:
"Get Grim, Get Grim, Get Grim."
Galvanised, the brave whose bones
Shivered with quiver-fugitives shouted:
"Vee Ma Gog, sacred Vee Ma Gog,
"You are the last of the Azarapo.
"You have led us to scalp-rich victory

"After scalp-rich victory.
"Now we will soon be gone,
"But we will always be with you.
"Lead us to one last glory: Get Grim."

For the first time and the only time
Vee Ma Gog faltered, torn between
A warrior's duty to die with his band,
And his band's demand that he cheat the flames
And fight on alone for them against a foe
More hated than their Sushone tormentors.
Still the death chant filled the forest but
As it slowly faded from the lungs
Of his wilting hatchet horde,
Vee Ma Gog glowered into the eyes of
His long-loathed enemy and nodded.
"Let me down. I want Grim," he said.
And he roared a last message to his men,
In a voice as deep and dark as a dragon's lair:
"My brave brothers, you all die as warriors.
"And know this: You will all rise again
"When I scalp Grim and hang his hide
"From the sacred Azarapo scalp tree.
"All who see it will smile and believe:
"Vee Ma Gog avenged his brothers.
"I am the very last of the Azarapo.
"But I vow to live until the day
"Grim the Greedy is squirming,
"Squealing and shrieking
"Under my scalping knife.
"Farewell my battle brothers.
"You will live for ever in my hatchet.
"You will haunt Grim the Greedy
"Until his blood greases the grass
"And I eat his lardy liver
"Before his lying, piggy face."

With that the Sushone cut him free
And ushered him, his body bathed in red,
To Asgeir and his spear band brothers.
Behind him, in the beat of a heart,
Seenaho calmly torched the chained.

Vee Ma Gog never flinched as the fire crackled,
Men screamed, Sushone jeered and the
Sickly smell of roasting flesh filled the clearing.
He never flinched; but he never looked back either.
His men had all died the day they were caught.
And now he was alive, reborn as a Viking.

Chapter 19

In the time it takes to gut and hang a stag
The Azarapo warriors screamed and melted
Until only blackened bones and grinning skulls
Protruded from death's smoking ash piles,
Leaving their women to the mercy of their
New masters and, worse still, new mistresses.
At sunrise they had been wives of warriors;
Now they were the slaves of the Sushone,
Envious of the village dogs which at least
Were free and fed better, cleaner scraps.
Such is the lot of losers the world over.
Many a Viking would value a raid here.
Gold the Black Hairs have none
But the flesh would fetch a fortune
In slave markets from Dyflin to Hedeby.

Vee Ma Gog sat impassive with Asgeir
Alongside the oar-strong in the long house,
Blanking out the sneers and jeers of his captors.
Asgeir turned to Hrolf Hardheart, Ketil Killfast and
His spear-wielders and nodded at the blood-lust
Of the Sushone, still not sated by the flaying,
The fires or the frenzy of their victory dances.
"We stay for the feast," he said, confidentially,
"And enjoy the fruits of razing the Azarapo.
"But we have business beyond this village
"And if we lodge long with Vee Ma Gog
"It won't be long before they forget

"We are their brothers and burn us too,
"As if we are nothing more than kindling.
"So, enjoy the feast but stand ready
"To strike for Stormmaster's sanctuary."

The Vikings lived up to their legend.
They had already rowed hard,
Sailed hard, and fought hard, and
Now they drank hard, ate hard and fucked hard.
There were two Azarapo women for every man,
And Hackasu was happy to see the Vikings
Humiliate his enemies and defile his foe.
If Valhalla is half as good, half as glorious,
Then no Viking need ever dread death.

But two of Stormmaster's strongmen
Shunned the trophies of their triumph.
Asgeir wanted only to lie with Mary
And Radnald Rogarsson, his cheeks
Still smeared with Hackasu's blood badge,
Had eyes only for his battle partner's daughter,
The girl he had nearly died for days earlier.
Then she had recoiled in revulsion,
But he had returned a hero, and
All knew he had saved Hackasu,
And the bear-scarred scalp-taker
Had blooded him as a brother.
So, with a dry nod from Hackasu,
Radnald wooed his woman with war paint,
His scalps and his white war feathers,
And this time she welcomed him and
Hugged him and kissed him until
Viking and Sushone were as one,
Brought together by war, lust and love.
No grunting here, no grief, no force,
Just caresses freely and fondly given

And repaid with mutual pleasure,
An oasis of peace among the carnage.

As the feast flowered on venison scent
One young Nordic spearman prepared
For the next battle, for the next foe.
Iggy Fjellason, only eighteen winters old,
Sat in a corner and fingered a file,
Paused and then took the plunge,
Shaving his teeth into sharp points,
Turning his smile into a terror grin,
A glimpse of Hel for his enemies.
Never did he flinch as the blood flowed,
Never did he cry as his teeth ached,
But never again would sweet, cold water
Cross his lips and cool his throat.
But why would a sea wolf care?
Dribbling senility lies not in store
For warriors for whom terror is all.

One Viking had a keen reason
To relish returning to the Sushone.
Broddi the Bloody was a thirsty man.
He had had a furious thirst
Since the last of the Icelandic ale
Was supped on a dark Atlantic night,
Replaced by the bitter salt of sea spray.
Broddi was as determined in peace
As he was brutal and driven in battle.
As soon as he arrived in Seenaho's realm
He had set about satisfying his thirst.
From the forest he gathered berries galore,
Berries left by birds and bears and savages,
Spared the frost by forest shelters;
He mashed them all in a big barrel,
Mixed in honey, herbs and magic,

Flinging an amulet in the freshwater sea,
And left all to bubble under an oak lid.
The day before he rode the deer sleigh
To the slaughter in the clearing
He lifted the lid, sipped and pledged:
"If I am denied entry to Valhalla,
"I'll toast our victory on my return."
And so, after sampling the prisoners -
Some things even mead must wait for -
He filled his horn, sipped and savoured,
And smiled with the pure joy of relief,
And thanked Thor for his magic trick
Of turning autumn's fruit into mind bliss.
Sweet red juice stained his beard
And he called out to the crew who
Were soon filling their horns with
The heart-warming water of the woods.
As they became boisterous, reliving
Their heroics, their scalps, their close-shaves,
Seenaho, Hackasu and Charmadu came over
And in turn were offered horns to down.
The tribe watched in awe as the chiefs
Sipped, rolled their eyes, then smiled
As they savoured the sweetness and
Felt the booze's throaty bite back,
And held out their horns for more.
Soon the other warriors were greedily
Dipping gourd cups in the claret and
Whooping with delight at taste and tang.
Lucky for Broddi, lucky for all
That he had made several vats,
Enough to drink for days,
A real winter wassailer's feast,
A real brightener for the dark days.
Broddi the Bloody earned a new name,
Just as battle worthy, just as brave,

But this time no-one had to die.
He just performed his party piece
Picking up a burning firebrand
From the heart of the longhouse.
He lit the brew with the flame
And roared as his horn breathed fire.
He held it aloft while wide-eyed Black Hairs
Whooped at his powers, and gasped
As he galumphed the brew, fire and all,
Tipped the pleasure bringer upside down
To prove he had swallowed the lot
And belched berry-scented smoke
Before bowing like a jester and
Recharging his horn with the red potion.
As Sushone shouted in excitement, Seenaho,
Already red-eyed, told the brewmaster:
"They say you make firewater from the forest
"And the braves call you Broddi the Fire-Eater."
And then he too scooped more battle-balm
And sank it like water from the lake, before
Licking his lips and holding out his horn again.
Charmadu alone held back, handing
Her cup to a warrior after just one taste.
To her it was too sickly, and its strength
Was something new and unnerving.
So she watched as Vikings introduced
Her brothers to nature's soothing mind massage,
But without warning of its skull-splitting price.
How could they? Why should they?
A man who is old enough to fight
Is old enough to drink like a man.
Warriors need no nannies.
Their only wet nurse is the
Horn hanging from their belts.

Viking and Sushone had bonded easily
United by so many similarities
Love of war,
Love of bravery badges,
Love of battle trophies,
Pleasure in punishing prisoners,
Worship of woodland spirits and
A great army of fickle gods,
Defiance of death, pain and fear;
So much they had in common,
But tonight, revealed a difference
Deeper even than their languages
Which remained alien to all but two –
Charmadu and taciturn Seenaho.
After two giddying horns of Broddi's brew
Vikings were just getting going,
Eager for a herd's worth of horns.
The Sushone were going somewhere else,
Their legs wobbly, their arms wild,
And even a foreigner could tell
Their speech was sluggish and slurred.
Four horns and Seenaho was on the floor,
Seenaho the Fearless, Seenaho the Invincible,
Horn spilled, claret trickling in the rushes,
And soon scalpmen, who, hours earlier
Had been formidable in the fight,
Were drooling in the dirt,
Eyes awry, well, for those who
Could still keep their eyes open.

As they fell like winter flies,
Broddi laughed and grinned:
"Ah well, all the more for us."
So the oarsmen upended horn after horn
While young warriors watched the prisoners,
And Charmadu agonised over the collapse of her kin.

She suspected poison but Asgeir and his gang
Had supped from the same vat, and were supping still.
Even Mary was downing draught after draught,
With no more sign of problems than the men,
Apart from florid faces, louder laughter and
A loosening of their lust to match their thirst.
Never had the Sushone drunk such a drink
That made men demand more, more, more
But left some for dead and others still standing.
So, she decided to even the odds and,
While Vikings were laughing at wasted warriors,
She slipped a pale powder into the vat,
Ground from wood-gathered mushrooms
Before winter's fingers shrivelled all they touched.
These mushrooms held magic properties,
The spirit key that unlocked the future
For secret-wise Sushone shamen
And warriors seeking to escape the world
From staggering sunrise to soothing sunset.
And then, spurning another brimful horn,
She watched and waited and smiled,
Well aware of what would come next.

And now Snorri paused and surveyed
The men who hung on his words
Or who would happily hang him.
A sip, a grin and he was off again.

Chapter 20

Asgeir and Mary were racing,
Running through the forest,
Fleeing the flesh-hungry
Two-headed trolls.
On the lovers ran, on, on
The rancid breath
Of the bone breakers
Hot on their hackles,
Even though their hunters
Towered as tall as trees.

And then a tree came to their rescue.
A hollowed out oak older than time
Offered sanctuary for man and woman
But no way in for the inhuman.
In they both dived, Mary clutching
Her chief's hardened sword-hand.
As their eyes embraced the gloom
They noticed roots arrayed like steps
Leading beyond the reach of the ravenous.
And so down they went, down, down
Parting cobwebs with their hands,
Brushing aside thick curtains of moss,
Sliding and tripping on this root and that,
Grabbing crawling creepers for balance
And feeling the chill rising from below.
Four days they descended, drinking water
Nectar-licked from the dripping cave walls.

The troll roars soon receded, but,
Once heard, were never forgotten,
Slowly replaced by sweet singing
Floating above the cold, damp air
Like a boost for the battered.
Four days they slid and slipped
Edging ever closer to the music,
Until the tunnel opened onto
A lake of serene beauty bathed
In a light of burnished bronze.
Starving now, the runaways spotted
A huge clump of mushrooms lit
By golden sunrays reaching through
The filter of swaying evergreens.
Without a word they picked them,
Washed them gently in the water
And then wolfed enough for
Stormmaster's men and more besides.
Dreamlike, they cast off their
Sweat-soaked clothes to bask,
Bare as babies, in the caress
Of the bronze light. Hand in hand
They walked into the water,
Warm as a summer's day,
As thick as a squid's ink
And just as secretive.

Asgeir felt Mary's silken skin
And soft, soothing curves, and
She his angular roughness and
Protecting muscle power.
With a sigh they sank into
The warming pool and swam
For the sheer pleasure of
The freedom water offers.
Little fish nibbled her toes,

Kisses from the welcoming,
And both felt they were flying,
Weightless in the inky black.
By now the bronze sky was purpling,
The songbirds playing above
Were pink and scarlet and crimson
And the sirens' song as soothing
And as light as a long-lost lullaby,
Floating over the lake, mistily,
From the pine island at its heart.

On they swam, though leisurely,
And emerged as one from the water
As if in a shaman's trance to pad
Under sweetly scented boughs,
On a carpet of pine needles,
The sharp made soft through unity.
And there, in a gold-lit clearing,
Were the most beautiful women
The world can ever have seen,
As freely naked as the lovers
And at one with golden nature.
"Welcome," smiled one,
Dark tresses tumbling over
Delicate, decorous shoulders.
"Drink with us and hear our song."
And so, they sat and supped
And savoured the siren serenade.
It was in a tongue unknown,
But no matter: it made perfect sense,
Just like the song of the sea to a sailor,
Or the peals of a nightingale to a skald.
And so, the warrior and his sorceress
Let the waves wash over them
And became one with the woods.

Bears foraged for berries without
Troubling Viking and lover,
Wolves licked their hands
And let them tickle their ears,
Big cats, bigger by far than lynx,
Rubbed tails against their legs,
Purring with pleasure and
Bringing plump rabbits
In the caress of velvet mouths.
The sirens served them,
Gliding over with glasses of
The sweetest mead for Mary,
Scented with heather honey,
Purer and kinder by far than
Broddi's rough-hewn barrels,
And ale of the gods for Asgeir.
This was not Valhalla but for
The lovers it was heaven.
How long the two were cossetted,
How long they cuddled under
The benign smiles of the sirens,
How long the damsels offered
Their favourite food and drink,
No-one will ever know.
But slowly the soothing bronze light
That bathed all in a golden glow
Turned darker, darker and
Gold gave way to crimson,
As red as a wolf's snarling gums,
Smoke rose over the forest,
Billowing over the beautiful
Whose faces sprouted hag's hair
From chins and wrinkling lips.
Under their gap-toothed glares
The lovers felt their nudity,
Felt dirty, felt depraved,

Shivered with shame,
In a stench of rotting fish.
They struck out for the far bank
In a lake as cold as ice
But burning like a bee sting
And boiling with bubbles
As sea beasts surged from
Submarine caves in a roaring rage.
Asgeir and Mary, hair matted
From chill lake and cold sweat,
Scrambled ashore, snow floating down,
Not the pure white gems of Norway,
But flakes of jet, lung-smothering
The forest like volcanic ash,
Like the dark vomit of Vanyajokull,
Death descending from the sky.
The blackening heavens rocked to
A haunting, goading laughter,
Not Stormmaster's merriment,
But the gloating glee of malice.
A wind from the floes of Svalbard
Blew clouds and smoke apart
And high in the Hel-ish sky where
Thor should have stood
Or Odin should have ridden
His magical eight-legged steed,
Was a familiar mean-eyed face,
Salivating with avarice,
And sneering snot bile
On the bare babes below:
"Enjoy the slut-bitch,"
Roared the disembodied head
Of Grim the Greedy,
"But ever remember, fool,
"I fucked her first.
"Pity the Friesian slut has fled.

"She used to enjoy her too."

Asgeir's right hand reached
For gutseeking Deathbringer
But the Dragontamer was truly naked,
No shield, no sword, no axe,
Nothing to fight this force of evil.
"Waverider is mine, from mast to keel,
"The Blood-Eagle banner is mine,
"Shieldsplitter is mine,
"And all the gold is mine,"
Laughed the haul-hoarder
Through the cloud flames.

Grinning like a wolf before a fawn,
He taunted his old spear hand.
"When white becomes green,"
Jeered the whip-wielder,
"And the shaggy walk once more,
"Where lake meets sky
"And meat rains on men,
"By the runestone of he
"Who fought before,
"There you fuckers will find me.
"Seek and chase, chase and seek."

He laughed like an earthquake rumble.
"But your crew will never catch me.
"You will never reclaim the gold.
"Shieldsplitter and all its magic is mine,
"Egil the Skinny is on my side,
"And guards the glittering loot
"For which you have so long lusted.
"Chase and seek, seek and chase,
"And I will always outpace you.
"With Shieldsplitter as my ally,

"I will always outfight you.
"The gold is mine, and
"I'm getting away, away, away…
"Seek and chase, always, chase and seek.
"Enjoy the whore, I fucked her first."

His voice faded, and his evil face
Was swallowed by the fires of Hel,
But lingered like the stench
In an overflowing long drop
After a midwinter meat feast.
Asgeir found himself coughing,
His lungs filling with acrid smoke.
He sat bolt upright, head hurting,
As if split by Deathbringer's blade or
Bludgeoned flat by Broddi's brew,
And through the fug, his eyes focussed
On a scene of carnage, corpses
Littering the floor like broken arrows.
Mary still breathed, her chest rising
And falling in sleep's soothing rhythm.
A nudge from Asgeir and her red eyes opened
On the chaos of the Sushone long house.
Still sitting cross-legged in a corner
Lost in an Odin-like trance was Vee Ma Gog,
While Charmadu's long blonde hair
Glowed like the halos loved by the skirtmen,
But the victors of the clearing were now
The vanquished of Seenaho's longhouse.
Asgeir's eyes began to unblur.
Still standing, sticky, red-stained horns
In loosening red-stained hands, was his warband,
Speech slurred and sluggish slow,
Swaying on widely-spaced legs
As if braced against a sea swell,
But still drinking, still swigging,

And as his ears filtered the hubbub,
He could hear them burbling,
Not the drivelling banter of every day,
But visions of red-fanged dragons,
Ghosts and ghouls,
Wine vats and Valkyries,
Black mountains and murder trolls.
They had sipped the same brew
As Asgeir and Mary and were gripped still
By its magic, trapped in the mayhem
Of their own befuddled mind rambles.

The booze fog began to clear, and
Grim the Greedy's spiteful taunts
Wormed their way into Asgeir's head.
He rose, marched into the middle
Of his crew's midwinter wassail
And abruptly broke the party up,
Knocking Broddi's drinking horn
Out of his juice-stuck, reddened hands.
Broddi reached for his sword,
Forgetting who was his chief,
But no sword was at his side
For his wayward eyes to find.
Hrolf Hardheart, Ketil Killfast and the rest
Were still standing, still speaking,
But their eyes were unseeing.
Ignoring their oaths and threats
Asgeir grabbed and emptied their horns
And took an axe to the vat of mind-mead.
His axemen howled like toddlers
Stripped of toy bows and arrows
As their vision-ship ran into the rushes.

Asgeir looked around the longhouse floor
And saw the undead stirring, the Sushone

Being reborn after Broddi's brew-bashing.
He shook Charmadu and hissed:
"What have you done to my men?"
And she hissed the same question to him.
"We meant no harm," he said,
"We fight and we drink, and
"Often we drink and then we fight.
"We thought the Sushone did the same.
"What Seenaho drank, we drank."
Charmadu glanced away. "No," she said,
"You drank more, you tasted our magic.
"I sprinkled wood mushrooms in the juice
"To help you see more clearly."
She smiled at the sea-borne,
Still confused by woodland spirits,
Spear-fights with snarling snakes,
And pipe-smoking bear skalds.
"Tomorrow morning, they will return to you.
"'Til then it is best to let the mushrooms
"Melt away and leave them to their legends."
Asgeir shook his aching, throbbing head,
Stroked his beard plaits and
Bellowed an order to sober the
Gold-lusters and the ring-lovers.
"Go to Stormmaster now, prepare to row
"As you have never rowed before.
"Grim the Greedy is getting away.
"It is time to get Grim. We seek and chase."
The longhouse filled with curses
As bleary-eyed Black Hairs struggled
To stand and mouthed Charmadu's
Explanation without any understanding,
All wincing at Thor's pounding head hammer.
Vikings grabbed shields, swords, axes, knives,
Radnald grabbed his girl, kissed her and
Pledged to her pleading eyes: "I'll be back,"

Before being swept out in a stumbling Viking wave,
From longhouse warmth to breath-clouded snow,
Racing and sliding with the shambling crew
To the brooding sanctuary by the crunching shore.
Vee Ma Gog alone did not run.
Pride never runs. Pride has its own pace.
He walked, head high, past snarling Sushone,
Steady of moccasined foot despite the ice,
And as he left the clearing he whistled,
Not a high pitched, piercing whistle but
A wavering fluting, blown just once,
But nothing more was needed.
Seconds later the giant sandy bear
Lumbered through snow-laden trees,
Collar shattered, revealing captivity scars
Around a neck as broad as two warriors' waists.
The Bear Who Brings Death was united
With his brother, the Bear Who Never Sleeps.
Two prisoners now free, two foes now friends.
Vikings never show fear but the bearded
Knew better than to embrace bears,
Especially bears reared on the bones of men.
But in Vee Ma Gog's broad hands
The bear was as playful as a puppy,
Purring like a kitten as he tickled its ears.
Vee Ma Gog whispered, it whimpered;
Vee Ma Gog smiled; it licked his lips;
Vee Ma Gog glanced to the oar-pullers
And his playmate rose on rear legs and
Opened its arms to awe-weakened warriors.
One by one they accepted its hug,
Breathing in its wet dog winter fug
As seething Sushone watched in awe –
In awe and well, well back.

Seenaho and Hackasu cursed the chief
But Vee Ma Gog strode to Charmadu
And in a voice troll-cave deep
Told her to tell the Yellow Hairs:
"This is my brother, Harbar.
"I am the Bear Who Brings Death.
"Harbar has brought many deaths
"And he and I will bring many more.
"These Yellow Hairs were my killers
"Now they are my blood kinsmen.
"They have welcomed my bear.
"Now they are my battle brothers."

Chapter 21

A Viking crew puts to sea without a thought.
Each man knows his job like he knows his name.
Even the idiots, and every crew has them,
Instinctively cast the ropes or ready the oars
Without an Asgeir telling them what to do.
But today Stormmaster's piddle-brains battled
Against Charmadu's mushrooms and Broddi's brew.
Bjerk Oddson and Odd Oddson – for Odd
Had followed in his brother's footsteps as a fool –
Lived up to their nicknames, Bjerk the Halfwit
And Odd the Other Half. And, as they always used
The wrong half, they wore this badge with pride.
Now you all know a Bjerk: fearless in the fight,
First to the shieldwall's front, slashing and stabbing,
The scourge of Saxons, Saracens and Scots,
At least, by his account, in after-battle revels.
Well, ale makes a warrior even of the weak,
And turns a coward into a cursing skull-splitter.
But brave talk over beer comes cheap;
Mead feeds boasts of combat close-shaves
Seen only by the speaker, never by the spearmen.
Through the long days of feasting, Bjerk regaled
All who would listen to legends of his bloodletting.
But Stormmaster's men just smiled and nodded
And turned their backs on his bragging
For they knew that when blood-bolts flew
Bjerk would be huddled behind the death-dealers,
Fit only to dig latrines or gut the deer

Or sharpen their swords or simmer their stew.
Soon he was left with only Odd to watch
His swordplay, his thrusting and swiping,
His ducking and dodging, his scalp-lifting triumphs,
'Til even Odd yawned and yawed to Broddi's brew.
And so Bjerk told his tales to booze-befuddled Sushone
Who understood not a phrase but knew a fraud on sight.
For they had eagle feathers, scars and scalps
And the Vikings arm rings, torques and brooches,
But balding Bjerk had just a pigeon's feather perched on his ear.
As the mushroom spell took hold, his tales grew wilder,
Until he slumped by the fire, his mouth wide open.
Soon his monk's fringe was smouldering stink smoke
And the Vikings were laughing, so Odd laughed too.
For Odd loved his brother but he loved fighting less.
This long streak of spite was tall as a tree but spineless.
Where warriors fight face to face, he whined behind their backs,
Fit like his brother only for the tasks even slaves sneer at.

When berry mead and mushrooms were long forgotten,
Viking and Sushone alike could remember Bjerk
Working with Odd on a longboat of their own.
Not for them a two-man rowing boat, a week's work
And a lifetime's service; no, Asgeir had a dragonship,
So, they too would have a war vessel, The Valkyrie.
Bjerk told Odd: "We grew up by a boatyard.
"We watched them build fleets of fighting ships.
"How hard can it be, bruv, with you to help?
"We'll build this beauty, and back in Norway
"We'll sell it and live off that and Grim's loot.
"We'll be as rich as Asgeir and twice as grand."

Black Hairs watched bemused as the brothers
Hacked down pine trees and sawed and swore
While Ketil Killfast quizzed them on their mission.
When he told them they needed tar for sealing

And wooden nails and fleece for fixing, Bjerk would
Scowl and swear and roar: "We know what we're doing."
So Ketil walked away, all too well aware that
Whatever Bjerk mumbled usually meant the opposite.
If he said he was a warrior, he was a weakling,
If he said: "To be honest", he had no honour,
If he boasted of bedding wenches, of 'Bjerk's going rutting',
As he liked to put it with a leer and a cackle,
All knew he had paid for the pleasure.
Even Azarapo women spurned this dribble-flecked oaf.
And Odd? He really had eyes only for himself
For Odd only really, truly, loved Odd
But hid behind his brother, two fools together.

The day came for the Valkyrie to begin her voyage.
Bjerk and Odd, helped by excited Black Hair boys,
Hauled her to the snowy shore and heaved her
Onto the water's edge, crushing the thin ice
Like an elk in search of water, pawing and pushing.
Bjerk slotted on the dragonhead, a ghoulish whore
Carved with the skill of a slave starved for days,
Hoisted the sail, hundreds of rags sown together,
A charcoal wild woman gurning from its heart,
And Bjerk urged Asgeir's men to climb aboard,
To test the newest warship of the fleet, the warship
That would bring Grim the Greedy to the blood-eagle.
But Ketil Killfast, Hrolf Hardheart, Broddi the Bloody
And all the rest of Asgeir's men stood arms crossed,
Knowing grins on their faces and Asgeir shouted:
"She's all yours, Skip, put her through her paces."
Bjerk did not know whether to beam with pride or
Bridle at the snub, so he and Odd did both,
Crashing through the ice till a breeze bit
And the Valkyrie raced like a greyhound and
Vikings ashore began to question their mockery.
Radnald Rogarrson, who for all his bravery

Was still a buffoon, even floated their doubts.
"By Thor's thunderbolt," he shouted, "we've got
"A new Viking ship. I wish I was on the Valkyrie."
But Ketil Killfast shook his head, Hrolf Hardheart
Looked to the heavens and Broddi the Bloody
Rolled his eyes in the presence of such stupidity.
And as the Valkyrie cruised offshore, Bjerk and Odd,
Two tiny figures in the sanctuary of the sea-donkey,
Learned that Thor's thunderbolts were being
Struck elsewhere on that day of vanity and folly.

The Valkyrie began to yaw and roll, and Bjerk
And Odd the Strange struggled to keep control.
Bjerk wrestled with the rudder and Odd with the sail
Which soon collapsed on top of him just as the rudder
Splintered from sea stallion's reins into worm-eaten wood.
As Vikings roared with laughter—Radnald laughed loudest—
Ketil Killfast told the throng: "It's about to get better."
And so they watched as the tar-less Valkyrie and its crew of village idiots
Sank serenely into the bone-chilling bath water of the ice bears.
Soon the lake had swallowed the wreck of wood and wishfulness
And Bjerk and Odd owed their lives to Black Hair boys
Racing out in birch bark canoes and hauling them home.
But as they shivered and shook, Odd sought someone to blame.
For Odd had one golden rule in life: Whatever mistakes he made,
The price always had to be paid by someone else.
In Odd's idiot world, it was always somebody else's fault.

But today the whole crew acted as if
The Halfwits had been their tutors.
Fingers got trapped, ropes got dropped,
Spears and shields slipped into the lake
As mead, mushrooms and sleepless nights
Made fools of the sea-wise, simpletons of the sly.
As Asgeir cursed and shook his loyalists,
Only Vee Ma Gog and Harbar the Hairy kept calm.

Then a great sandy arm scooped down and a paw
Like a pail hurled ice water onto the slipshod.
As any Viking will tell you, there is nothing
A face-full of winter water cannot cure.
So, from bear hugs to bear showers,
From addled to active, clumsy to composed,
The hungover hauled the Ice Bear sail high,
And the big spirit bear who never sleeps
Began to use his brawn to earn his keep.

Despite days of drinking and dreaming
Grim the Greedy was easy to follow.
A weak sun had replaced the winter chill
Leaving a clear trail through the ice where
Grim and Waverider had fled the fighting.
Asgeir, Mary by his side, chased the channel,
And when Ketil Killfast asked where they were going
Asgeir looked towards the setting sun and said
"We go ever westwards. We go where Grim leads."
He told his crewmates of Grim's mocking message,
The search for a runestone where white turns to green,
Where meat rains from the sky, where the shaggy stalk again.

They lost count of how many days shivered into nights
On this vast freshwater lake whose forest shores
Gradually shook off the white cloak of winter.
High above the honking of long-legged wide-winged birds
Beating a steady path northwards despite the furring frosts
Pointed to warmer days ahead, as did the first dawn birdsong,
Serving as a soothing wake-up call for the weary.
Warriors who struggled to row through winter's rust
Were now back to full fighting fitness, and lusting
After Grim's blood-soaked gold and his blood-eagle fee.
Several days into the voyage, the water trail vanished
As ice floes scattered in a melting breeze,
But forests faded into flatlands of grass leaving

No hiding place for the hunted, though elk and deer
Provided fuel and thrills for the hunters.
After days of silent squatting, Vee Ma Gog
Drank the land-fleeing breeze,
Sniffed it, tasted it, savoured it,
Read its unwritten runes.
And rose on stiff legs to gaze forward,
Staring with cold, unspeaking eyes
At log platforms on treeless plains,
Lures for vultures and buzzards
Which vied in feather flurries
For the feast strapped aboard.
Were these bodies bribes to the gods,
A gift to the bonebreakers
Or food kept from foragers,
Safe from the fangs of wolves?
Vee Ma Gog knew, but could not tell,
Cursed to silence by Sushone slaughter,
His forthright tongue made mute,
And Norse as foreign as Frisian.
But his hands could speak as fluently
As a skald who has supped from Odin's cup.
A growl, a nod and steady hand gestures
Steered Asgeir and Stormmaster's power shark
Ashore where spring's pale green shoots
Were poking through the last snow crystals
Towards the caresses of the warming sun.
Ashore at last, the wolf pack swayed on a land
Which stretched away in waves of brown and white
Like the swell of an ocean frozen in spite by Loki.
Above them on rough wooden poles was a platform
Bedecked by painted shields and bloodied scalps,
But the sickly-sweet stench of death told its own tale
Before huge long-necked black birds, ravens' rivals,
Rose in a flap of feathers, guts glistening on bald heads.
Vee Ma Gog's hands described a feather head-dress,

A scalp-shaver slain in battle, helped heavenward
By his tribe and armed with bow and arrow
To hunt and fight in the afterlife of a true warrior.
Vee Ma Gog shielded his eyes against the shimmering sun,
Once more sampled the air and scanned the horizon,
Pointed westwards and growled one word: "Grim."
Then he grabbed Radnald and before he could resist
Silently play-scalped him, a hand for a hatchet,
And held the fantasy trophy to his chest.
All wanted Grim's loot, all wanted Grim's hide,
But all knew now who would hack off his
Steaming, scrawny scalp and guard it for good.

The grasslands gave way once more
To woodland where smoke rose lazily
From birch bark longhouses while
Black Hairs in gaudy bark canoes,
Shaggy cloaks over their shoulders,
Rowed out to shadow the fur faces and
Their giant dragonship of death.
Vee Ma Gog ignored them
But they saw him staring ahead,
Hands free and scalp secure,
And saw him as proof the marauders
Were no real threat to their realms.
Half the sea-rovers rowed while
The rest stood to arms, ready
For any sudden move,
Any bow strung,
Any stone slung
Or spear flung.
In clearings they could see
Women at work, planting crops,
While painted warriors spearfished
Or stalked spring-coloured waterbirds.
Shepherded by sheepdog canoes

They coasted into an inlet,
Sliding onto a sandy shore.
Asgeir gave no orders
To the well-drilled who
Were already on their guard.
But he leapt onto the shingle
And bought new friends with
Amber beads from the Baltic.
He whistled to Vee Ma Gog
Who came like a dog,
Not like a cur but like
A king's hunting hound
One step behind the stag.
For some time now Vee Ma Gog
Had been as silent as the dead.
But now he spoke and proved
He had been listening all along.
"Good Black Hair," he said.
"They like them," and pointed
To the see-through stones
Strung around Asgeir's neck.
Asgeir's eyes opened wide,
And saw he held the key
To unlock the locals' hearts.
To Ketil Killfast he shouted:
"Get the amber. Bring the beads."
And he commanded Vee Ma Gog:
"Where is Grim? Get me Grim."
Vee Ma Gog, face still as ever,
Let his hands do the talking.
Without speaking a word
He pointed to the snow,
He pointed to Asgeir's face;
He pointed to the yellow grass
He pointed to Asgeir's hair;
He took a stick and

Sketched in the sand
A great dragonship
With single sail,
And soaring eagle
Flying at its heart.
He held one hand
Flat to his forehead
To scan the horizon
And let his left
Surf the sea,
Riding like a dolphin.

The painted devils,
One had a red face
With a black wolf
Masking his eyes,
Another a black hand
On each bronzed cheek,
Jabbered and blathered
And gestured westwards,
Always setting sun-wards.
They bowed to Stormmaster,
Brandished the amber,
Tapped their breasts
And pretended to paddle.
Vee Ma Gog, still unsmiling,
Mouthed: "They want to come."
The Wolf hefted his hatchet
And fought an unseen foe,
And the Hand howled
Like a wolf and slashed
The warming air with his knife.
"They know here. They help,"
Said Vee Ma Gog who had
Begun to repay his rescuers
By finding Asgeir native guides.

Chapter 22

Snorri had been standing and skalding for hours
And his audience had been drinking for longer.
The longhouse was hooked, caught in Snorri's spell,
And the sun's winter rest had turned day into night,
Night into day, so sleep came only at beer's behest,
The body's rhythms as confused as a cripple's dance.
But Snorri had more to tell, and felt the hangman's halter
Tightening every time he saw a befuddled warrior wilt,
So he turned to Sven, sipped from his leather tankard, smiled
And said: "Grim is still out there. Asgeir and Vee Ma Gog
"Are still seeking him, and the day of reckoning is due.
"But I have talked long and you have listened well.
"With your blessing I will stop now and rest awhile,
"And return you tomorrow to the land of the Black Hairs
"And the exquisite beauty of the Blood-Eagle.
"As you feast on venison, and quench your beer thirst,
"You will learn how the long-bearded met their match,
"And how long it takes to die from the bite of the Blood-Eagle."
As Sven nodded, and his widow-makers rose
To steam and stain the snow with their frothing piss,
Snorri commanded his captors: "Before you sleep
"Let me leave you with a riddle, a poser,
"A challenge to chew over before Asgeir returns:
"Is a man who fights for his life a hero?
"Or is a hero he who fights
"For another's life when
"He could walk away?
"Or can heroes be created

"Not by bravery but by skalds?
"And who is the hero then?"

Chapter 23

Sleeping with a noose around your neck
Is never easy even for the fear-free.
But on his hay pillow with rats as bedfellows
Snorri could hear treachery in train,
Wersil whispering to his henchmen,
Fragments of phrases, wine-slurred,
Wafting through pine-wood walls.
"Hang him now," said one.
"Save him, 'til Sven gives the nod,"
Stumbled another, belching.
And then Wersil's hissing hatred
Boiling over like a blackened cauldron.
"Hang when I say… Fuck Sven, the old fool.
"You've a new younger warlord now."
And Snorri? Did he quail? Did he quiver?
No. He smiled. He turned to face the fire
And slept the sleep of the stringpuller.

Hours later, when axe-head hangovers
Were soothed by another barrel of beer,
And the healing aroma of meat roast,
Sven led his ringmen, his killers,
Into the heart of his longhouse
And a boy summoned Snorri with
A blast through a bullhorn
Just as Odin wakes the war dead
For another day of feasting and fighting.

The horsehair halter
Told Snorri he had
One more song to sing
To save his neck or dance
From the gnarled snow oak
Beyond this theatre of doom.
But if he was afraid,
He did not flaunt it.
Showing fear feeds death,
So he grinned, fox-eyed,
Like one who knows
What soon must come,
Like a mushroom-wise
Sami shaman.

My lord, he began, ladies, blood-letters,
Boys and, glancing at his empty tankard,
Worthy wenches, will you walk with me
Back to the land of the Black Hairs,
The land of endless skies and eternal steppes,
The land of bear and bison, of gore and glory,
The land where Grim the Greedy hoards
His loot and where Asgeir steers Stormmaster
On a hunt now nearly five moons old?

A murmur, a grumble, shuffling benches,
A growl over spilled ale, and a low chuckle,
Revealed the fear-dealers were his again,
Hypnotised by his word-spell, seduced
By the saga of Asgeir and his gold quest.

Stormmaster had no need to live up to her name.
By now the gales of winter were long gone,
Ice floes melting into the lake's blue green,
And oars replacing wind as she nosed
Ever deeper into this hostile land.

But Black Hairs ashore shrieked
At the sight of this ghost ship.
The gurning skull of a Holy Man
Grinned from the dragonhead,
Scalps flapped in the light breeze
From the top of the sail mast,
Brightly painted Sushone shields
Vied with Viking round shields to
Save the sea-rovers from war wolves.
The porcupine quills of arrows
And spears bristling from shields
Provided proof of past battle honours.
And, back leaning against the mast,
Was a new sign of devilry – a furred
Sandy bear roaring defiance
Through fangs longer than daggers
At a sun-stirred brother bathing
In the reborn, silver-glinting wetlands.
The Wolf and the Hand were in thrall
To the majesty of the wind-gorging
Ice Bear, to the muscles of the oarsmen,
To the might of Stormmaster but
In mortal fear of Harbar the Hairy and
Nervous of Vee Ma Gog the silent,
Whose huge strangler's hands
Could kill as easily as they could speak.
Asgeir had placed his faith in Vee Ma Gog.
The sole survivor owed his life to Asgeir
Who in turn knew his life lay in the hands
Of the brooding Black Hair if the Vikings
Were ever to survive in the wilderness.
Asgeir led by instinct, guided by hunches,
But he took help wherever it was on hand.

And so he turned to Mary,
His soulmate and sorceress,

To read the runes of the Fates.
Her necklace, her magic bone
And her own witch's wisdom
Were all she needed to keep
Asgeir and Stormmaster on course.
And so, behind the vast pine mast,
In the shadow of the sandy bear
And below the Ice Bear banner,
She rolled the spirit-speakers' bone
And slipped into a sleep trance
Before rising, green eyes closed,
But all-seeing as always.

"Vee Ma Gog guides you well",
She told her lord and lover.
"Tomorrow, round these headlands,
"Where white becomes green,
"And the shaggy stalk again,
"Where lake meets sky
"And meat rains on men,
"By the runestone of he who raced before,
"There you'll find your gold looter.
"There your seeking can end and
"The gold-chasing can begin.
"But beware. I can only see so far
"But I do know Grim is grinning.
"He is gloating and goading,
"Guarded by scalp-hungry Skraeling.
"The Haul-Hoarder is far from ready
"To give up his gold just yet."

It was Asgeir's turn to grin.
"Grim will never be ready
"To give up his gold but
"I am ready to grab it back from him.
"Deathbringer and Doublefang

"Will drink his sticky blood.
"We will take our summer's spoils
"And when the swallows patrol
"Norway's midge-rich pastures
"And the sickle-winged scream
"Over the swaying treetops
"We will wassail under the pines
"Of my paternity once more."
With that he strode to the stern,
Turned his back on Stormmaster's
Faint white wake racing away
Towards Norway, towards home,
Faced his blade pullers and
Told them to prepare for battle.
But this outer boldness belied
An inner turmoil. As shieldmen roared,
Asgeir's brain raced: How, just how,
Could meat rain from the sky?

Dawn kissed the sea-lake
With a white mist no taller
Than Stormmaster's mast.
Slowly the sun burned off night's veil
To reveal a sow bear on the beach,
Fur still long and flowing
After so long as an ice-shield.
Tripping and rolling close behind
Were the jewels of her sleep:
Two fat cubs play-fighting
Like Viking boys drilling
For life's battles ahead.

A hundred oar strokes beyond
Was the biggest bear ever seen
Even by wood-wise Vee Ma Gog,
The Bear who Brings Death.

Even Harbar the Hairy,
The huge Bear who Never Sleeps,
Paid tribute, backing closer to
The sail-mast, as if to keep a
Healthy distance between him
And the growling devil bear's
Long fangs and sceptre claws.
On and on rowed the sea masters,
Grim's guts and gold always
In the forefront of their minds.
On the light westerly breeze
Came another calling clue -
A rich longdrop stink like
A winter's worth of waste
From a stale cattle byre.

After the next headland
The culprits came into view:
A sea of slow-moving
Shaggy maned, mud-caked,
Big-skulled, boulder-large bison,
Spindly-legged on
Barrel bodies just like
The beasts of the Rusland,
But bigger and more brutal,
With eyes strangers to mercy.

The herd stretched to the horizon,
Scattered across the sweeping steppes
Like a vast forest of shrubs that
Foraged and fed, lowed and snorted,
In defiance of this cruel world.
Caressed by the sun's warmth,
A red cliff rose from the lake
Sheer above a rocky shore.
Beyond, the rolling grasslands

Rose higher still, forming a bowl
Above the edge of the red crags.
Lurking on the bowl's fringes
Were wolves, bigger than any
That stalk Scandinavia's woods,
Lying in wait but for what?
The Hand and The Wolf prickled
Like guard dogs at a broken twig,
Reaching for hatchet and knife,
Their palms and their fingers,
Their arms and their faces,
Telling all there who could read
To be ready for battle.

And then the whole Earth shook
Like the dawning of Ragnarok,
Making even the lake quake.
A thunder beyond even Thor
Filled the darkening sky.
No lightning flash, no drum roll,
But a relentless, rolling roar
That grew louder and louder
As a cloud of dust rose
Towards Odin's beer halls.

Carried on the cooling breeze,
Like a ghost army's caterwauling,
Was a whooping, fast and frantic,
Growing ever more fever-frenzied,
As thunder pounded the steppes.
And then, right over the grassy ridge,
Charged scores of bug-eyed bison,
Whites of their leering eyes clear,
Even to Waverider's water-girt guards,
Who watched, eyes, axes and swords sharp,
Three arrow shots from the shore.

The shivering bulls, cows and calves
Careered headlong into the bowl,
And the wolves howled them
Into a funnel of fear which
Made them stampede still harder
Until, snorting and roaring, they
Tumbled over the precipice,
Head over heels,
Horns over flailing hooves,
Legs still lunging
As they plummeted
Onto the leering rocks
In a sickening
Series of cracks
And clumps
And crashes.
And then
There was
Silence
Broken only
By agonised lowing
From the last lungfuls
Of life in foaming beasts
Which moments earlier
Had been grassland giants.
And then in the bowl above
The devil wolves threw off
Their pelts and whooped,
Exposing buckskin-clad
Braves, faces and bodies
Painted for battle, trumpeting
Their triumph. On the foreshore
The rocks came alive and
Unleashed arrows and lances
Into any bison still struggling
To cheat the hunters who

Were already slitting open
The bellies of the beaten and
Hauling steaming, blood-red livers
Out into the chill spring air and
Ravening on them raw while
The blood trickled down their cheeks.

"The meat", Asgeir told his silver-seekers,
"Has clearly rained from the sky."
Pointing to the last snow pockets
Surrendering to a sea of new shoots,
He grinned: "The white has become green."
Pointing to the endless horizon of
Their widening waterway through this
Alien, warlike world, he said:
"The lake has met the sky.
"Now, all we need is the runestone
"Of he who raced before and
"Grim will be in our grasp.
"But Frigg only knows where
"A message could be hidden here."

Vee Ma Gog's fingers and thumbs
Spoke swiftly of lost carvings
To the Hand and the Wolf
While Mary, eyes closed,
Consulted her necklace.
Minutes passed, minds probed,
Until as one the war-painted
And the witch pointed to a hill
And the last of the Azarapo
Slapped his palms together,
Destiny confirmed by a clap.
And so Grim's pursuers rowed
Two miles beyond the bloodied rocks,
Ignored by red-armed Skraelings

Focussed only on the fresh meat
That would break winter's stark fast.
Starvation can make a man blind,
Even to death, such is desperation.

Beaching, oar-raising and arming
Was the well-oiled work of a moment
And all bar five axe-wielders went
To find the key to Grim's fortune.

Well, five and Harbar the Hairy.
Every man has tasks to which
He is suited and big bears
Are best left behind when creeping
Through the land of scalp-cravers.
So Harbar climbed quietly aboard,
Making Stormmaster his cradle.

The Hand and the Wolf led the band.
Hatchets at the ready, hawk-eyed,
They pushed past shoulder-high grass,
Up slopes, down into hollows,
'Til they reached some high rocks.
Like wolves seeking wounded prey,
They sniffed the wind and read the sky
Until the Wolf howled and pointed
To a rock face scarred by carvings.
Scratched in stone at a giant's height,
Their outlines painted blood red,
Were stick men with sticks for spears,
And hunting hounds pursuing bison.
The feather-bedecked tribe danced
In circles of men and women round
Bears, wolves and huge hedgehogs with
Quills as long as war lances.
The Hand nodded, the Wolf howled,

And wafting on the breeze were the whoops
Of the feasting bison-disembowellers.
But Asgeir, Ketil Killfast and Hrolf Hardheart
Merely shrugged at the childlike sketches,
Shaking their heads in open despair
Of ever finding the sign they sought
In this endless wasteland so far from home.
The Black Hairs were so crestfallen,
Even their white feathers wilted,
Whimpers replacing whoops of triumph.

As Vee Ma Gog's hand signs struggled
To set these hunters on a true scent,
Mary spoke with her spirits.
A rub of the necklace bone,
A calm sprinkling of soil, and
Her clear emerald Irish eyes
Closed to become all-seeing.
The wind was rising swiftly and
To the south, over the grassy sea,
The skies were darkening like
Billowing smoke after an attack.
"Stay here," she muttered, eyelid-blind,
"A storm is coming, twisting and turning,
"Watch where it leads, watch well,
"And your quest will be complete."
So, in the shelter of the red rocks,
Stormmaster's tough men tensed,
For the storm that would be their master.
Clouds as black as Whitby jet
Snarled across the plain like
A stampede of snorting bison.
Thunderbolts fizzed and dazzled
All around until a lone spark
Set the brown grassland ablaze,
Spreading panic through the steppes,

Sending deer, bison and war-painted
Into a headlong dash of death.
For all the darkness no raindrops fell,
Just more lightning, more rolling thunder,
Until high up in the heavens
Hraesvelg the Corpse Gulper
Beat his great eagle wings and
Cracked the whip of the gods
Which scrambled from the sky
In a twisting, roaring funnel of fury,
Blacker even than the clouds,
Changing course by the second,
Crushing and killing all it kissed,
Sucking all in its path skywards,
Until bucks, boulders and bison rained
On the flatlands below, ripped from
The trail of devastation and dumped
Crudely on the whim of the winds.
Asgeir and his men watched and waited
And never have Odin, Thor and Freyr
Heard so many heartfelt entreaties
From men fearless in battle but
Openly fearful of this divine wrath.
All begged deliverance as death
Raced relentlessly towards them,
Rattling up the slope just like
Waverider's Whitby raiders,
Spewing boulders longhouse large,
Devouring all with its spinning grin.
Its malevolent black heart had
The quaking axemen firmly in its sights.
But as Mary and Vee Ma Gog chanted,
Mercy songs shaped by different shores
But united by man's universal bond,
The beating, unquestioning lust for life,
The funnel of fear turned, sped down the slope,

And as suddenly as it appeared, disappeared.

Too late, though, for Asgeir. Like a true warlord
He had stood at the head of his men.
No shieldwall this time, no axe-wielding,
But a warlord who skulks is worth no more
Than a dragonship that leaks or
A stylish sword that shatters on impact.
So Asgeir confronted the wind devil,
And the wind devil repaid his defiance
By sucking and flicking him towards the gods,
Twisting and turning and tumbling him
As if he were as light as an autumn leaf.
Deathbringer and Doublefang offered no
Protection in this malicious maelstrom.
The only death bringer dealing here was
The bottomless spite of the storm gods.
Mary screamed as she saw her lover,
Her leader, lifted rapidly heavenwards;
The desperate crew cried out in grief
As Dragontamer met his match.
And Vee Ma Gog? His face was still,
Always still, but his eyes flickered,
Not that any of the storm watchers saw.

Chapter 24

On the shingle the seasteed's shieldmen
Watched in awe as the wind rose and
The sky darkened like a sun-kissed sea
Clouded by ink from escaping squid.
Skidi Njalson, Vog Cnutson, Einar Hrolfson,
Fine fighters all, bold and sure, plus
Bjerk Oddson and Odd Oddson,
The Halfwit and The Other Half,
Had never felt so far from the fjords.
Mesmerised by the might of furious gods,
These guards failed to do their duty
And soon found that storms
Can be a fighter's friend.
The first to learn this lesson
Was Skidi, skewered by a flinthead
Through the skull, loosed off
From the gloom of the shore-woods
By a bowman buried in the shadows.
As the rest scrabbled for swords
And shields, axes and lances,
A flying hatchet smashed Vog
Full in the well-travelled forehead,
Splitting his leather helmet and
Showering wild-eyed Halfwits with
A hot fountain of metal-flavoured juice.
Arrows rained down and ended
Einar's adventures in a writhing agony,
Though he died with his sword in hand.

Bjerk and Odd's duty was simple:
To protect Stormmaster, to save
The way homeward for their brothers,
Or die heroically in its defence.
But when the time came to fight
The Halfwits opted to flee,
Fumbling with their weapons
Like raw boys before men.
But there was nowhere to run.
Behind them lay the lake,
Before them an unseen foe
Who saw their every move.
And so, screaming they ran
Into the horny-handed embrace
Of blood-red savages slavering
At the torture that lay in store,
Licking their lips at fresh new flay-fodder.
As wiry, iron grips dragged them off
Into the eye of the blackening storm,
Other Black Hairs howled at
The pleasure of slicing off
The still warm scalps of the dead.
But the hair was not trophy enough;
For them a true scalp came complete
With the face attached, so they took
The spirit as well as the life, letting
The battle valour of the vanquished
Boost the fame of the crowing victors.
But these eight steppe stalkers,
Bodies sinister in red and gold,
Faces ochre and black, white and green,
Eagles' feathers fluttering proudly,
Wanted more glory, more acclaim.
Stormmaster, the biggest canoe
They had ever seen, offered renown
And the chance to soar skywards

On warbirds' feathers in the fuming eyes
Of warriors left to sulk and skulk at home.
So, undaunted by Stormmaster's battle jewels,
Skulls and scalps,
Shields and arrow stubble,
One by one they climbed aboard,
Hoping to make Stormmaster
Dance to their curt commands.

Asgeir's sea beast creaked in protest
But landsmen cannot read a dragonship.
So they prodded and probed
Until one patrolled the stern and
Rummaged in a thick black rug.
But this treasure trophy proved
An alluring piece of loot too far.
It sprang to life, rose up in a frenzy
Of fur and claws, snarls and fangs,
Towering well over two men tall,
And the last thing the Black Hairs heard
Was a roar, unlike any that ever raced
Across the rolling grassland, a roar
Wilder and shriller than a hurricane,
A roar that tore heroes to shreds.

The shelter-seekers on the hilltop
Were bereft at the loss of their leader.
So far had they sailed, so many battles,
So many storms, so many perils defied,
Struggling together, surviving together.
But now they were alone in a wilderness.

The crew was awash with heroes.
Ketil Killfast, Hrolf Hardheart, Broddi the Bloody,
And Oddo the Hairy, all were bravery embodied.
All were in their prime, all in their twenties,

All wore silver arm rings won in battles
Since their teens, all carried tattoos
Thanking Thor and Odin and warding off
The dragons of Hel and the tricks of Loki.
All were loudly praised in saga and song
By Vikings, from Varangians to Vardalanders,
Gotlanders to Greenlanders.
But it is one thing to wield weapons;
Quite another to command killers.
Stabbing and slashing is easy,
It just takes guts to take guts.
But leading is another skill,
Another level,
Another talent.
Asgeir had come from nowhere
But he had been born a warlord.
He knew when to attack,
When to wait,
When to reward,
When to rebuke,
When to reprieve,
When to retreat,
And when to kill,
And he always knew,
Which way to lead.
His words were few,
But worth waiting for.
Whether in this alien world
Or lost in the rollers
Of the black Atlantic,
His crew always followed.

For magical, mystical Mary,
His loss was cataclysmic.
He had given her freedom.
He was the first leader to treat

His slaves like humans
And not like chattels
Fit only for flogging or fucking.
He had let her gifts grow,
He had trusted her despite
Crew doubts and complaints,
Even risked his command,
And she had repaid him,
With her sorcery, her spells
Her foresight, her shape-shifting,
Her loyalty and above all,
Her love.

But to the others she was
And always would be
A wench, a slave, a slut.
Tough it is for anyone
To escape their past,
Especially the lowly.
With Asgeir gone, so too
Had her future flown.
But with Asgeir gone,
The rest were lost too,
Alone in a fierce land,
Norway's fjords and forests
Evaporating for ever
In the pained mists of the mind.

Vee Ma Gog alone was unmoved.
Then, he was ever unmoved.
This was his native land and
He could read nature's runes
Better than blundering Yellow Hairs.
The Wolf and the Hand
Were nervous, more concerned
For their own safety so close

To the bison hunters than
For the scalps of ghost faces
Met only a few days before.

Vee Ma Gog, tribal top knot
Floating in the warming gale,
Watched the twisting wind tunnel
Stagger drunkenly and gutter
And die by a green mound
Of grass and rocks, much as
Children hunt the end of
A rainbow for its treasure.
As Mary wept and axe wielders
Grieved Asgeir's shocking loss
Vee Ma Gog rose cross-legged,
Slowly, painstakingly, to his feet
And pointed to the devastation
Littering the middle distance.
He said two words, only two,
But they were enough to breathe
New life into the near lifeless.
"Vikings," he said, "look."
And as the twister wilted to
Faint weakening swirls,
A figure landed gently on
The mound, as if lowered
By a giant, tender hand.

He stood there, sword by his side,
Axe and shield held high,
Hair wild like a Highland bull
Battered by storm and spray,
But still alive and staring back.
Mary blinked tear-bleared eyes,
Battlemates narrowed theirs
And then roared as one:

"Dragontamer, Dragontamer,
"Dragontamer is back.
"Dragontamer is back."
They raced and stumbled,
Sliding down the rocky slope,
Vee Ma Gog slower, always slower,
But steadier, storm-proof, cooler,
With long, loping strides and
As keen to see his saviour
As the raiding, cheering veterans.

The Wolf and the Hand
Dropped onto their knees
Stricken by Asgeir's magic.
Amid embraces and back slaps,
Asgeir told how he had ridden
The wind tunnel, flying over
The rolling, waving grasslands,
Swirling and tumbling faster
Than a leaf in an autumn gale,
Dodging bison and bears,
Deer, elk and wolves,
Black Hairs and boulders,
Barely able to breathe
In the furnace of the funnel.
But now here he stood,
Battered and bruised,
But unbeaten by Thor's rage.
In his belt was a Black Hair hatchet,
Prize and proof of a skirmish
In the middle of the whirl-storm,
High in the heavens in full view
Of the welcoming gates of Valhalla.
Ketil Killfast laughed and said:
"You were already Dragontamer.
"Now you are reborn as Stormrider.

"What will be your next name?
"Whatever will you do next?"

Asgeir smiled and pulled Mary over.
"This," he said, and picked her up,
Kissed her, hugged her and held her
Like he would never let go.
With an arm still round her waist,
He added: "And this". He nodded
To a large stone sitting on the mound.
The fates had found the key to their quest.

Chapter 25

To some the stone meant nothing
A boulder dumped on a rise
Overlooking lake and river,
The eternity of the grasslands
And the twister's trail of wreckage
Across a pristine landscape.
But to rune-readers like Asgeir
The spidery red lines carved deep
Into a pink-grey rock offered hope,
A welcome link with home but also,
As clear as a spring moon, a warning.
This was as good a runestone
As any in Norway or Gotland.
And its gaunt graphics showed
That Charmadu and Seenaho
Had told the truth, not that
Asgeir had ever doubted them.
For the benefit of death-dealers
To whom runes were ghostly scribbles
Asgeir read the script aloud
In a low voice full of reverence;

"From far Norway came
Olaf Blodason and
His warrior-rich dragonship
Roving under the wolfhead.
Here they fought a painted foe.

Here they won with Odin's help.
Here they"

But the message, the voice
Reaching across generations,
Died there, silenced for ever.
The first five lines, so bold,
Were enriched with red
But the rest were rough-cut,
Stark bare stone, unfinished.
Asgeir scanned his men who
Looked back, and all knew
Olaf's bloody fate well before
The Wolf howled and the Hand
Led Vee Ma Gog through the grass
To a dry, whitened pile of sticks.
There, riddled with arrows,
Were grinning skeletons,
Scattered, far from complete,
After decades of feeding wolves,
And the few skulls that were left
All shared the same sharp scars,
Shaved from forehead to nape
By the scalping knife of fiends.
Odin may have helped them once,
But he forgot the rovers that day.
Perhaps his ravens, Hugin and Munin,
Spread their wings elsewhere that day,
Perhaps that day they flew east not west,
Perhaps that day they swapped
These Badlands for deserts to watch over
The wealth of the caliph of Baghdad.
Perhaps Olaf had angered the gods
Or perhaps his luck had fled,
And left him and his men to be overrun.

But warriors die every day.
Even fear mocking seafarers
Like Olaf Blodason feel
The bite of a battle-axe's
Glory sooner or later.
All who hold a sword
All who sail on a raid
Know the price to be paid.
No time to mourn these men.
Life is only for the living.
The living can only
Learn well from the past
Not waste time wishing
Its bumpy path was altered
Or else they all risk
Their skulls following
Their long gone forefathers
In death's mocking grin.

Now the dream had nearly come true.
The white had turned green,
The shaggy were stalking once more,
The lake had met the sky,
Meat had rained on men,
Not once but twice,
But where, then, where was Grim?

The rune-fed crewmen
Descended to the grassy plain.
A glance from Asgeir, and
Ketil Killfast scaled the rise
To scan the vast horizon.
Nothing. Silence. Heaven.
The head-high yellow grass
Flowed in the breeze like
Sognefjord on a summer's day.

But difference there definitely was.
An arrow rushed, swishing
Through the air, stinging
Ketil in the small of his back,
Sending him sliding, dazed,
Head-first into the feet of Asgeir
Who watched the arrow quiver,
Stuck in Ketil's chainmail which
Was more than a war-match
For this copper-fanged widow-maker.
But there was no time to thank
Bodo of Hedeby who had forged
This lifesaver, this metal blunter.
As Ketil struggled to breathe
And felt the bruise spread on his back,
Three feather fletches harpooned the Hand
In his chest and his ribs, left and right,
No chainmail for him, no metal,
Just a chest plate of porcupine quills.
A second was all it took
Before he staggered and fell
Into the flowing grass so far from
His farm in the lakeside woods.

The Wolf whooped his war cry
And from over the ridge emerged
Fifty warriors whooping their reply.
At once Asgeir shouted: "Shieldwall!
"Shieldwall! Back to the boat."
But as Vikings formed a shuffling circle,
Other braves blocked their way,
But a short spear throw away.
No runestone would rise
For these bison-bearded
In this ruthless wilderness.
No saga would be sung

By glory-loving wassailers.
Lost at sea or slaughtered
In a foreign fight, that's
What their families would think.
All knew that soon their
Bones would be feeding bears
And their Nordic scalps would be
Bloodied trophies for a
Tribe they had never known.
But the brave ever have hope.
If a man can fight, he can hope.
He can hope for heroic life,
He can hope for heroic death.
For they who fight, death
Is but a fleeting interlude,
A stepping stone to the
Beer halls and feasts of Valhalla.
So, the shieldbearers unsheathed
Their swords, brandished their spears,
And prepared to win Odin's welcome.
Hrolf Hardheart went further.
The shield-biter barged beyond
The sanctuary of his shipmates
And stood ten steps out in front
Spinning grim Double Death,
His two-headed axe, his bulging muscles
Making light of its skull-splitting weight,
As he defied death one last, glorious time.

The Black Hairs could no more
Read runes than Vikings
Could read bison tracks
But if they could, they
Would have trembled at
The tattoo on Hrolf's forehead.
"HEL" it proclaimed and

That is precisely what he promised.
So, he defied the fear-pleasers,
Their arrows, their spears,
With his pre-battle display of
Axemanship, unmanning taunts
And disembowelling threats delivered
In his acidic Nordic tongue
As he had done so often before.
The Black Hairs held off
From loosing arrows at the hero,
Seeming to welcome the chance
To wage war man to man.
A Black Hair accepted the challenge.
In one hand a hatchet,
In another a long stick,
Feathers and scalps
Fluttering down its length.
The painted face crept up to Hrolf
Like a cat stalking a mouse,
Watching his every move,
And as Double Death smashed down
He darted in and, as it rose,
Touched the Viking with the stick,
Gently, a baby's kiss on the stomach,
And leapt back, whooping, jubilant,
To the brotherhood of his band.
Hrolf and the sea-battlers
Were bewildered but he
And Double Death kept on
With their dance of defiance.
Another Black Hair crept forward,
Timing his leap to perfection,
And dabbed Hrolf on the foot
Before howling his triumph.
Emboldened, a third ran up,
But in his haste, he tripped,

And gave the huddled Vikings
Their last chance to cheer.
As the scalp chaser staggered,
Hrolf split him in half
From head to quill-covered chest.
Splattered with blood,
Hrolf licked his lips and
Roared his death taunt:
"No-one mocks Hrolf, no-one.
"Read my forehead, you fuckers."

But defiance is never enough.
As the pile of broken Black Hairs grew
Asgeir chilled to hear a familiar cackle.
And right up on the rolling ridge
Beside an eagle-feathered chief
Whose headdress grazed the grass
Asgeir could see Grim,
Grinning and gloating,
Much as Mary had warned.
And overhead, cronking their calls,
Two ravens flew lazily past.
Asgeir had sought and chased.
He had pursued the hated ring hoarder
But his prey had become his predator.
Asgeir had pinned his hopes
On Stormmaster's protectors
Running to the rescue of the hopeless.
But he knew this was a nonsense.
Only three of them were fighters.
The Half-Wits were as much use
In a battle as a sword made of celery
And three men could not fight through
So great a horde of face-flayers.
And soon the Black Hairs bored
Of feeding Double-Death and

Moved in for the kill like wolves.

Words cannot relate the rage
Unleashed in the shieldwall
As painted faces closed in
On the tattooed dragonmen.
But death was not their destiny,
Not yet, anyway,
Not now,
But later.
That's right. Later.

Soon warriors were overpowered,
Weapons wrenched away by
Wiry hands and war lovers
As lean as wolfhounds.
Instead of hatchet thrusts
Or sharp scalping knives
Blessing with their death kiss,
Vikings were flicked
By long scalp sticks,
And taunted shrilly
By wild, elated whooping
Like the howls of dogs
Guarding a clean kill.
The sailors' hands were bound
With animal sinews
Well soaked in water
Which would shrink
And tighten and make
Weaklings of the strong.
Nooses around their necks
Were linked with hempen ropes
And slave-taking warriors learned
How it feels to be a slave,
And freedmen rued their return

To a life of vile servitude and
A life forever haunted by death.

Chapter 26

Warriors carried weapons
Forged in Hordaland
But Doubledeath, Kneecleaver
And Gutgorer were now
In the hands of the painted,
And the land-caged seamen were
At the mercy of squat, spitting women
Who mocked them, shamed them,
And brandished rusting blades
Near their rapidly shrinking balls.
But Asgeir held his head high
And defied the brutal clubs
That battered his head
Every time he reminded
His wilting warband
Who they were – warriors all –
And where they were from.
"Heads high, banish fear,"
He preached through the pain.
"We are Norsemen and
"No men are braver.
"They crave to break you
"And see you cudgel-cower
"But time there is plenty
"To make them crawl.
"Let them threaten
"Let them taunt
"But you will laugh loud yet.

"We are death's fearless defiers
"And pain is our pleasure.
"Remember, always remember –
"As long as we live,
"We can always fight and
"As long as we live,
"We can kill."

His words rallied all,
Though the Wolf and
War-wise Vee Ma Gog
Were now walking unseeing,
In a wordless, worldless trance
As if already long dead
And nothing could hurt them now.
What did they know that
Asgeir and his men did not?

The tall grass gave way
To closely grazed steppes
Littered with dry bison pats.
The death dealers and
Their unwilling playthings
Soon caught up with the
Footsore, snail's pace progress
Of the scattered, travelling tribe.
Dogs, working like donkeys,
Were dragging fresh, dripping meat
Piled high on long land-rafts,
Whose whitened bone-like poles
Bounced along the tussock plain,
Sending chattering rats skittering
And leaving ski tracks in their wake.
Women with shiny black hair
And fat babies on their backs
Also hauled the hunters' booty.

And always stalking the warband,
Skulking black shapes prowling,
Tongues long drip-drooling,
On the crests of the rolling land waves,
Were packs of small, lean wolves
Waiting for a lone forager's chance
To raid and steal and loot like Vikings.

Asgeir smelt the village
Well before it flooded his eyes,
A sickly-sweet stench
Floating over the landscape,
And then, breaching a yellow ridge,
They saw below, by a shallow river,
Fringed with birch, willow and juniper
A forest eagle-flown from Lappland:
Clusters of tall, cone-like tents,
Taut bison skin stretched over
Long protruding poles,
Painted child-like with
Stick-men pictures
Of warriors and bison,
Bears and weapons,
Brightening the grimness.
The simple tents looked like
The summer homes of the Sami
In Norway's remotest north,
The reindeer herders
Who track the treeheads
Wherever they wander.

The scalp-takers were hailed
As feather-worthy heroes,
Heavily-laden as they were
With meat, weapons and prisoners.
Even the strays barked their tribute.

Leading the welcoming party
Were two bejewelled men
Weirder than any wonder
Witnessed by well-travelled Asgeir.
One walked backwards and
When the others whooped
He wept and hissed.
When they sat down
He promptly stood up.
When they sang victory chants
He chose a mournful wail.
Where the rest sported long hair,
He was as bald as a goose's egg.
Though they wore very little
In the warmth of the spring,
He shivered in wolverine furs.
Stranger still was the master
Of the village's welcoming party
Or was he really its mistress?
Taller by far than any Black Hair,
He had the body of a man,
But walked like a woman,
Moved his arms and hands
With the grace of a swan's neck
And spoke in a soft, high voice.
His eyelids were lined with black,
His lips painted blood-red.
His nails, too, were decorated,
And round his neck was a delicate
Necklace of sea-shells, pink and peach,
To prettify his women's buckskin.
His hands looked soft as silk,
His arms thinner than a girl's.
No white feathers for his head,
No fighting had worn him down,
Yet the hatchet-bearers beamed

On beholding him and basked
In his lady-like approval.

When he saw the walking dead
He shrieked and pouted,
And slapped them weakly,
One by one, on the cheek,
Pausing only for Hrolf Hardheart.
Then he clapped his pretty hands,
Waved coyly to the women and
Languidly lisped out his orders.
No womanly mercy would come
From this she-man shaman.

Asgeir heard the Halfwits
Far before he saw them
And knew then that no rescue
Could come from Stormmaster.
Their screams filled the camp,
High-pitched, haunting and shrill,
Followed by groans of deep agony.
But high or low, they never slackened.
In the heart of the tatty village,
Hung from a scaffold by their wrists
Over the glowing coals of a fire
Were the guards who had fled.
Their running days had fled, too.
The feet of the latrine diggers
Were being slowly roasted
Like swine for the Althing feast.

Watching them, with sick glee,
Savouring their suffering,
Was gold-grabbing Grim,
Brandishing the sacred sword
Stolen from Egil the Skinny.

"Welcome, you mutts,"
He laughed. "So magical
"To see you so far from home.
"My new friends and I
"Have laid plans for you.
"I hope you all love them
"As much as we will.
"Soon you will see just
"How they play with prisoners.
But please don't worry," he leered,
"You will, you soon will."
Some yards behind him stood
The rest of his crew, Thorfinn's men,
A ragged, gaunt-faced mob,
So unlike their plump leader.
A few looked how Asgeir felt,
Sick to his writhing stomach.
One had red eyes and
Kept wiping his nose
On a once-white sleeve.
Another had given up
And just let his nose run
'Til he looked like the
Snotty-nosed kid he
Had not long left behind.
He sneezed and earned a cuff
From his skipper who
Had never been known
For his kind-hearted charity.

As the sun began its sleep
And flames from a fire
At the village's beating heart
Replaced its fading light
The festival of fear began.
Boys began to drum and

A menacing, animal rhythm
Drove a long wailing dirge.
Warriors, torsos painted,
Wearing only loincloths,
Emerged from a lodge,
Following the white steam
Billowing from its turf door.
Glistening in the fire light
The braves began to dance,
Slowly, then faster, faster,
And as they whirled and wheeled,
Arms out wide, wild eyes
Blanking out the stars above,
Others grabbed Vee Ma Gog
And waylaid the growling Wolf,
Lashing them back to back
To a huge blackened pole,
Taller than two tents,
Wider than two warriors.

Grim erupted in fury,
Like the fire-fountains,
The lava mounts, of Iceland.
"Not them," he fumed,
"Not them, you fool!
"Kill the Vikings first.
"You can kill those idiots anytime."
And he shoved one of his snivellers
Towards the torturers, telling him
To make them leave the Black Hairs
'Til last. But in Norway, a guest
Treats his host with respect
And so it was with these
Wild men of the wilderness.
So, the sniveller's insolence
Was seen as an insult.

A massive club smashed his teeth
And sent him scrambling, stunned,
Snot flying, his mouth spilling
A gobletful of man's red wine
Over Grim's grubby sheepskin,
His reward another cuff in rebuke.
As he whined, the painted flap
Of a cone tent was flung open
And the flames revealed a tall chief,
Muscled chest and arms bare,
Scalps bedecking buckskin leggings,
And down his back a bison skin
And on his head the beast's head,
Complete with sharp curved horns.
The Vikings had never seen
Such a devilish headdress,
But they had heard of them,
The crowns worn by Hel's trolls.

The Halfman-Halfwoman
Greeted the bisonman with a bow
Like a benevolent host at a feast,
Not grief's harbinger at a funeral.
The Hornhead grabbed the sniveller
Slapped his face, swore and
Threw him among the women
Where this callow, cowering Viking
Lowered his head in plain shame.
Bisonman did not even glance
At Grim and his silent fuming,
Marching instead to the pole of torment,
Running his hands through the prisoners' hair,
Relishing the scalps that would soon
Join the top knots strung from his clothes.

All the while the Halfwits kept up
Their own musical accompaniment,
Wailing and whining like women,
Out of time with the drumming
Like amateur whistlers at a wedding.
And each time they screamed
The squalid children laughed
And piled more wood on the pyre.
Then the Wolf and Vee Ma Gog
Faced their toughest test.
Warriors formed a line before them
And took turns to fling knives
And tomahawks or stretch their bows
And unleash rushing arrows at them.
But the aim was not to hit them.
The aim was simply to terrify
With skin-flaying close shave
After hair-clipping close shave,
And their aim never missed.
It is a nerveless game played out
By captors and captives
All over the war-torn world.
Captors terrorise their prisoners
And the already dead torment
Their torturers by refusing
To cower or quail. So can
The victim become the victor
Even as he succumbs slowly,
Even as he writhes in silent agony.
The Wolf and the last of the Azarapo
Well knew war's rules
And played their part,
Staring unblinking into the eyes
Of each hatchet hurler,
And never once flinching
Even as thudding blades

Scythed through hair,
Shredded leather leggings and
Quivered below balls.

All the while Asgeir
Watched as women
Heat-whitened knives
In a spitting fire near
The tower of torment.
Cold steel is trial enough
But few can long forebear
The test of a white-hot blade.
At this point Asgeir scanned
His broken, downcast warband,
Scowling pride back into the slumped,
And he realised one was missing,
Radnald, Radnald the Ringless,
The brainless spearman,
So powerful in battle,
So pointless in peace.
Asgeir's whispered questions
Drew weary shrugs from his crew,
'Til one, a freckle-faced Dane,
Bjorni Long-Teeth, nudged
Hrolf Hardheart and said:
"Last I saw, he slipped off.
"He went away for a leak."

Chapter 27

Snorri now paused for breath,
Or did the skald stop for beer?
But his thirst sated, he asked
Sven's hunter-killers, if, perhaps,
They wanted a rest, a piss-pause.
But the wolves replied with roars
And Snorri resumed his saga-song.

With a woman's gentle grace
And a killer's gloating grin,
The man-woman led Hornhead
To the Black Hairs' prize prisoners.
Not Asgeir the Dragontamer,
Not Asgeir the Stormrider,
Not Asgeir the ocean's overlord.
They knew nothing of his heroics
And they cared much, much less.
No, with a few leisurely words
And a fleeting lady-like caress,
He – or was it she – led
Doubledeath's master,
The slaughterer of so many,
To the Bisonman and, with a kiss,
Raised Mary slowly to her feet.
So, it was the turn of Hrolf Hardheart
And Mary, Asgeir's miracle-maker,
To face the tests of their new masters.
Hrolf, hands tied, was given the honour

Of being hanged, not by the neck,
But by thick bone hooks thrust
Into his chest muscles and then hauled
On ropes high above the Halfwits' fire
And spun round by death's mistress
As the warpainted chanted and jeered.
Blood slicked his torso but silence
Ruled his mouth. No groan, no cry,
No satisfaction for the scalp-throng.
Hrolf had seen the chest scars
On every man – every man
Save the Halfman Halfwoman,
And realised this was a warrior's
Rite of passage. Like a true Viking
He faced Hel without fear,
Winning hard-faced nods from
His would-be spirit-stealers.
And as he span and pain filled
Every part of his bloodied body,
Shooting stars skidded overhead,
Like the stars exploding in his brain
Until, blessed relief, he blacked out
And twisted and turned limply like a leaf
At the mercy of a lazy, summer wind.

Mary was manhandled like a beast
And Hornhead held her chin
In his calloused hands as if
Her skull was already his.
Mary glared into his soul,
A hatred burning bright as fire.
No helpless glances to Asgeir
Who ignored her as if she
Was worth no more than a dog.
His coldness was kindness,
A ploy to protect his woman.

Wanting is weakness;
Reveal your greatest treasure
And your enemy covets it more.
Hornhead snarled and, with a flourish,
The leering queen of torture
Tore off Mary's top
To bare her whiteness and
Trigger hissing gasps from
The sun-burnished Black Hairs.
She, like Hrolf, was now near-naked
And at the mercy of the merciless.
But round her slight neck still,
Hanging from her leather thong,
Was the small plain bone.
No carvings marked it out,
Nothing of beauty this, but
It was hers and hence
The Halfwoman wanted it
Like an unreading Viking
Craves a monk's books.
So, he or she snatched at it,
Held it in its palms and then…
Well, what then? What then?
Halfwoman thought she was in control,
That the prisoners were her playthings,
But now Mary's magic took over.
And the all-conquering Black Hairs
Began to descend into Hel,
A Hel to be recounted in terror
For as long as eagles soar and
Bison are hunted on the plains.

The Halfwoman simpered and seized
The small bone, Mary's wondrous map
Through the world and its mysteries.
The Halfwoman grabbed it, held it tight,

Grinned and widened her eyes in pleasure
Only to scream, a high feminine squeal.
She screamed and screamed, as her hand
Turned to ice, turned blue and broke.

Four fingers dropped like daggers into
The tribe's well-trodden ground,
Giving off an eerie blue glow
That lit the misery around Mary
Like a copper-fed forge,
As the mixed-up shaman
Hopped and moaned and Hornhead
Reached for his hatchet.
But just then an uproar broke out
All around the bloody pole of pain.
The Idiot had walked backwards,
Spoiling to join in the war-sport.
He grabbed a bone-handled knife,
Turned his back on the tower, and
Took aim over his wide shoulders.
The Wolf watched in private horror.
The Wolf stood firm, eyes forward,
But knew death was seconds away.
No man could master a knife
With his back turned to the target.
He breathed his last and braced
To earn his place with his ancestors,
On hunting grounds rich in bison,
Sweeping to an endless horizon.
But where the other warriors had
Rained blades on prisoners rapidly,
The Idiot liked to take his time,
To put on a shaman's show.
Still shrouded in furs, he was shivering,
Shaking from head to mocassined toe,
Sweat streaming down his grotesque face,

And, just like Grim's snivellers,
Snot dripped from his hook nose.
Then, knife at the ready,
He sneezed and sniffed
And sneezed again,
And coughed and choked
And sank to his knees.
He knelt there helpless,
Whining like the Halfwits,
Before slumping onto his front,
Face-first in the filthy floor.
His hands loosened their grip
On his grisly scalptaker
And with a rasp and a rattle
His chest heaved its last.

The Black Hairs watched bemused.
The Idiot always did the opposite
To other people, and they were
Accustomed to his contrariness.
They thought it was another stunt
So one prodded him playfully
And pressed the fool to stand up.
But the Idiot kept up the act.
So another turned him over
And found oblivion's blessing –
Eyes redder than a salmon's
Hauled from a river harvest
And a body floppier than a fish.
Cries bawled out, men backed away,
And then one of the women
Started sneezing, and another,
Warriors too, until Black Hairs
Began to drop like birds
Frozen in an Arctic ice storm.

All the while Asgeir watched,
Sitting among the condemned,
Waiting to see what torture awaited,
Seeking salvation from any source,
And as baffled as the Black Hairs
By the twists of fate before him.

Confusion had claimed the captors
And Mary was left trussed and standing
As hosts hared from one side of the camp
To the other, spears and hatchets in hand,
Ready to fight the invisible foe.
Seconds earlier they had been victors,
Comfortable with brutal cruelty,
Relishing the shame and agony
Of the Yellow Hairs from the lake.
Now they were panic-stricken
Like chickens in Halfdan's hen-house
When the red coated raider breaks in.
And then the Bear Who Brings Death
Did just what he was born to do.
Vee Ma Gog showed that the tautest sinews
Cannot hold the stronghearted.
He roared like a beast of the forest
And from the bleak depths of his spirit
He summoned his blood brother
With barks, grunts and growls
To make the hair of even the scalped
Come back to horror-haunted life.
From the darkness came the reply:
Silence. But for the first time
Vee Ma Gog's granite face,
Crowned by knives and arrows,
Cracked into a knowing smile.
Still bound, still a target, but he was free.

As Black Hairs tried to revive the snotheads
Hornhead rallied his chaotic scalpmen.
Calm returned, or so he thought.
And then Vee Ma Gog's smile broadened.
The night air was broken by a breeze
Like an arrow loosed off by a boy,
A slow rushing noise followed by a thud.
And, rolling neatly to the feet of Hornhead,
Feathers of courage still attached,
Was the bloodied, mangled head of
The leader of the lakeside ambushers,
The killers of Stormmaster's guards.
The Bisonman held his hatchet tight
And looked frantically from hewn head
To the Halfman-Halfwoman to The Idiot
To blue blades freezing the soil and on
To the shivering, frothing and sneezing
And then to Asgeir, all in a second,
As another head flew towards the fire
From the other side of the camp.
Over a few murderous minutes,
The losers flew into their village.
One more, then another, from a further quarter,
And another, until it was raining skulls.
No returning heroes, these, then.
And now Vee Ma Gog got his reply -
A roar from the deep, blank darkness as
Harbar the Hairy told the Black Hairs
Of his unsated hunger for heads.

In this cauldron of madness
Asgeir felt a hand on his shoulder
And a knife slit his sinew chains.
Radnald the Leaker had returned
To free his Ringstripper, the chief
Who nearly surrendered him

To the Sushone revenge-seekers.
No words were swapped, but Radnald,
Pointless in peacetime, was superb
Whenever war's trumpets came calling.
So, crouched low, he slid and slashed
Down the line until the Black Hairs' bondsmen
Were free to turn the tables on their torturers.
Many warlords would long for twenty-five warriors,
All battle-hardened, all foreigners to fear,
Fervent for revenge, sword-fodder in their sights,
But what use are Vikings without weapons?
Their axes, swords, knives and shields
Were scattered, held as trophies by
The whooping plunderers of the plains.
And waiting in the wings, his face aghast
Was Asgeir's trophy, Grim the Greedy,
And his ragged, heavily-armed oarsmen.
Freedom means nothing at all without
The power to protect it – so Asgeir
And his spearless crew were still prisoners,
At the whim of the warpainted and, worse,
Their fellow Norsemen, knowing
That mercy and Grim were strangers.
And then another roar, a loud crashing and
The flames cast light on the redeemer.

Chapter 28

Blacker than the night,
So black he stood out
Like a shapeshifter's shadow,
Harbar the Hairy loomed,
Drooling over the eagle-feathered,
Before racing over the river
On all fours, fur ruffling,
And claw-crashing through
The spear wall that bristled
To keep his blows at bay.
The Black Hairs were no cowards,
Reared, every one, on warfare,
Well, everyone but the manwoman,
And they let their arrows fly,
But so winter-lush was the bear's fur still
That these death-stingers tickled not killed.
Trampling and mauling all in his way,
He growled straight for Vee Ma Gog,
Leaned on the tower of torment,
Flattened it as its prisoners flailed,
And with one cleave of his claws
Cut clean through the hide ropes
That had for so long held them.
And in his rage, he tossed the tower
Towards Asgeir and his toothless crew
Who hurried to harvest the metal crop
Which had made outlines of The Wolf
And Harbar the Hairy's human brother.

The Vikings were whole once again –
And so, the slaughter began.

The feather wearers were worthy foes,
Forbidden to show fear
And trained in battle-skills.
But an enemy in retreat,
An enemy in shock,
An enemy falling to
An unknown killer
Has no chance
Against the shieldwall-wise
Craving long-sought vengeance.
The Black Hairs had havens
Ever waiting in the wilds,
But Viking boltholes there were none,
So Asgeir and his warfarers fought
For their freedom, for their fame
And, with Grim standing before them,
For their hard-won fortune.
I could, of course, give you gore
But better to give you glory.

Snorri snubbed the bloodlust
Of the carnage caressers,
Suppressing their roars
With a shushing of his lips.

First to fall was Hornhead.
Like all who are learned in war,
Asgeir knew by instinct
The golden rule of raiding:
Kill the leader and
The rest will run;
Fight the foot soldiers and
Your battle will be long.

So he looted the tower.
Asgeir grabbed a hatchet
And set it flying, tumbling,
Glinting in the moonlight,
Splitting the chief's chest,
And as the fountain flowed
The Dragontamer pounced.
He seized Hrolf's sacred axe,
Dropped by Hornhead
In his writhing death throes.
He hurled dreaded Doubledeath
To Ketil Killfast who returned
With relish to where Hrolf Hardheart
Had left off before being overrun
On that blood-slicked slope.
With Hornhead twitching his last
His warriors whooped and turned
And ran headlong with the women,
Leaving blades forged by the fjords
To be reclaimed by the bloody-bearded.

Now I won't bore you ravens with the battle,
How Radnald Rogarrson parried and punched,
Stabbed and slashed through painted ranks,
How his spear feasted on fleeing Black Hairs.
Or how saw-toothed Iggy Fjellason, the fang-filer,
Blooded his weapon by biting braves
Like a fox in a hen house, killing at will,
Throat-ripping, vein-loosening, heart-stopping,…
No, you've heard it all before, haven't you?

As some shouted: "No, we haven't,"
Snorri grinned: "Oh yes you have,"
Before returning to the warfare.

Nor will you want to hear how Vikings also
Had to pay a blood price. Bjorn Nilsson,
Sigi Fire-eater and Gritti Big Knees
All fell to hatchet hacks or the sting
Of death barbs unleashed by Black Hair bows.
But they died in the furnace of the fight
And are now being served by mead-maidens
In Odin's hall of heroes, his home of the brave,
Happier in Valhalla's land of the free
Than ever they were fishing on the fjords.
And every ring-worthy raid-fighter knows
No battle worth the name is ever blood-free.
Their scalps were saved by their shipmates,
Their trophy-seeking killers shaved instead
By Radnald, Broddi the Bloody and rib-recovered
Ketil Killfast. Battle is the best cure for bruises.
But you old war-worshippers don't need me
To paint a picture of the blood and bones,
Sweat and spittle, roars and screams,
Vomit and shit stink of every sword clash.
But in the time it takes to ready a dragonship
The Black Hairs were broken and a dust cloud,
Billowing in the breeze, hid their headlong retreat.
Torches, too, lit from torture fires
Created a sickly smoke screen
As tents were put to the flame,
Hides hissing in the heat.
But not everyone fled, not all escaped,
And cowering in a bison-skin tent was
The host of their torture, the Half Man Half Woman.
Simpering smiles and coy glances are no defence
Against sword and spear when scores are settled,
But Asgeir spared the mistress of murder.
As Broddi prepared to skewer the worthless
Asgeir stayed his spear-arm, saying:
"I have plans for her. Slavery is a worse penance

"Than a warrior's swift death and this snake
"Does not deserve to die like a warrior."

As Asgeir cut Mary loose
And cloaked her beauty,
Broddi the Bloody
And Oddo the Hairy
Lowered Hrolf Hardheart
To a muddy mattress.
The Wolf howled his death taunt
And Vee Ma Gog fed Hornhead
To his hairy, human-hungry, rescuer.

And so, another race began
As fast as summer sports
In the lush mountain meadows
But with life not laughter
As the victor's trophy.
Grim was furious, horrified.
He had Asgeir in his grasp.
He had found allies crueller
Even than he to finish off
His former band of loot-robbers.
But he had borne the seeds
Of his own disease-defeat across
The ocean in his sickly crew.
Black Hairs fight without fear
But an unseen killer is too much
Even for these skirmish-masters.
And so, months and thousands of miles
From home and hearth in Norway,
Grim faced Asgeir over the carnage
In their fight to the finish,
In their private Viking war,
To own the hard-won hoard.

Asgeir's men, battle-friends reclaimed,
Formed their shieldwall, and Norse nous
Brought to this land of darting raids
The grinding, slashing tactics of dragonmen.
Teeth gritted, bloodletters gripped,
They watched Grim curse and cuff
His crew into their own battle bastion.
But where Asgeir's men slipped silently
Into position, spears poking through
The arrow-spiked sword-blunters,
Waverider's warriors shuffled and swore.
The Viking shieldwall is unforgiving.
Valkyries take even the strong
As shins are hacked and shield cracks
Yield to let swords stab the brave.
A shieldwall exposes all
And warlike resolve is all.
No hiding place lurks there for
Waverers, worriers or weaklings,
The uncommitted, the questioning.
Doubt and you will die.
Dare and you might just live.
A shieldwall stands on unity
And implodes on dissent.
Stormmaster's men could see
They had won well before
The first clash of iron on ash.
Grim's men all knew it too,
And the sour smell of fear-sweat
Wafted over, piercing the fire smoke
Like acid through lard grease.
But before every battle
The old rules must be observed
Even by the raven fodder.
So Asgeir and Grim marched out
From the safety of their man forts

To show their contempt for their foe
And their indifference to death.
Brandishing the stolen sword,
Egil the Skinny's Shieldsplitter,
Grim launched the death ritual.

And two jet ravens alighted
On the prone tower of torment.
Silent, all-seeing, spectres.

In a loud clear voice,
The hacksilver hoarder
Breathed bile and hatred.
"Look around, loot-lovers,
"And learn where your bones
"Will bleach after your flesh
"Has fed the moon-howlers.
"You will pay your mutiny toll
"By blunting our blades
"With your scrawny skulls.
"Better still that you die
"Than you dodge death
"For the blood-eagle awaits
"Any snivelling traitors who
"Avoid Valhalla's welcome.
"In the seconds it takes
"To slaughter a lamb
"Your bowels will feel
"The thrill of cool air.
"Remember, I have Shieldsplitter,
"Egil the Skinny's legendary sword,
"Never beaten in battle,
"And what do you dogs have?
"A whore who I had long before you."
And, thrusting Shieldsplitter aloft,
Grim turned to Waverider's warriors

And gave the roar that Asgeir
And his rovers had heard so often,
The battle roar of the monk-raider,
The roar of the death-dealer.

Chapter 29

Asgeir stepped shieldless over Black Hair bodies,
Strode right up to Waverider's shieldwall,
Belly-slasher scabbarded by his side,
And stared boldly into the eyes of his enemies,
One after another; and one after another,
They blinked and looked away first.
Grim lurked back in the middle, Shieldsplitter itching
In his hardened hands, but Asgeir was no fool
And held himself a good spear lunge distant,
Time enough to leap and parry and unleash
Deathbringer from his worn leather shelter.
Stepping back so all Grim's men could hear him,
He gave them a death grin, the salivating smile
Of wolves closing in on a wounded deer.
"You know what awaits you. In a few moments
"Your chests will rise no more, your eyes
"Will mist over, never to see again,
"Like the glassy eyes of a hook-hauled codfish.
"Your last lifeblood will trickle away,
"Staining this sour soil, to be trampled on
"And pissed on by scalp-loving women.
"And for what?" He faced his old skipper.
"For him? For this goblin of greed?
"Don't forget that we know him well.
"He is the master of self-sacrifice.
"He will sacrifice you and save himself.
"Ask his most loyal man, his protector,
"Ask Aethelfrith the Vile, his slavering guard dog.

"Oh, but you can't: Loyalty cuts one way for Grim.
"Your master slashed off his head in a fury
"And Aethelfrith's skull now rides our longship,
"A warning to any who tie themselves to Grim.
"And if you win and if you live, your only reward
"Will be life under the lash, all work and no pay.
"Your arms are bare. Look at my men's arms.
"I am Asgeir the Ring-Giver, Asgeir the Rewarder.
"And he is Grim the Greedy, Grim the Goldhoarder,
"Grim the Ringkeeper. Fight for him, make him rich
"And you will stay poor and oppressed and his spearfodder.
"Don't kid yourselves that Valhalla awaits.
"Odin welcomes only warriors who die in glory.
"No glory here. Only gore. Your gore. Yours alone.
"Your leader has angered the gods. Even a troll
"Would respect the Death Fleet but not loathsome Grim.
"He brandishes Shieldsplitter like a secret weapon,
"But you know it is not his. You saw him steal it
"From Egil the Skinny's eternal sea-bed.
"All know of Shieldsplitter's fame, how it
"Slaked its thirst on Saracen and Saxon skulls.
"But swords are like dogs,
"Loyal to one owner,
"Untameable by impostors.
"It is one thing to stand to arms.
"It is another for those arms to stand to you.
"Shieldsplitter is no stranger to war and its wiles.
"It can tell between a campaign king and a coward,
"A ring-giver and a greed glutton, a chief and a cheat.
"Invincible in battle once, certainly, but no more.
"And when you all knock on the doors of Valhalla
"Do you think Odin will welcome men who served
"A defiler, a desecrator, a despoiler of the Death Fleet?
"No, you all know the answer. I can see it in your twitching eyes.
"So, your choice. Fight and in a few moments
"Our starving steel will feast on your guts and you,

"You will be heading for Loki's sister's ice sanctuary.
"Your choice: Live or die. Valhalla or Hel.
"Rot here as raven fodder or return to the fjords' embrace."

He waited to let Waverider digest his words.
And then, in his forceful voice,
He offered the men honour.
He said: "A Viking does not fear death.
"A battle's blood unlocks
"The gates of Valhalla
"And leads to Odin's hall
"And its Valkyrie shield-maidens.
"But what Viking wants to die
"For a futile, wasteful gesture?
"Wise is the warrior who
"With his Lord by his side
"Lives to sail and fight again."
Another pause, pregnant with death.
"That," he glanced at Grim,
"Is not your gilded lord.
"Gilded, yes. Lord no.
"He longs to be a lord,
"Craves the glorious title,
"But his greed makes him unworthy.
"But I, Asgeir Dragontamer,
"I am a worthy warlord."

He walked one last time along the front rank
And his gaze met only the glistening of fear sweat.

He returned to his cheering spearmen
And the shieldwall swallowed him
Like the sea closing over a shark fin.
Asgeir knew the battle was almost won
Without a single clash of steel on steel.
All knew he never shirked from bloodletting

But he had a bigger victory in sight.
A warrior who dies fighting is a winner.
Better to break Grim before his men,
To harm him by humiliation, to show
Him for the self-seeker he was
And condemn him to an eternal death,
His name blackened by cowering.
And so Asgeir dragged Grim back
To the beach below Whitby's black cliffs.
Hidden behind the shieldwall
Asgeir breathed life into the lungs
Of the headless henchman.
"Waverider beware," came a wail,
Sing-song and light, a taste of the Tyne
On the grasslands of the bison,
"I am Aethelfrith, I was Grim's man,
"Now I am headless and my skull
"Is doomed to roam the seas
"'Til the Kraken ends my misery.
"For Grim I gave all, for Grim
"I whipped and killed and wielded
"Axes across the wild northern seas.
"But as his gold piled up
"My only reward was food.
"As his silver glittered
"My only wage was murder.
"Why, master, why did you
"Whip off my head without
"Once waiting for breath?"

Grim's eyes darted in every direction,
As his reddened, weather-racked face paled,
White waning through his greybeard,
And he began to scream abuse
At the slave brother he had slaughtered.
"Shut your lying mouth," he shouted,

"Stop your carping, you little shit.
"I am your leader. I alone decide,
"And I alone, who lives or dies."
But his voice wilted with every word
And his bravery drained with the blood
Sliding from his head to his shaking hands.
Foam formed on his lips, his eyes widened,
And, Shieldsplitter still in his right hand,
He covered his ears to silence the spectre.

But Aethelfrith the Vile's stringpuller
Was far from finished. In faltering Norse,
The slave-Norse learned on the longboats,
He said: "A warband lives on loyalty
"But you are loyal to you alone.
"Waverider, learn from my betrayal.
"Live to ride the waves once more.
"Choose what you do wisely.
"Go with Grim and, win or lose,
"Death and despair are all that waits.
"Ditch the despoiler and see how
"A true warlord rewards his warriors."

A shuffling surged through the shieldwall,
Whose rumblings belied the stony gaze
Of Norsemen bracing themselves for
The rasping death of raw steel.
Sweat soiled the cheeks of soldiers
From Shetland, Iceland, Stromfjord and beyond,
Thrown together for trade and loot,
Bartering and battle, hacksilver and slaying.
But Grim was not their warlord.
Thorfinn the Bald's skeleton
Had been picked snow-white clean
By sea's scavengers months ago,
Within days of Doublefang slicing

His legs off on the Orkney shingle.
Grim could hear the muttering
And smell the fluid, shifting sands
Of his mercenary oarsmen.
No Aethelfrith in this throng,
No guard dog to defend him,
Fed on scraps and lies of freedom.
So he did all that was left to him.
He growled at his men and grabbed
The bruise-headed sniveller, holding
A bejewelled knife to his scrawny neck,
And roared: "Fight or bathe in his blood."
But even as he spat out his threat
It was his red wine that watered the soil
As a Danish blade slashed his hamstring,
Hobbling him like a Saxon horse.
As he screamed the sniveller leapt
To a snot-filled freedom of shocked shame.
Asgeir and Stormmaster's swordsmen
Watched Grim's men turn on their whipmaster.
But the goldhoarder had one, last, desperate,
Roll of Loki's dice to throw, a last chance to live.
He staggered clear of the shield fort and
Held Shieldsplitter, sword of eternal fame,
And brandished it above his head,
Hefted tightly in gilded gauntlets,
Looted long ago like all he owned,
Pledging vengeance on any rank-breakers,
Threatening to unleash his invincible brother
On any shieldwall side-switchers.
"Shieldsplitter has never tasted defeat
"And never will. He has skewered and slashed
"His way across the world and, I can feel it,
"Here, in my hands, he laughs at this little band
"Of looters, this whining pool of piss.
"He fears nothing. I fear nothing.

"With Shieldsplitter we will win
"And the battleworthy will be rewarded."

At last, at long last, Grim had grasped
The laws of leadership, using glittering bait
To bolster his ranks, to put fight into the fearful.
But such lessons are best learned early,
Not after years of flogging and theft.
Grim was the sort of father who would
Welcome guests to his daughter's wedding
And send them away empty-handed.
No wonder he had no wife waiting,
No bairns to return to for winter's rest,
Doomed like the Death Fleet to roam
For evermore, homeless and haunted,
Counting his gold his sole consolation.

As Grim glowered outside Waverider's shieldwall,
Holding Egil the Skinny's battle brother aloft
Like a torch in the depths of a tortured night,
The sky darkened once more and a wind arose,
Whipping across the grassland in a rage.
Above the whistling of the gale came
A familiar chorus, the howling of the Halfwits,
Still roasting over the slumbering fire.
They had failed their fellow fighters,
Fled instead of safeguarding Stormmaster,
So Asgeir was in no rush to rescue them.
A blood-eagle beckoned, if he could
Only fracture the fragile war bond
Between Waverider's wavering crew
And their crumbling, limping commander.

The collapse had already begun.
As black clouds blotted out
Spring's golden life giver and

Shifted broiling day to shivering night,
Waverider's biggest warrior,
Kjartan the Oak, guaranteed
The blood-eagle would fly.
This vast veteran barged out
Of the bowel-loosening shieldwall,
Sheathed hungry Gutgorger,
Fingered his broad cheek scars
And strode calmly to Stormmaster.
This striking grey-flecked beard
Roared defiance before defecting,
Deaf to Grim's wailing traitor taunts.
"I am Kjartan the Oak, and well-named,
"Son of Bjorn Haraldson, son of
"Harald Bjornson, warriors all,
"Warriors right back to the Kellings.
"I shit on death, I never run,
"But this fight is not mine.
"This ringhoarder is not my master,
"And never will be, never could.
"Death scares me not. Death,
"Heroic death, is my duty,
"Heroic death is my door key,
"To Odin's hall of heroes.
"But there is no heroism here,
"Just a hack fight to the death
"To make a rich man richer.
"Grim is greed, greed and greed,
"And I am not ready to die
"For Grim the Greedy."

In the sweat-filled fug of Sven's hall
A rumble enveloped the beer-bearded.
Men fight for gold and glory,
For their lives and, most of all,
For their friends. A true warrior

Would rather die in gut-spilled agony
Than betray his true battle brother.
True, men fight well for a warlord,
But only if he acts like one and
A true warlord rewards his wolves.
Fools see generosity as a weakness
But for a warlord generosity is strength.
And over many long loot-summers
Spearmen had grumbled and rumbled
That Wersil the ring-keeper had much to learn,
That Wersil was no match for Sven Ravenfeeder.
And for the first time since Snorri started to skald
A flicker tickled Wersil's icy, heartless face
And a grin softened Sven's narrowed eye.

At the Skraelings' camp, the stench of death
Curdled the air and where Kjartan led
The rest of the death-facers rapidly followed.
Waverider's sea-farers stepped forward,
One at a time, and then in a flood
Until they were exposed, naked to
Stormmaster's disciplined spearmen.
Asgeir considered the choice – chop
And kill and slash and slaughter
And then reclaim his crew's gold
With no newcomers to nag for a share.
But he had promised them their lives
If they left Grim the Greedy for him,
He had promised them a return
To the fjords if they swapped sides
And Aetheling the Vile had promised
Them ring-giving in return for serving
Stormmaster well. And a promise
Must be kept just as gold must be given.
And besides, many months of fighting
Lay ahead before any would see fjords

Rising from the pale blue of Norway's seas.
So Asgeir gave the order and the shieldwall
Parted to swallow its new bloodletters.
But ever after Asgeir was on his guard:
Once a defector, always a defector.
Loyalty, once forfeit, fosters new betrayal.
Switch sides once and you'll switch sides twice.

And what of Grim? For months
He had fled Asgeir's embrace,
Risking the great unknown and
Running the gauntlet of
Tribes more animal than men,
All for the sake of shaking off
His one-time war-colleague,
Now his relentless wolfhound.
And, at last, the race was lost.
Grim may well have been greedy,
Grim may have led by the lash,
But Grim could not be called a coward.
And as the blood-eagle beckoned
He readied to win Odin's redemption
And die fighting, sword in hand,
Not squirm, face down in the dirt,
And let his lungs be torn
Clean out of his bony back
And woven into crimson wings.

Shieldsplitter held high,
He retreated to a mound
To make his last stand
And on the trampled tussocks
He roared taunts to his hunters,
To his turncoats, to his killers.
So set was this friendless fighter
On paying the blood price

For a seat in Valhalla's beer hall,
That his red mist blinded him
To the Whitby-black sky and
The swirling, wispy wind devils
Dancing around his death stage.
But Waverider and Stormmaster
Marked the change in heaven's mood
And stood off, half-watching Grim,
Half-guarding against the plain-stalkers,
The trolls, ghouls and giants hunting
Human flesh in this unforgiving land.
Grim saw this, saw Broddi the Bloody
Hammering four stakes into the soil
And hauling a sharp boulder to the middle,
Grim's belly pillow for the blood-eagle,
And cursed their craven cowardice,
Hoping to provoke a swift death wound
And deny the gloating traitors their sport.
Grim was in full battle rage,
A cocktail of courage and anger,
Bile and frothing wrath and,
Yes, death dread and,
The greatest dread of all,
Of dying a shameful death,
Cowering instead of clashing,
Screaming like a woman
Rather than roaring like a man.

But Grim the Greedy missed his nemesis.
He had expected death at the hands of men
But worse, much worse devils awaited him
And it never dawned on him
Even when the wolf pack
Scattered in a clang of metal.
So he raged and roared and ranted
And laughed at the fleeing torturers.

But sometimes it is best to check
Before you think it clever to laugh.

Chapter 30

Bile poured forth from Grim's frothing lips,
As he showered shame on the lung-lusters,
Needling them with slurs to stoke their anger
And trick them into killing him quickly.
They were, he raged, worse than women,
Snivelling shield-cowerers and spear-shirkers,
Back-row warriors, goreless glory-hunters,
Soft in the sword – in battle and in bed.
Asgeir and Kjartan the Oak were traitors,
Violators of the sacred oath of loyalty
Between warlord and unquestioning warrior,
They were all bum boys, buggers,
Arse-bandits, cock-suckers and prick-pleasers,
And Mary? She was a slut, a whore, a harlot,
Who'd fucked him every way he wanted,
Her wantonness making animals seem moral,
Only truly happy when debasing herself,
And, he leered at Asgeir, evil in his brow:
"Whatever you do with her, remember,
"I did it with her first and better."

And so, he sang his death song,
So full of energy for one soon to sleep,
Not a hero's farewell, but a ballad of hate
Designed to dodge the death he feared.
But spears and swords, arrows and clubs,
Came there none; no-one stepped up
To seize the quest-target, the hate-hulk.

Well, I tell a lie. Grim's time on Midgard
Was ebbing, like a retreating spring tide,
And some there did step up, did strike,
But they were not of this world, oh no.

Even Sven stopped drinking and chewing.
Even his wolfhound dropped his bone.
The cattle in the byre ceased their lowing.
The wenches waited instead of waiting.

But in the wild, dark wastelands the ravens
Watched and waited, ready to fly to their master.
And a drumbeat grew, but not from drums.

In his frenzy Grim had failed to spot
The shifting backdrop of his death.
Well, when a man is about to die
He stops admiring the scenery
And his mind narrows
To death's snarling teeth.
So, when Waverider and Stormmaster
Scattered and flung themselves flat,
He continued raging and ranting,
Egil the Skinny's Shieldsplitter
Held aloft, his only friend,
But soon to be his hellish foe.
As the sky darkened ominously,
The swishing drumbeat strengthened,
Dust twisters danced and grew
Into gale gusts, wind whippers
Strong enough to roll a longship.
Black Hair tents flapped in flames
And the Halfwits swayed like
The newly strangled on the gallows.
A rumble, a roar and from the lake,
From Stormmaster's mooring, rose

A waterspout, spinning heavenwards,
Spraying gulping, gasping fish
All around. But this was no bounty,
Rather a warning, like a tattoo
Beaten by Thor's mighty hammer.
And as Grim cast his curses
In all directions, like the dying fish,
Huge dark shadows surged over.
Broad wings, long barbed tails and
Scimitar fangs bared in scaly mouths
Became clear in the fading light,
The drumbeats revealed as wingbeats –
Two dragon guards of the Death Fleet,
Led by Asgeir's battle rival, the sea-struggler,
The dragon he heroically tamed so long ago.
They circled once and then swooped
One after the other and, without landing,
Took exactly what they had come for.
One swept down, wingbeats like a north wind,
And with one bite, one sickening slice
Tore off Grim's head. The Greed-King stood,
As a red fountain like a volcano of wine,
Pumped, pulsated from his thick neck,
Glowing bright against the blackness.
Then Asgeir's debtor slid through the slipstream,
And with a scaly hand, jagged with thorn knuckles,
Ripped Shieldsplitter from Grim's gilded gauntlets,
And then, and only then, did the Gold-Hoarder
Sink to his knees, sway, arms twitching,
And collapse on his chest, blood-writhing.
The head-biter swept back around and
From treetop height spat out Grim's skull
Which bounced and rolled to the silent feet
Of Vee Ma Gog, who looked into its blinking eyes.
As Harbar the Hairy flayed Grim's body flesh free,
The last of the Azarapo grabbed the tribe traitor,

The battle-shirking, oath-breaking self-server,
Held his head with his foot, and his cold knife
Claimed the scalp he had coveted so long,
Vaunting his vengeance with a war whoop
That still haunts the wide steppes
On wind-battered winter nights.
And then the sword-reclaimer flew back,
Leisurely flaps now, no need to race,
A slower, lighter, fading drumbeat,
And basked before Asgeir, hanging
Like a wind-hover over his sea-partner,
Shieldsplitter in hand in a soldier's salute.
The Viking crews were standing now,
Shocked but safe, at least for a while.
Broddi the Bloody shouted:
"Dragontamer, he's hailing you.
"You won his war-respect."
And then the two dragons
Paid their respects,
In a special underworldly way,
By pissing on the war gang,
From a great, great height.
As they banked and flapped back
To their eternal watery patrol
Their golden piss, fish-fed and oil-rich,
Smothered the Halfwits' smouldering embers
And smear-stained the Vikings' Norse clothes.

The crews stood there stinking and dripping,
Wiping the salt stench from their lips,
And then Asgeir began to laugh,
A long pent-up laugh of relief,
Months of command tension released
By a victory he had long craved
But which had come with
A humiliating sting in the tail.

Dreams can come true
But never as we dreamt.
And as their lord laughed,
The others laughed too
And Hrolf Hardheart came to,
His hanging hell behind him.
His skewered chest was red with blood,
A flood unleashed by bison bone hooks,
But, as he wiped away the dragon soap,
The deep cuts healed, leaving only scars,
Bedroom battle honours to woo the women.
The Halfwits, too, took the piss.
Broddi at last cut the whiners down
And their feet, burnt to the bone,
Grew back before his wide eyes
But would for ever more always be black –
So no bedroom battle honours for them.
And Grim? His body was melting inside
Harbar the Hairy's belly, his tough flesh
Ravened by the bear's fighting fangs.
But from his dirt pillow the plunder poacher
Was still ranting, still raving, still raging,
Even as his head bled from scalp and neck,
Earning a kick in the mouth from Vikings
Sick of his avarice and remorseless bile.
Some men, you see, never learn to keep their heads.

Chapter 31

Dragon-drenched sweat-soaked Viking garb
Was cast off and Black Hair dead stripped,
Months of sea-salt and strife swapped
For bison buckskin steeped in torture,
Soay sheepswool for beaded shirts and
Hempen hose for leather leggings,
Scalps flapping from the sooty seams.
Radnald Rogarsson took still warm
Blackened firebrands and painted his face,
Yellow clay the only relief in his war mask.
Others followed his lead, each face different,
'Til Norsemen wore New World savagery,
Only their flaxen hair and beards pointing
To their long yearned-for fjord homeland.
Even flame-haired Mary wore war paint.
Asgeir, his face now red and blue and white,
Grabbed the trophy he had so hard won:
Asgeir the Dragontamer,
Asgeir the Stormrider was now
Asgeir the Horn-Headed,
A shaggy headed helmet of pride
Crowning the great chieftain's command.
He also rescued from the camp blaze
The spirit-sapping face scalps
Of Olaf Blodason and Sea Ruler's crew.
Their yellow hair and shrivelled features
Would never more be flaunted as
Savage-savoured signs of triumph.

They were heading for home,
To rest forever beside the fjords.

Vee Ma Gog and The Wolf watched
With wordless faces but the latter
Gave his approval in his familiar way,
Throwing back his head and howling.
And from the hills all around his brothers
Joined the grasslands' ghost chorus.

Spears, shields, axes and swords reclaimed,
Hatchets, clubs and scalping knives looted,
Scalp sticks brandished; bison skins slung
Over broad oar-built Dagafjord shoulders,
The two crews stole as one to their dragonships,
Grim's severed head still hurling kin taunts.
Stormmaster lay beached still, intact,
Straining on the shingle, bodies littering
The blood-stained, conifer-lined lakeshore.
Kjartan the Oak, face striped red and black,
Led the way to Waverider, shore-shelved
In the next bay. "So close, so close,"
Cursed Asgeir silently to himself.
Had he sailed only another hour,
Round that high, shielding headland,
Past the witchhead hill,
Waverider would have been his,
Without a fight, without a war,
And all his men would still live,
And all Grim's gold hoard would be Stormmaster's,
Not shared with a mutinous horde of fight-fleers.
But a promise is a pledge,
A pledge is a promise,
Norway was many battles away,
And gold doesn't glitter for the dead.

The four guards prepared to die with honour
When they saw the painted devils approaching.
No Halfwits these: when they spotted the Hornhead,
They beat swords on shields and harnessed spears,
But a call from Kjartan the Oak was enough
To make them lower their death-shafts unfed.
Crews, not battle, were joined, fight-foes
Made brothers by shared need not shared deeds.
The four were offered the life option:
Stop being hunted and fight for the hunters,
Or fight and die now and stain the shingle red.
Wisely they chose life even though Asgeir demanded
They lead him to the loot and hand over the hoard.
Grim alone objected, his dribble-filled skull
Still barking out orders under cover of
A shirt soaked in stinking dragonpiss.
His warlord's voice might still be strong
But his days of command were long gone.
The guards had done their job well.
The hoard lay not on board but was buried
On a flowered hillside overlooking the lake,
Nine paces north of an old oak sentinel
That stood out alone on the grassy slope,
Its bark shine-polished by generations of bison,
And host to body parts of Black Hair victims
Picked clean by slick-headed black vultures.
Two crews worked together to raise the sack
From its grave, to give new life to the gold,
But one man would decide its fate, one warrior,
Asgeir the Horn-Headed, Asgeir the Ring-Giver.

Two crews licked their lips in anticipation
But two crews felt their throats dry, too,
As they waited to see who was favoured,
Who was tolerated and who had failed.
Some, the battle-brave, glanced, smugly,

Towards the Halfwits but the Halfwits
Gurned and grinned and rubbed their hands,
Ready for their reward, ready for payment,
For this pair always felt entitled,
Always believed rings were their right.
Bjerk Oddson, the head Halfwit,
Had even been heard boasting how
He and his brother had laughed at the fire,
Had refused to fail Stormmaster's men,
Had borne themselves like heroes,
Hanging defiantly, like Odin from Yggdrasil.
Bjerk the Black-footed, Bjerk the buffoon,
Even brandished a scabbed scalp
Which all knew he had stolen
From a Black Hair scalpstick.

But so it is after all bloodletting.
The biggest battle-boasters
Have least to brag about.
He who sings of his own bravery
Is ever blind to his own cravenness.
But Asgeir saw all and knew all,
Like all wise warlords,
And he prepared to smile on some
And to exact a penalty from others.

Lookouts posted, he spread out the riches
Which glittered under the kiss of the golden sun
And called forward his heroes one by one.
Each bead, each bangle, each torque, each ruby
Recalled a raid, like a map of the monk houses
Sparkling along the bleak, windblown Saxon shore,
Idling hoard-houses of jewels and wealth.
Here was Whitby, there was Dunwich,
Here was Jarrow where Fuldo fell.
Each spoke like battle veterans to the raiders.

But for now, misted memories gave way to glory
As the chieftain chose his battle brothers.
Ketil Killfast, Hrolf Hardheart, Broddi the Bloody
Stepped forward and each stepped back
Their muscled arms bulging under silver rings.
Others of Stormmaster's crew were rewarded,
Some with rings, some with silver,
For not all fight with equal distinction,
And not all expect the same salute,
And returned to their ranks smiling.
Even Mary was called to account
And her magic, her shapeshifting,
Was held up as a weapon as sharp
As any warrior's gutfeasting war lance.
"She," said Asgeir, "has saved us so often.
"Broddi owes her his lungs, we owe her
"Our sea feast, Radnald owes her his life,
"The Sushone owe her their supremacy,
"And without her there would be no treasure."
She returned with a jewelled necklace
And an ornate, needle-sharp hairpin,
Ransacked from a rich woman's wardrobe.
And then Harbar the Hairy shambled forward,
The skullhurler taking bison meat as his medal.
Asgeir called Vee Ma Gog and The Wolf
But both declined, preferring still-wet scalps
As their hard-won, bloody battle badges.
And then it was the turn of Waverider,
The turn of Grim's oarsmen and axe-wielders.
Kjartan the Oak was first, and he returned
Ring-proud, a silver serpent on his forearm.
Asgeir called forward the snotty-nosed youth
Who had sneezed death on the torture-captors,
Despite Grim's repeated beatings and bruises.
Asgeir towered above him and barked:
"Boy, what is your name?" The greasy-maned lad,

Wiped his nose on his sleeve and began:
"Nag Hakonson, son of Valdar of Vik,
"Son of…" Asgeir stopped him to say:
"Yes, yes, yes. You are now Nag Wetnose,
"Our secret weapon." As the crews laughed
Nag Wetnose grinned at his fame
And cherished a thumb ring,
Small reward for a warrior
But plenty for a poorly pup.
But others were less well rewarded,
Having to settle for hacksilver,
A paltry return for months of rowing
Against the perils of storm and spear,
Arrows and whips, starvation and pain,
And staring down death every day.
But then Asgeir called forward Radnald.
"Waverider," he said, "you want more.
"But you know you have to earn it.
"I don't know any one of you.
"All I know is that you flee well,
"That you have swapped sides once
"And once switched you can switch again."
A murmur arose, but Kjartan scowled
His boatmen into grumbling submission.
"You abandoned Grim, a move well made,"
Continued Asgeir, his bison horns adding
To his height as he stood on the mound,
"For he never earned any man's trust,
"He never even bought a man's trust.
"But you must win my trust like true Vikings,
"By showing your grit in the ordeals ahead.
"Do so, and your arms will glitter, and all
"Will know you to be valiant among Vikings.
"Learn from Radnald Rogarrson here,"
And he nodded to the man whose spear use
Was second to none in the shieldwall

And a liability when peace prevailed.
"This warrior was always in the front row
"Of the shieldwall and has warred with me
"For years, raiding across the Norwegian Sea.
"I could never ask for a braver brother.
"But his lust nearly got us all killed
"And only Mary's magic saved us all
"From bloody Black Hair vengeance.
"He was once the most silver-sated
"Of all my Valhalla-proud war-raveners,
"But I stripped Radnald of his honours and
"The lance-leader became the warband's lowliest.
"But when Black Hair irons were warming
"For Hel's torment, Radnald rescued us
"And led the rout, hurling us our arms
"And scalping like a native-born Black Hair."
Asgeir stepped two paces forward to embrace
The sometime bruiser, the sometime fool,
And gave him two gold dragon rings.
"Radnald is redeemed," shouted Asgeir.
"By your deeds you too can be redeemed."
He paused and scanned the crews,
Holding up in both hands a golden ring
Hailing heroic Sigurd's victory over the serpent,
And roared like the lions of Barbary:
"Remember: I am the ring giver
"But what I give I can take away.
"You would all be ring grabbers.
"But what will you give me back?"

All the time the Halfwits were beaming,
Ogling the beauty of the loot,
Bjerk nudging Odd as Radnald was reborn.
"It's our turn now," whispered Bjerk
To his scrawny soulmate, "rings galore for us."

Chapter 32

"And now", smiled Asgeir, "We come
"To Stormmaster's gallant guards.
"The heroes of the lake harbour,
"The scourge of the scalpers,
"The death-defying spearmen
"Who laughed over the torture fire."
All eyes turned to the Halfwits,
All felt the cruel relish of watching
Another receive a chieftain's wrath.
In the blazing fire fed by the guards,
Two knives were already glowing white.
All guessed what was coming,
All, of course, but Bjerk and Odd.
Bjerk grinned and winked at
The long thin streak of gloom
Who, as usual, stared blankly,
Awaiting the reward, he believed
He had earned just by being born.

"Well," purred the Bisonhead,
"How could I possibly repay you?
"What could ever be a worthy
"Battle badge for such bravery?
"Rings? Gems? Maybe dirhams
"Brought from Baghdad's bazaars?
"Well, I'll tell you how we'll decide."
Bjerk could not hide his pride.
If he had been a dog

He would have wagged his tail.
"We'll ask your battle brothers
"What your blood prize will be."
Bjerk beamed at the crews
And even Odd began to dream.
"We'll ask, let's see, I know,
"We'll ask Skidi Njalson, Vog Cnutson
"And, oh, yes, young Einar Hrolfson."
Bjerk's brow began to furrow,
And Odd began to fidget
As the truth began to dawn
Even on this duo of dolts.
"Oh, but we can't ask them,
"Can we? Their raven-scoured bodies
"Lie lifeless by Stormmaster's keel,
"Their scalps and faces scraped off.
"They died doing their duty, defending
"Our only way home, our lifeline,
"Our key to the Easternway to Norway.
"But you two still live, you two still breathe,
"You two still have your scalps,
"You still have your flatulent faces.
"So why do your fat hearts beat
"While wolves feast on your brothers?
"Why were you taken unharmed?
"Where were your weapons and
"How did the Black Hair warriors
"Find us so swiftly and in such force?"
Bjerk began to splutter, spit flying
As he defended his battle failure.
Odd began to whine, blaming all,
All but himself. Anything that went wrong
Was always somebody else's fault
Just as anything that went right
Was always claimed by him as his.
But Asgeir, bison horns on his head,

Silenced the Halfwits with a shieldwall stare.
He lifted his head and his voice:
"Watch and remember, Waverider.
"See and marvel, Stormmaster.
"Fight well for me and rings will
"Glitter on your oar-muscled arms.
"But let me down, run like mice,
"And you will pay a blood price."

The weather-beaten Halfwits paled,
Sun and wind-whipped tans
Turning to ice bear snow
As Asgeir delivered his verdict.
"You put your lives first,
"You put all our lives last
"Just to save your vile necks.
"You are self-serving cowards both,
"Craven, wavering, whining cowards.
"Now all will see what rats you are
"Just by reading your wretched faces."
Hrolf and Ketil, Broddi and Radnald
Seized the struggling shieldwall-shirkers
And from the furnace of the firwood fire
Asgeir drew the white-hot knife of justice.
Hrolf held Bjerk's howling head still
As Asgeir brand-gouged the letter C
On the blubberer's sweaty forehead and,
Lest he grow long hair, on both cheeks.
And then he pulled the other knife,
Fizzing, humming and dazzling with heat,
And shame-scarred Odd the Simperer,
Odd the Screamer, in the same way,
Carving the badges of cowardice
On his forehead and beardless cheeks.
Most men would have learned
But Bjerk had battled hard

To be hailed as a Halfwit
And still struggled to grasp
His guilt as a fight-fleer.
So, he let his bile boil over
And from the foggy bowels
Of his malice-muddled mind
He dredged up all the slurs
That had ever been levelled at him.
"You fucking scumbag," he bawled,
Froth forming on his leathery lips,
"You cunt, you steaming pile of crap,
"You're no man, you fight like a nun.
"Look at you with your baby's beard,
"That's no beard, it's bum fluff.
"I bet you were bullied as a boy,
"And no wonder, you're thicker
"Than a winter's pile of pigshit.
"Grim was more of a leader than you,
"Yes, and he's not the only one
"To have slotted your slut.
"We all have, we've all fucked her,
"She'll do anything, three of us
"At a time and still she wanted more, more…"
And then Asgeir's ring-festooned fist
Parted the fool from his yellow teeth
Which fell to mingle with the shingle.
Asgeir spat: "You make it so easy, arsehole.
"String the bastard up by his blackened feet
"And we'll see how hungry Harbar the Hairy is."
And as Grim garlanded Bjerk's bravery,
Hailing the hole-digger as a warrior,
The Halfwit swang in the cooling breeze,
Still raging, still ranting, still stupid
While the last, sweet, Sushone honey
Was smeared over his tattooed head and arms.
All the while Odd watched in silence.

All his life he had hidden behind his brother,
Too soft to fight for himself but happy
To let his brother menace and maul.
So, did he protest, speak up for the oaf,
Offer himself for Harbar in his stead?
No, of course not. He watched with
Cold, dead eyes and a sour smirk.

Vee Ma Gog finger-whistled and
Harbar the Hairy lumbered over
To leer at the selfish whiner.
Grim's flesh still filled his belly
But Harbar had a whale's hunger,
And soon sniffed the sweet honey
And drooled over the fruit of the hive.
Bjerk, arms hobbled behind his back,
Jerked and wriggled the gallows dance,
Desperate to dodge the dagger fangs.
But Harbar held his head,
Paws clinging, claws biting
Into the greying, cloying skin,
Licked Bjerk's stricken face
And then sniffed his fat arms,
Before biting a honey-soaked chunk.
But even bears, even hungry bears,
Have their limits, and Harbar howled,
Staggered back, spat out the feast
And vomited under the villain
Before groaning back to the boat.
Bjerk had performed the impossible.
Sushone honey was the purest,
Sweetest any Viking had ever tasted.
But Bjerk the bitter, Bjerk the yellow,
Had turned sweet into sour.

When Bjerk had finished screaming
He flaunted his foulness like a virtue
And taunted Asgeir once again.
"You cunt, you can't kill me,"
He sneered, "I'm invincible."
But Asgeir, eyes glinting,
Half-grinned at the Halfwit.
"Oh, we can kill you, scum,
"We can kill you in so many ways.
"I have one hundred ways for you to die,
"All slow, all sordid, all scream-filled.
"Laugh while you can, fight-fleer,
"Your lease on this world is up."
As he talked, two ravens landed
On a branch at Bjerk's eye level.
"Do you truly imagine Hugin and Munin
"Will speak well of you to the tree-hanger?
"Do you seriously think the Valkyries
"Have selected you for Valhalla?
"Hel, and its icy eternity,
"Is your destiny, yours and all cowards.
"While warriors fight every day
"And feast every night under Odin's eye,
"You will shiver and starve with the worthless."
A murmur whispered over the waterside,
Growing to a chant to chill even a moron;
"Blood-eagle, blood-eagle, blood-eagle…"
Asgeir let it rise, let Bjerk believe his lungs
Would soon be flying from his back,
Let him beg and plead, blubber and bawl,
Before silencing his men with a hand held high.

"No, this war dodger is not worthy.
"Grim the Greedy merited
"A man's death, a blood-flight.
"He was a bastard but

"He knew how to fight,
"He knew how to loot,
"He knew how to raid.
"This oaf can't do anything
"But dig shallow holes
"For us all to shit in.
"He has earned a shit's end
"And that's what he'll get."

As the spear-dropper span on the tree
Asgeir carved up the two crews,
Making Ketil and Kjartan commanders
Of Waverider; with them went
Nag Wetnose the rewarded,
While Dragontamer and Hrolf safeguarded
Stormmaster and her golden hoard.
Both crews were mixed up
To keep mutineers in check
So Stormmaster's battle brothers
Could watch for Waverider unrest.
Wise was Asgeir, wiser than the owls.
Loyalty that is bought
Can easily be sold again.
And what of Grim the Greedy,
Grim the Malign, still raging
From the dark of his ragbag?
Asgeir called over Broddi the Bloody.
"One skull crowns the dragonhead
"And scalps fly from the mast ropes.
"Now put Grim up where he really belongs,
"Right up on the rear of the boat
"So he can gaze at the dragon's arse
"All the long seaway home and the wind
"Can carry away his ravings so
"Only the sea spirits will hear him."
And so to laughter from the crew

And loud, bitter protests from Grim
His bloodied head was slid
Over the dragon's flexed tail.

Chapter 33

By now Asgeir's authority was absolute,
Two crews cowed or courted by his power.
But Kjartan the Oak, Son of Bjorn Haraldson,
Himself the warrior son of Harald Bjornson,
Was as bold as his blood-loving forebears.
And ever since Stormmaster's dawn raid
On the shingle of the fire island, ever since
Waverider had fled to the sanctuary of the sea,
He had wanted to know why the hunters
Were so tenacious, so relentless, so tireless.
Before climbing aboard his seasteed,
He bearded Asgeir and asked coolly:
"Asgeir the Dragontamer, why have you chased
"So hard, so long and so far, and fought so many
"So ferociously? There's plenty more loot
"Festering for the dragonships on the Saxon shore.
"What then is in this chest you cherish?
"Is it true it holds a gold ring loved by Odin,
"A ring craved by the Valkyries, a ring
"That confers control over night and day
"On whoever wins it and wields it?"
Asgeir looked unflinching into his eyes,
And snarled through his bushy beard:
"Fuck magic rings. If one really exists
"It did Grim fuck all good. Look at him,
"Grim the Arse-Grinner, Harbar's hunger cure.
"So much for magic rings or troll talk.
"We chased so hard,

"So long and so far,
"And fought so many so hard
"Because that gold hoard is ours.
"For its glitter we risked all,
"Sculling on the high sea.
"We raided, we fought, we looted,
"But Grim grabbed it all for himself.
"No-one steals from me. What's mine
"Is mine and no other man's.
"Take mine from me and you die.
"Fight well with me and
"What's mine will be yours."

He turned to the two crews and
Pointed to the bleating Blackfoot
Spinning and screaming in the breeze.
"You are Vikings. You fight. You die.
"If you live you win. If you die you win.
"Valhalla and the Valkyries await
"The valiant war-dead warriors.
"Every time you set sail,
"Your tawdry life is forfeit.
"Death is your brother.
"You opt to put yourself
"At the mercy of man,
"Sea storms, Kraken-fang rocks,
"Sea serpents, arrows, axes,
"Spears and swords and, always,
"The woven fates of the Norns.
"Every new dawn is a bonus,
"Every new dawn you are reborn.
"Look around: Not one of you has seen
"Thirty winters. Raiding is for the young
"But raiding rarely makes old bones.
"Raiding makes you rich,
"Feeds your fame,

"Wins you women,
"But war makes widows,
"Haunts the home weepers.
"So, when you climb aboard, live for today.
"You flee no-one until your lord commands.
"You fight. You die. You fight for fame,
"You fight for arm-rings, and, above all,
"You fight and die for your brothers.
"And those who cower or carp?
"Their craven names will be known
"As far as the fjords reach and beyond,
"Wherever Vikings trade and fight,
"Condemned as cowards until
"The black clouds of Ragnarok
"Wreck our battle-proud world and
"Odin breathes no more,
"Broken in the fangs of Fenrir."

He spoke to the wretched rhythm
Of Bjerk's mercy-begging.
Hrolf looked over and asked
How they were to kill the Halfwit.
Then, alert sentries sounded
The alarm and a whooping climbed
Steadily over the trampled hillock
Overlooking the lake. Asgeir gave
The order and all scrambled
Waverider down the shingle,
Two war crews, one dragonship,
Shields up, helmets on,
Oars rowing well beyond
The range of savage arrows.
But they could see Bjerk the bullshitter
Twisting and jerking on his death-tree.
Scores of painted warriors crested
The corpse-hill and swarmed towards

Their old captive, left for their pleasure.
Bjerk's hoarse voice screamed for mercy
From his "mates" on the shrinking ship.
And then the Black Hairs halted as one,
Turned and ran and melted back over the mound.
Bjerk began to laugh, a laugh of triumph and relief,
And his voice, defiant and rough once more,
Floated over Waverider's wake:
"You see, you cunt, you can't kill me,
"You can't kill me; you can't beat me."
But, being a Halfwit, he hadn't paused
To ponder why warriors had run away
From the wreck of a fat fight-fleer hanging
Unarmed and head down from a tree.
But all aboard Waverider knew it was not
Bjerk's battle-fame, his war renown,
That had scared the scalp-takers.
It was left to Radnald, glee-fuelled,
To help Bjerk grasp the horror ahead.
"Behind you," he shouted. And shortly
His spear-friends piled in and
A chorus of calls winged over the water
To the smirking, jeering boat-bodger.
"Behind you," shouted the shieldmen,
"Behind you, it's behind you."
Bjerk wriggled round and his smirk
Turned to terror, to a scream
Like a stuck pig at midwinter.
For behind him was a bear that made
Harbar Grim-eater look like a midget,
And from far out on the tranquil lake
The Vikings could see that his sap
Was rising like a spring sapling
And Bjerk was about to learn
How so many women had felt
When he took them in raid rampages,

Claiming fleshly trophies won
By the fearless fighting of others.

The ravenous big brown bear,
Snapped the rope and dropped
Bjerk onto the pine-needle bed
And with one swipe of its claws
Ripped off his filthy rags and
Buggered the buffoon
Over and over again.

Sympathy, there was none,
Not for a brother betrayer,
And soon all were taunting him,
Singing a song made up by Ketil
On the spot. As the bear pumped away,
The poem reached Bjerk the brainless:
"Bjerk is bear-bait, Bjerk is bear-bait.
"He talks bollocks, he breathes bollocks,
"He was Bjerk the Bonehead
"But the bear ravaged him rigid,
"So now he's Bjerk the Bear-Buggered."
Even Odd Oddson managed a grin,
As he edged towards the Half Man-Half Woman,
The only other outcast on the boat,
But it rebuffed him with a fierce hiss.
So Odd sank deeper into Waverider
As it left Bjerk to be pleasured by the bear
And bore the war bands to Stormmaster.

Chapter 34

Stormmaster loomed round the headland,
Mutilated Black Hair and yellow hair bodies
Mingling on the blood-soaked shingle.
The shore tremble-sang in pebble cracks
As Waverider beach-glided from the lake.
The crews split up and made haste to leave.
Bjerk and his bear would not tarry the torturers long.
But as weapons and war-booty were loaded,
Under the shelter of the limp Blood-Eagle sail,
Ketil asked when they would finally get their fun.
He said: "Asgeir Stormrider, when will prisoners
"Ever feel our fury? We've sailed, rowed and fought,
"Slaughtered and scalped, even wassailed,
"But not once have we made a captive scream.
"The Sushone skewered their scalp slaves,
"The dragon got Grim before we could,
"The bear buggered Bjerk, Odd isn't worth it,
"And the Half Man Half Woman won't care.
"So when will we see the blood-eagle fly?
"Who will we ever bless with blood-red wings?"
Asgeir smiled, put his hilt-hardened hand on
Ketil's oar-shaped shoulder and fed his bloodlust:
"Fear not, widow-maker, fear not.
"The blood-eagle will fly and soon.
"I know just the man and always have."

And so, two ships with one warlord
Sailed ever eastwards. The loot secured,

Asgeir's veterans felt free to honour
A vengeance-vow they had all made
On the blood-showered Orkney shore.
When sails swelled with oar-resting wind,
The gold-searchers sheared their bison beards,
A sea-borne sheepfold from Fjordland.

Their wiry winter fur catching
On the brusque spring breeze,
A Norse lining for forest nests,
Their skin faced the sun once more.
But Asgeir's knife nestled in its sheath.
Hrolf, human now after months as a beast,
Found his chief at the dragonhead,
Long hair and beard flowing like a banner
As he watched Waverider racing alongside.
"We have got what we came for, Dragontamer,"
Hrolf smiled, "Why not trim your beard and
"Leave being a bear to Harbar the Hairy?"
Asgeir looked back. No smile parted the face-pelt.
"For you and the boys the pledge has passed.
"But I have other bitter scores to settle.
"There is much more to do, more blood to shed
"Before my chin can redden again in the sun's rays."
Hrolf frowned and as he opened his mouth
Asgeir replied unasked. "You are my battle brother.
"You are part of me, and I part of you. We are one.
"If you are cut, do I not bleed? But ask not,
"And when the time comes you will know.
"But this beard stays, my hair stays uncut,
"My sword stays sharp, gut-slashing sharp,
"Until my rightful destiny is determined."
He turned to face the onrushing wind and
The weary, savage-ridden, storm-riding way home.

There isn't time to tell of their homeward heroics,
How they fought a tribe of three-legged trolls,
How shields soaked up spider-poison arrows,
Unleashed by Skraelings with ears as big as bowls,
How the green, blue and yellow lights of the gods
Spread through the night sky and danced on the lakes,
Caressing the vast, brooding, fir-coated forests,
How Vee Ma Gog wrestled a bear bigger
Than Bjerk's lover and turned its pelt
Into a second sail that outstripped Waverider,
Or how… well, so many wild adventures,
So many close shaves, so little time.
But one I will relate. How Asgeir showed
Brain is better than brawn, wit better than war.

Riding rapids, the dragonships bounced
Into a boiling water-swirl below and
Turned to race the river to the next lake.
But blocking their way was a giant Black Hair
Taller by far than Bjerk's insatiable bear, who
Is probably still buggering him as I speak,
Backed by hatchet-wielding henchmen,
Smaller by far than Vikings but outnumbering
The Norse by five to one. So had The Norns
Lured the gold-stalkers to their death stage?

Vee Ma Gog, himself no dwarf, spoke
With his hands to the scalp-seekers.
Even his face paled as he told Asgeir
Of the price of the passage to safety.
"The giant wants a trial of strength,"
He said in his beer barrel voice.
"You and him. You win, we all live.
"You lose, he eats us all."
"And if I refuse and we fight?"
"Look around," replied Vee Ma Gog

Who nodded to the arrows trained
On their hearts, death in a flint,
Flighted on a shaft of ash,
Faster than a stooping peregrine.
"Then fight I will," growled Asgeir.
And Grim laughed with glee
As the drumbeat began again.

Like all Black Hairs the giant was beardless
But his arms bore battle scars and a seam
Of stitches ran down his chest while his hair
Hung rank over murderous eyes and his hands
Crushed rocks between palm and fingers.
He towered over Asgeir, his biceps bigger
Than the Ice Bear banner swollen with wind.

When Asgeir went ashore he searched
For ways to win, to outwit, to outwise.
The giant roared, his dwarves jeered,
And the ordeal began with a display
Of power to make a volcano proud.
Lying by the river as it entered the lake
Was a boulder as big as Harbar the Hairy.
The giant heaved and hurled it one-handed
High in the sky and it flew in an arc until
It landed at the far shore, forming an island,
Sending waves crashing back to crews
Who could already feel the giant's foul fangs
Crushing their weak and feeble flesh.

Asgeir, war-sweat rolling off his forehead,
Looked around for a reply as the giant
Ogled Mary and licked his fat lips.
Asgeir saw his salvation in the shingle
And realised that his childhood had readied him
For this moment. All he needed was calm,

All he needed were still waters and the wind
To drop, at least at first. Soon the stars
Were aligned and he stooped to pick up
A small flat stone, the size of his palm,
Perfectly round, and stepped forward,
A throw that offered life or death in
The flick of a wrist, skill not strength.
And so, he skimmed the stone and
His crews, the Black Hairs and the giant
Watched as it scampered across the lake
Leaving a trail of circular ripples in its wake,
Like a water boatman chasing limpid prey,
To the giant's new island which it struck
Before splitting in two, both stones
Rebounding back across the water,
Bouncing together 'til they skittered
To a halt at the feet of the Viking-eater.
The giant's spittle rage erupted in a roar
And his dwarfish devils cowered
In dread of his random retribution.
He picked up another rock, smaller,
And flung it, growling, so it flew until
It plunged onto a distant slope.
The giant parted his rancid hair,
A waft of filth floating down, and
Rubbed his swollen, sweaty belly,
While leering cruelly at Mary.
She shrugged off the lust-gaze
And guided Asgeir's eyes to the swallows
Surging northwards to summer meadows.
A net was commanded and Asgeir waited
'Til a swarm of swallows was grass-skimming
Before he cast it wide and caught fifty
Of the chattering, joyful, spring-bringers.
With threads he tied their legs to a small rock,
Lifted the net and set them free.

As one they rose and resumed their route,
Unrelenting in their laboured race
To reach the tundra's insect feast,
Swarming together in warming marshes
In nightless days well beyond the forests.
And so, all watched as they crested the hill
Where lay the giant's stone and then
Disappeared, like a fading cloud,
Over the hazy, smoky blue horizon.
The giant howled, ranted and raged,
Plucking a dwarf from the floor
And flinging him headlong into the lake.
Asgeir took on the latest trial,
Grabbed his own angry dwarf and
Flung him into the icy flood.
The giant snapped a birch in half
So Asgeir reached for Doublefang,
Razor-sharp skull-splitter of northland fame,
And with one swing felled a fir
Which crashed onto the giant's feet.
More roars, more rages, more raving,
As he stepped back and trampled
On two of his friends, flattening them
Like wrinkled shirts under a woman's iron.
By now Asgeir knew the ordeal would never end.
He had matched or beaten the monster
At every turn but the beast wanted his feast
And would find new trials 'til he won
And could pluck the crews like chickens.
Worse, the sweat-stinker had had enough
And proved a giant's word is worthless.
Another snort, another roar, another shriek,
And a ham hock arm crashed down
Like toppling timber and seized Asgeir's jewel.
The giant grabbed Mary in his left-hand while
His right hand uprooted tall trees

And drool dripped from his midden-mouth.
But, fatal mistake, Mary's arms were left free,
And as he roared, she slipped a hairpin
From her red tresses, a plunder pin,
One of her shoreside battle trophies,
And when he moved her to his maw
She stabbed him boldly in the eye and
Flicked it out like a whelk from its shell.
Screaming, he dropped her into the lake,
Staggered and stumbled, a red fountain
Clouding the clear chill waters as his
Agonies curdled the landscape's calm.
Mary swam back to be hauled aboard,
Joining Asgeir back on snarling Stormmaster
Whose wooden water wings were already
Spreading and biting the river for a race
To safety on Asgeir's given command.
The giant still straddled the stream
But in his pain was blind to the boats
And, as they passed under, Radnald
Displayed his spearman skills
Hurling one lance deep into
The giant's unguarded groin,
Tumbling the ogre like a tree
And guaranteeing no man ever
Had to pay his blood price again.
As the dragonships pulled away
Mary gave Stormmaster a new trophy,
Nailing the death-eye into the dragon-neck
To join the scalps, skulls and beaded shields
Of the buckskin-clad crews' battle boasts.

Chapter 35

The days were getting longer,
The nights were getting lighter,
When the dragonships approached
The black lake of the Sushone,
The vanquishers of Vee Ma Gog.
But one last hurdle lay in wait
Before the haven in the wilderness
Swapped foes and fear for friendly faces.
Around midday cloudless skies
Darkened, vast mountainous clouds
Lit only by jagged lightning streaks,
As if Thor and Mjollnir threatened
The sea-farers' long pined for peace.
And from nowhere came canoes
Powered by war-painted muscles
Pounding paddles through the spray,
White war feathers flattened by the wind.
Up went Vee Ma Gog's great bearskin sail,
Stormmaster bucked and strained
Before skimming the surface like a
Swan running over a lake for lift-off.
Waverider wallowed briefly in the wake
Before Kjartan cast the swallow net
Across the path of the howling pursuers
Whose boats were briefly buffeted and
Turned sideways until canoes collided
And savages spilled into the inland sea.
It did not halt the hunt but bought time

And let the Blood-Eagle pull away,
The wind driving the dragonship on
As the oar power of the predators
Tired before resuming their mission.

But when Waverider closed in on
The command ship a new menace
Reared its head and revealed
The trap set by the scalp-cravers.
A flock of skuas circled overhead
Mirroring the whirlpool that swirled,
Bubbled and roared in the lake-heart,
So wide that escape was there was none.
Asgeir had to turn now and fight
Swarms of whooping hatchet hordes
Or be swallowed in a spiral of doom.
Even Vee Ma Gog wore his death mask.
"Manahee, Manahee," he muttered,
"Kill all, no captives, scalp lovers."
Broddi the Bloody ruled the rudder
And was all set to tack away
From the looming mouth of the lake grave
When Mary, dragonbone hand-gripped,
Dropped down to her knees and,
Eyes closed and lissom body shaking,
Shouted "Straight on, straight on."

No time to talk,
Only time to trust,
So Asgeir,
Sword in hand
Spoke the command
To mount the maelstrom
As Mary shouted: "Shields flat,
"Oars up, oars flat, oars out
"Stormmaster will do the rest."

The benchmen bent into it,
And braced themselves for death
As Stormmaster raced into
The turbulence's outer ring.
The dragonship sped up
In the spinning waterwheel of death
And girded itself for a battering,
Flattening its sails as
The breeze swelled and embraced
Shields, sails and broad-bladed oars
Just as the swirling lake's spite
Spat the ship out and flung it skyward.
Stormmaster flexed its neck and
Straightened its tail as if
It was riding a hurricane
And suddenly was sea-free,
A dragonship floating and flying,
Just like a Death Fleet dragon,
And banked over canoes
Of cowering warriors.
A Viking never skips
The call of battle
So, the loot-lusters
Loosed off a flurry
Of wailing death-needles,
A strafing snowstorm
Of defeat and death.
Waverider soon followed,
Kjartan commanding
Warriors to sprout wings
And the dragonship duo
Drove brave Manahee
Into their own death trap.
Stormmaster and Waverider
Worked as one and
Swiftly fed the whirlpool

With their foe-sacrifice.
Battle won, death defied,
The dragonships glided gently
To Charmadu's shore,
Once winter's ice shelter.

Women and children
Ran screaming from the
Majestic battlebirds
That floated down,
Landing with a coy curtsey
Before crunching ashore
And shifting side by side
In the scented pine shade.
Drums rang out once more,
Summoning the war-keen,
Guard dogs barked and yowled,
Growling their own alarm.
Instantly bows were strung,
Spear-arms stretched taut,
As trusted bloodletters
Were trained on the lake fliers.
But when tall Asgeir unlashed
His helmet and leapt ashore
Swordless, threats turned
To whoops of relief not war.

Chapter 36

Vikings seeking the solace
Of sweet Sushone women
Were swiftly disappointed.
Hackasu the bear-scarred
Commanded the arrow-armed
And grim as ever, was in no mood
For welcoming smiles or embraces.
Even while his hunters
Howled their salute
He sent out scouts
To sniff out an attack.
A night hoot, a screech,
And Charmadu emerged
From the forest's depths,
Her hair a flash of gold
In the glade's green gloom.
Her Norse, faltering at first,
Soon flowed free again,
Loosened like a thawing stream,
And Asgeir learned again that
A warrior's work is never done.

Guards stationed by the dragonships,
Sushone and Vikings stalked
Back to the willow-bark village
Which was attack-ready tense,
Prickling with weapons and
Crackling like the humid air

Of a summer thunderstorm.
Even newly weaned pups were taut,
Play-fighting long forgotten
While their pack prepared for war.
And as two worlds' warriors
Slid silently into the sanctuary,
Charmadu detailed their disaster.
"Seenaho is lost," she said.
"Seized by Manahee marauders.
"When we massacred the Azarapo
"The warlike Manahee moved in
"And our triumph has turned
"Into more and more war.
"Seenaho and five men
"Went scouting ahead
"A day's march from here
"And tumbled into a bear pit
"Set in the trail by the Manahee.
"Four lie still in the pit,
"Arrow-stiff, scalp-flayed.
"Somehow Seenaho survived,
"But was carried off into captivity
"To face the living death of fire-flames.
"And the fifth, a puny pup
"Failing on his first raid,
"Was freed to skulk back,
"His ears hacked off,
"To tell of Manahee triumph.
"Hackasu is rallying a rescue raid,
"But Seenaho is as good as dead.
"Vengeance is all we have left,
"A slaughter to satisfy our bloodlust."

But through his stallion's mane
And wild, bushy, bison beard
Asgeir urged war-wise caution.

He looked at Charmadu closely
And offered swords and deception
As a life-saving solution.
"The Manahee have set a trap,"
He told her, "and want to wipe out
"Your best warriors just as you
"Butchered the leaders of the Azarapo.
"Kill a wolf and another will replace him.
"So, it is with tribes. Flux breeds flux.
"Their warriors are hate-waiting for you,
"Hidden and hatchet-handed.
"They know the way you fight.
"They know how you hunt.
"But they don't know us.
"We are Vikings, night-hunters,
"Sea-raiders, plunder-grabbers,
"Sword-slashers, spear-stabbers.
"We appear from nowhere
"And melt away like sprites,
"Safe with our loot long before
"Our foes can find their shields.
"So, you lead us to Seenaho
"And we will bring him home
"With or without his scalp
"And the Manahee will never
"Trouble your territory again and
"Sushone will savour another summer.
"But after the venison-victory feast,
"We Vikings will return to our sea-road.
"We have old scores to settle
"Wrongs to right,
"Skulls to split
"Scum to clear,
"Back across the sea,
"Beyond the death fleet,
"Beyond the sea dragons,

"Back home, in Norway,
"Back where we belong."

He paused as Charmadu
Explained all to Hackasu.
Sour-faced, he roared in rage.
Sushone fight for Sushone,
Outsiders should keep outside,
Was his war message.
Words weren't needed.
Frowns and fury
Form a one-world language.
But Asgeir's words won the day.
He held Charmadu's hair
Up against his lion's fleece.
"Tell Hackasu," he said,
"He is a great fighter,
"The fearsome defier of bears.
"But we are as one.
"We are Sushone.
"Sushone are Vikings.
"Our blood is shared.
"Our blood is your blood.
"Your blood is our blood.
"Together we are brothers.
"Let's unite the best of both."

So, Norsemen readied for a new raid,
Sharpening swords, axes and spears,
To ease their slashing and slicing
In the blood slaking of battle.
But on Asgeir's command
They continued their conversion
From Norse to natives,
Copying the canoe crews
That cast them to the lake's maw.

Each man, each man save Asgeir,
Each man save the sulking Halfwit
And the Half Man Half Woman,
Who were sent with the women,
Shaved the sides of his head
Leaving a bold brush of hair
Bristling from forehead to nape
And bronzed their pale scalps
With bilberry juice to join
Sun-browned, beardless faces.
Big Vee Ma Gog then gave them
Gut-rippers and skull-splitters,
Taking local hatchets, shields,
Bludgeons and bows and arrows.
And then Radnald led them in
Lighting their faces, the colours of Hel
Until Sushone warriors bridled
At so many Manahee in their midst.

Asgeir called for the raid's sole survivor,
The callow battle-virgin, the ear-shorn pup,
But Charmadu said he could not be brought.
"He awaits his fate," she said.
"He is tied, alone, to a fire pole.
"He failed us; he failed his tribe.
"Better that he died fighting
"Than run home bawling like a baby.
"He will burn, and we Sushone
"Will be the better for that.
"Warriors fight, warriors die.
"Warriors never run – never."

A roar shook the skald hall
And none roared louder
Than they who had run.

We all hate most what
We know is our weakness.

Snorri smiled, sipped, and resumed,
His magic working its word spell.

Hackasu's face was stone-set,
Pitiless as a ship's dragonhead -
No compromise, no compassion.
But Asgeir's mercy sprang the pup
From the Sushone shame-furnace.
"A disgrace he surely is and
"A disgrace deserves to die.
"But only this rat knows where
"The Manahee hold Seenaho.
"Let him be our raid guide,
"Let him lead us to the Manahee,
"Let him rescue his name,
"And if he lives you are free
"To burn the boy one hundredfold.
"But without him Seenaho burns.
"This battle-pup is our last hope."

And so, the shaking Sushone was brought
Before the Manahee mimics, and tremored
To see so many ear-takers in his camp.
But through Charmadu's assurances,
Asgeir gave him a golden chance
To reclaim his name in battle,
If not escape the black fire pole.
Blood pumped once again through
Veins frozen for so long with fear
And the hand-enfeebling trembling
Faded away to renewed resolve.
Frightened Deer bade farewell to fear.

The warband left at dawn,
Shrouded in ghost mist,
And for two troubled days
The battle-scarred boy,
Barely old enough to fight
But easily old enough to die,
Led Vikings and Sushone silently
Through sun-starved forests,
And every birdsong,
Every branch break,
Every scrub scramble
Brought the brutal menace
Of a Manahee ambush.
But the boy could read
An invisible trail
Like a bald monk reads
A braided, gilded manuscript.
To Vikings the trees looked the same.
To the boy each tree told its tale.
Each tree sang its life song.

As the sun set on the second day
The boy began daubing mud
On his unlined face, a death mask.
But for whom? Boy or Manahee?
With Charmadu back with the women,
Vee Ma Gog's manly hands spoke
For Vikings and his hated foes.
But before they set off
He told them both he was
With them as if with his own.
"Azarapo gone. I happy Viking now.
"Sushone Viking, Viking Sushone.
"Manahee scalp Azarapo
"Azarapo scalp Manahee.
"Viking kill Manahee.

"Now Sushone kill Manahee.
"We fight same foe.
"We fight same way.
"We all, all the same."

Hackasu's stone face
Barely flickered but
His death glares died.
The last of the Azarapo also
Shared his battle knowledge
Of his malevolent Manahee foes.
"Azarapo, Sushone and Viking,
"Our gods live all around us,
"The sly wolf spirits,
"The talking trees,
"The singing streams,
"Manahee too. But Manahee
"Worship one god above all,
"And this fear-god can be our friend."
The warrior whispered to Asgeir
And his hand signs gave the word
To hatchet-faced Hackasu.

All the time the two forces
Misted through the forest,
Harbar the Hairy made up
The raid's rear, halting only
For honey or root feasts.
But now the time to fight
Had blossomed at last
As Sushone followed
Frightened Deer's lead.
Battle-ready, the boy nodded
To a curtain of sentinel trees,
Sniffed the air, and shuffled
In his silent war dance.

Words there were none
But hands can command
As easily as growled orders.
Ruthless, Vee Ma Gog gave
Hackasu the battle brief.
Slowly, stealthily, Sushone
Fanned out and soon
Sent the sentries to Hel
In a series of noiseless slaughters.
And in the forest's fading light
They themselves replaced the guards,
While Vikings girded themselves swiftly
With Manahee arms and shields.

Asgeir had hatched his plan
And for once this warrior
Led from the rear – and wisely.
His mane and beard pledge
Meant he had to be hidden
Up to the hunter's moment.
He and Hrolf Hardheart
Stayed veiled in the shadows
With the Sushone braves while
His painted sea band slid towards
The innocent scent of woodsmoke
Wafting through the tree-screen.
As when the winter deer
Led them to snow battle
The Vikings launched their killing
Under the cover of the night
When victorious Skraelings
Prefer feasting to fighting.
But tonight, endless torture
Formed the Manahee's delight,
With Seenaho their sole sport.

Asgeir and glowering Hackasu
Watched the painted sea-pirates
Pad along a moonlit path
And slip one at a time
Into a clearing lit by
Dancing flame shadows.
And there they mingled with
Manahee with eyes only
For Seenaho's death parade
Presided over by a brute,
A true giant, arms bulging
Under bone-rings, his ridge-hair
Crowned by a flourish of feathers.

Seenaho's noble chest and limbs were
Streaming with a red-sheen of blood.
His yellow hair was long gone
Dripping red from a scalp stick
Brandished in his bruised face
By a fat boy little bigger
Than Frightened Deer.

Humiliation hurts more than death,
But it was Seenaho who was humiliating
The Manahee by his manly demeanour.
No cries, no pleas came from his lips,
Just spit and sneers and death defiance,
Goading them with his taunts
To do their worst as he stood
Bound tightly to the firepole
On flame-hungry, bone-dry faggots,
A stray ember from eternity's inferno.
Broddi the Bloody nodded his approval.
Warriors can die weeping in fear
Or they can die defiantly
And frustrate their foes

And turn death into victory.
In the clearing's forest fringe
Hackasu held Frightened Deer
And forced the weakling to watch
This lesson in fear-free courage.

For the smiling Manahee
Secure in their clearing
The sport was all-absorbing.
No-one noticed the new braves
Back from the scalp hunt and
Masked by the flame-flickers.
But then the Vikings began their rescue
With bravery beyond saga words.
A Berserker burst out of the woods.
Hrolf Hardheart, as bare as he was born,
Spinning Double Death round and round,
Making the axe as light as a mere birch branch.
As the shocked Manahee howled and
Muscled towards their widow-makers,
A shout shook their clearing-camp.
The warriors swivelled westwards
To see axe-wielding Asgeir
Right opposite his sea brother,
Blurring fearsome Doublefang
With a matching death display,
But with a bison mane and beard
Framing his ferocity on the
Forest's dimming, darkening edge.
And then a southern apparition
Stepped into the flame-light.
Ketil Killfast, span sword
And hunting knife, a blur of blades,
Only for death to rage from the north.
With a red-hot roar that chilled
Once warm Black Hair blood.

Harbar the Hairy, scenting fresh flesh,
Slavered and swiped, raked and ravened,
Fangs and claws glinting in the moonlight,
Like a one warrior battle horde.
As one, Manahee dropped to their knees
Foreheads kissing the pine-needle floor.
Even their giant chief flung himself
Face down in the dirt, mercy pleading.
And then the Manahee learned that their god,
The big ghost bear of the lake-woods,
Had betrayed them and their kind.
Harbar the Hairy roared and lumbered
Among the cowering cutthroats,
Slashing worshippers with bear blades,
And let the Vikings do what Vikings do.
The dreaded Manahee died meekly,
Like Christians kneeling before their shrines.
A few hotheads, heretics, tried to fight,
But the rest were cowed by their creed,
And fell as fast as weakling monks
Praying for mercy from their marauders.

Night-time is fight time for Vikings.
Night-time is rest-time for Sushone.
But one raging Black Hair broke
In fury with tribal tradition.
Frightened Deer raced from the shadows
To face down the Manahee giant,
Who, now risen, hatchet in hand,
Was easily twice his height
Twice his size,
Muscled where the lad
Scarcely had sinews,
Biceps bearing battle honours
Where the boy only bore
Battle shame as his name.

But brain beats brawn and
Righteous revenge beats all.
Without flinching, Frightened Deer
Hammered his hatchet into
The brute's raw-boned shins
Before cleaving him cleanly,
Gizzarding him from groin to guts,
To ensure no more bucks
Were born to the Black Hair.
With two brave blows,
Frightened Deer had become
Raging Stag who Fights,
A feather-worthy warrior,
Who had cast off his cowardice.
But the boy was new to war and
Had not learned the rules of battle:
Attack hard, then pull back,
Attack hard, then pull back.
The first he did fearlessly
But the second he forgot,
And, before death's dry rattle,
The giant jabbed a bear knife
Into the boy's fresh face
And so both died together
Intertwined
United in blood by
The chief's failure
And the tyke's triumph.

Chapter 37

As their blood mingled in the pine needles
And Vikings indulged their battle rage -
Sea raiders still sing of Hrolf's double kill
With one swirling, gut-ripping axe swipe -
Asgeir made sure of the mission
And unsheathed an impassive Seenaho
From his flame grave firepole.
Seenaho's skull was bare to the bone,
His chest a blood lake,
His arms knife-flayed,
His legs war-slicked
In flowing, metallic claret.
But the second he was freed
He grabbed back his scalp,
Broke loose a blade from
A mutilated Manahee
And knelt right over
The tribe's writhing chief,
Spitting frothing defeat
Deep into his dying eyes.
With a devil wolf's howl
He scalped his persecutor
And flung it in his face
So the giant's last sight
Was blood-dripping proof
Of his eternal humiliation.
Then Seenaho cradled
Frightened Deer in his arms

And whispered quiet words
Of comfort and congratulation.
As men screamed and blood sprayed
The last sight savoured by the smiling boy
Was his father's overt, overbearing pride.
In death Frightened Deer was reborn,
Lifted from coward to warrior
And lives still in Sushone songs
With all their other battle braves.
So it is with Vikings. Death we vanquish
By the courage and daring of our dying.
And so, we ride with Valkyries to our Valhalla
To live and fight and wassail for ever
Just as the Sushone fallen fly to theirs.

They returned true heroes,
Bearing the raid booty
Of fire fodder prisoners,
Painted scalpsticks strung
With spiky trophy pelts
And weapons tempered
By Manahee scalp-juice.
All the long walk back Seenaho
Led the fighters as a chief should and
Told how his band was ambushed,
How he watched his men murdered,
His son fight heroically until seized
To suffer ear-slicing by the chief
Only to be spared a slow death
For a warrior's worst destiny -
To be sent home in shame
Mournless, hateful shame,
As a sole survivor
Of warrior slaughter.
Back he bravely went
Knowing slow death and

Long disgrace awaited;
Back he bravely went
Sacrificing his life
To save his beloved father
By leading his Sushone
Back to the Manahee horde.

But on that long walk back
Thanks, came there none
From scalp-sore Seenaho,
Not to Asgeir and his Norsemen,
Nor to Sushone saviours.
Perhaps thanks showed weakness,
A nod to Seenaho's raid-party failure;
Perhaps gratitude was wrong
Because rescuing was right.
Why thank for what you would do,
For action without question?
Perhaps thanks make easy words
And deeds are worth much more.
So, as the pirates approached
The safety of the Sushone
Seenaho held back and
Let Asgeir take the lead.
Only then did Seenaho follow,
Pulling Frightened Deer
On a birch branch litter.
Frightened Deer the boy
Was no more, manned
And redeemed in death.
His mother could dry her eyes
And smile once more.

The feast that followed
Vaunted the Vikings
Who were war-honoured

With white feathers
As proof positive that
They were worthy warriors.
Asgeir then displayed
The fair, fading scalps
Of the forefathers of
The fair Sushone siblings,
Seenaho and soft Charmadu,
And told of the gory fate
Of Olaf Blodason
And his glory grabbers
On the rolling grasslands
At the hands and hatchets
Of the painted bison-hunters
And howling wolf-runners.
For three days and three nights
The forest fed the victors
While the silent vanquished
Awaited their flames of defeat.
But before the Sushone
Sharpened their death-shafts
Or gathered their fire faggots,
Asgeir gave Seenaho notice
That Norway called him home.
Even hard Hackasu was moved
To embrace the outsiders
So making them insiders
On the day they parted.

But one man held back.
Radnald Rogarrson was he.
Asgeir's spearguard,
Shieldwall legend,
Life deliverer,
Crew rescuer,
He had long since crossed

From Norway to New World,
And looked more Black Hair
Than Norse Blood Hero,
With Manahee hair tuft,
A forest of feathers
And faded buckskin breeches
Bearing hard-secured scalps.
His face permanently painted
And scalping blade ever sharp,
He was Sushone now.
Only his regained arm rings
Recalled his true origins.
But Radnald's reason
For remaining was timeless.
This hard-hearted fighter
Had been softened by love.
The comely girl for whom
He had run the gauntlet,
The comely girl for whom
He had nearly died
Had stolen his heart
While his ruthless heroics
Had soothed Hackasu's.
And so, while Stormmaster
And Waverider readied
For sea passage perils,
He opted for forest life
With his new blood band.
"Nothing and no-one
"Waits for me in Norway,"
He told wise Asgeir. "Here
"I have my woman,
"I have my meat aplenty
"And war waits all around.
"I never really liked
"Sea storms much anyway."

Asgeir gave him silver,
A last arm-ring blessing
But Radnald spurned
New battle honours, saying:
"Gold and silver
"Have no value here.
"What we all want
"The wild forest provides.
"Only leave me with
"My spearshaft and shield
"And I'll make Vikings proud."

But as a little bit of Norway
Opted to stay behind
A little bit of New World
Opted to sail away.

Vee Ma Gog had gained
The right to remain,
His mauling of the Manahee
Showing all Sushone
His valour and value.
His defiance on the firepole
And Asgeir's battle approval
Had laid the pale ghosts
Of legions of the scalped.
Asgeir, who knew men
Much better than most,
Had let him decide,
Knowing valiant Vee Ma Gog
To be a leader, not a follower.
Blind obedience did not
Flow naturally through
The legendary Black Hair,
But let him ponder the options,
Let him think them through,

And he became oak-strong steadfast,
A narrow-eyed warband stalwart.
"We leave now," explained Asgeir
"For our mountain homeland.
"We would be happy and proud
"With you as one of our crew.
"But the salt sea that awaits
"Is a thousand wide lakes across.
"The waves are ever rough,
"The wind will be winter cold,
"Even under summer's sun,
"Dragons lie in wait, unfed,
"Far from land-sight,
"And death will stalk us all
"Across the blue, green and grey
"Of the seaway's heartless whims.
"And there will be no coming back.
"Climb aboard and bid farewell
"For ever, for all time
"To your beloved homeland
"To your wild woods,
"To your deer, your rivers,
"To your berries, your birds.
"You will bury your proud past.
"If you decide to stay
"Stay with our blessing.
"We will smile and wave
"And wish you well.
"Your well-won place in our
"Warriors' pride parade
"Is safe should you stay,
"Safe should you sail."

Vee Ma Gog paused,
But his impassive face
Hid his grit and guile.

By now his ship-learned Norse
Flowed as freely as Seenaho's.
"You are great tribe chief,"
Said the bear-big Black Hair,
"I speak freely, openly,
"As a fellow chief.
"Since Viking fighters came
"My homeland is mine no more.
"Once I knew these woods,
"These deer, these rivers,
"These berries, these birds.
"But now they are strangers.
"I buried my proud past
"When I left the firepole.
"I am Viking only now,
"I am Vee Ma Gog the Viking.
"I am The Bear who Brings Death,
"And this bear will bring death
"To our foes wherever we go,
"For your enemy is my enemy,
"Your friend is my friend,
"And I sail where you sail.
"Death may well follow,
"Death may well lie in wait,
"But death lurks here as well
"And death holds no fear for me.
"Better to die bravely
"Fighting as a Viking
"In a vast new world than
"To die an outsider
"In my lost old world."

Chapter 38

Farewells were fond
But when the sun
Crested the vast sky
Asgeir gave his order:
"Norway next! Pull hard!"
Men heaved, men pushed,
And in a cacophony of
Creaking, grating and cursing
The dozing dragonships
Were reborn on the water.
But before the sails
Were freed to feast
On the light westerly,
Seenaho's war canoe
Came close alongside and
Charmadu stood up
And handed back
The sacred scalps
Of Olaf Blodason
And his long-lost men.
"Take them home,
"Return them to Norway
"Where they always belonged.
"We don't need their scalps,
"Their death misery reminders.
"Better to remember them
"As our fearless forefathers.
"Their spirits live well here

"Through Seenaho, me and Radnald."
And then the pale canoe turned,
The dragonship sails billowed
And Norse and natives parted.

The Ice Bear and the Blood-Eagle
Bore the Vikings ever eastwards,
Every minute taking them
Closer to home, mead and mistresses.
The quest out was easier
Than the long struggle in
As the lakes and broadening river
Led steadily towards the sea.
But the benchmen still had to
Manhandle Stormmaster
And Waverider round rapids,
Through forests and around
The roaring thunder of the
Waterfalls of the trolls
Whose spirit spray clouds
Could be seen from miles off,
Rising like steam from
A giant's copper cauldron.
Only on land were the crews
At risk from scalpbands
And two unlucky men fell
To toxin-tipped arrows,
Writhing and frothing,
Nurturing the wilderness
With precious Norse blood.
But before the days
Began to shorten
The ships kissed the sea,
The slowing river widening
And its banks blurring
Into a purple distance,

Sweet freshwater mixing
With stinging saltwater
In a familiar ferment of foam,
Chill rollers and swells,
Pluming peaks and troughs
That only a sea stallion
Can truly plough with relish.
The wave-shearing dragonships,
Blessed with spent arrows,
Bucked with pure pleasure
As they welcomed the waves
And revelled at returning
To their true home-haven.

And now, said Snorri,
The noose itching his neck,
I have spun long and
You have listened well.
More, much more, awaits,
But, as ever, the best drama
Will be saved 'til the last.
But this climax,
This exposure
Of a spearman's
Faults and strengths,
Of the Valhalla-bound
And the Hel-doomed,
Is best heard
With a clear, cool head.
So, my lord, I beg leave
To break briefly now and
Skald for my life tomorrow
When all will learn
That old legends are more
Than myths. They master
The deepest, darkest

Desires of dread-men.
And if boredom should tire you,
Your death tree stands ready
And this nagging necklace
Will strangle my song,
And make me dance
Odin's lonely jig of death.
But should my word spell
Work its mind magic
I will flaunt for ever
This halter as a reminder
Of Sven my saviour
And as proof positive that
Well-picked words can be
As sharp as sea-raiders' swords.

With that the Icelander bowed
And Sven nodded assent.
With his barrel-rumble voice,
Sven gave his command.
"We retire happily now, skald.
"You have held our minds
"You have nourished our night.
"But be sure when you return
"That you do not slip up.
"This time tomorrow
"You will be a master skald,
"Free to stay, free to wassail,
"Free to wander at will,
"Or you will amuse us once more
"Squirming from Hel's oaken scaffold
"As we praise your last performance."

To Sven life was pure sport
And death was his plaything.
Pity and compassion were

Complete strangers to his jet heart.
Painful death he ordered on a whim,
For fun, to while away an hour.
In his warband he was judge,
Jury and heartless hangman.
But he did not know
What Snorri knew
And therein lay
The key to unlock
Who would live and
Who would die,
Who was Valkyrie-blessed
And who was cold, Hel-cursed.

Chapter 39

Snorri rose for his day of decision.
Outside in the bone-numbing day-night
Fresh snow shrouded the northern woods,
Muffling all movement and noise.
Cloud blotted out the moonlight, leaving
Just a faint snow glow in the gloom.
No-one was coming, no-one could leave,
And so, as wenches swept away
Feast-fallen waste into the straw,
Snorri and his horsehair halter rose
One last time to mix myth and morals
Into a cocktail headier than mead and ale.

The killers were belching and farting
Making a winter feast fog familiar
To any Norseman grounded by the sun's
Dreary desertion of the Northland.
Their dinner tributes mingled with
The aroma of roasting mutton,
The murk from winter's cattle byre,
The sourness of beer and wine breath,
The staleness of sweat and trampled straw
And the sweetness of wood smoke
Offering relief from the man-beast stench.
It was in this fetid pit of menace
That Snorri skalded for his life —
Not that he let the stress show.
Instead he inhaled deeply and

Spoke calmly, with a smile,
Like a woman delivering bad news.

As Snorri stood, Sven commanded more beer
And while slave girls served the fighting class
The chief gave his guest's noose a gentle tug,
Earning cheers from his chosen men.
The churls were hoping for a heroic saga
Followed swiftly by a good hanging.
After a long summer of slaughter,
Wan winter can soon pale and bore
And bloodlust once unleashed
Is never easily quenched.

Bitter beer, summer's sun in a bull's horn,
Soothed Snorri's secret nerves and
Smoothed the killers' hackles.
And so the white-haired one resumed
His steady descent to destiny.
Soon he would know
Which web the Norns had spun.
But so too, he smiled, would Sven.

You have heard well, Snorri told
His congregation of monk-slayers,
How Asgeir fought and gulled
His way to wealth and fame.
He is now sailing home
With two growling dragonships
Where once he had none,
Ships laden with wealth
And shieldwall soldiers
To deploy just as he wished.
But let me ask you legends this:

A warrior has gold and silver
Dirhams and amber
And bejewelled bibles.
He has white walrus ivory,
Slaves and mistresses galore,
Swords, shields and spears
Ships and crewmen by the score.
Yet still he yearns
Yet still he burns
Well, what could he want more?

Answer this and Asgeir's quest
Will become clear.
Merely answer this and
The blood-eagle will
Make its belated bow.

The bear-skinned and bearded
Spilled beer and benches to chant
"Blood-eagle, blood-eagle",
As if the booze-bile of their shouts
Could sharpen their battle-blades.
Sven purred to feel their ferocity
Undimmed by frost and rest,
Boding well for the raiding season,
Before bidding them to sit down.
Wersil the schemer sat frozen-faced,
Merely narrowing his snake's eyes
At his battle slaves' fervour.

Then, nodding to a slavegirl for a refill,
Snorri climbed back on board
Stormmaster as the Ice Bear
Strained in the Norse-wards wind.
Stormmaster and Waverider,
He said, were racing eastwards,

To escape the clutches of
Long-clawed sea-monsters,
To moor once more in Norway's
Soothing late summer sun.
And as they jostled for the lead,
Pride pushing the looters ahead,
Hrolf told of his time twisting on the tree
Over the torture flames of the Black Hairs
And the vision shaped by their torment.

As pregnant sails gave life
To sea speed and salt spray,
Hrolf held court to the idle-handed.
Pain, he said, promises death or wisdom
So, when our captors pierced my chest
And hoisted me high, skyward,
Like summer-caught cod
Drying and spinning in the breeze,
I thought Odin's hand maidens
Had chosen me for his endless feast.
Nine hours did I spin -
Or was it just nine minutes?
But searing, scorching pain
Soon surrendered to blackness,
Which battled with swirling clouds
And blinding, flashing lights
That split my skull like axes.
And there I saw my destiny,
Our destiny, all our destinies:
To endure nine ordeals before
We can get what we want,
Before we can earn the right
To be hailed as returning heroes,
Before we can sit by our hissing fires
And savour a snow season of serenity.

One of the men, a Waverider
Switched to Stormmaster
For safe keeping on the sea,
Spoke for many when he shouted:
"But you've got what you want.
"You've got the gold
"You've got the glory
"What more could you crave?"

Hrolf nodded politely
But his eyes sent out
A plea for silence
To let him relive his trance.
"Before my firmly closed eyes,
"I saw all," he continued.
"They all came to me,
"Our ordeals appeared,
"Past, present and to come.
"We have had the hunt for Grim,
"The hard voyage to brutal lands.
"Along the way Asgeir gained
"Eternal fame by taming the dragon.
"I saw him fight his scaly foe
"In a wild frenzy of sea-foam
"And I beheld the beast
"Bowing in submission.
"But I watched from on high, wheeling
"Like a fulmar above the foment.
"Third to emerge before my eyes
"Was our bloodletting in the snow
"And our revenge raid on deer sleighs
"As Mary flew like an eagle overhead.
"Fourth ordeal was Asgeir's storm-ride
"And his skirmish in the sky
"With skulking scalp-hunters,
"A wind-ride which led us to

"The bones of Olaf Blodason.
"Fifth was the Hel in the grasslands
"Which Radnald alone escaped,
"Luckily for us, of course.
"And then, in my searing agony,
"I saw the horrors lying ahead.
"But only now, only now,
"Are these hallucinations returning,
"Now I have had time to think.
"I saw the sixth, it was foretold,
"The giant who blocked our journey
"And who spear-sharp Radnald ensured
"Will never sire another monster.
"And the seventh, too, was foretold:
"The maelstrom, and the oarsmen
"Mastering the sky as they rule the sea.
"The rescue of Seenaho did not register.
"We rescued him as we'd rescue each other.
"But two more ordeals must we defeat
"Or die in the defying before we can
"Wassail as warriors at our leisure.
"The eighth is almost upon us:
"A storm that must scatter us all
"To lands unknown
"Where men eat men
"Before we muster for
"A furious sea battle.
"And then there's the ninth:
"I have seen the ninth.
"The risks are Asgard high.
"The rewards are great.
"But the outcome remains
"A mystery known only to the gods.
"But this destiny we cannot dodge
"This destiny we must confront.
"It is a destiny that every day

"Draws nearer and delivers
"Death for the vanquished
"And raven-riches for the victors."

A rumble arose among the crew.
Perils aplenty were their companions
But home was now their hope.
They had faced enough foes
For ten decades of raiding
Without defying new devils.
Asgeir well knew his soldiers.
He knew their life-limits
So he swiftly slew the spectre
Of Hrolf's rambling fables.
"What will be, will be,"
He said, "but we will sail
"Ever onwards, ever eastwards.
"Norway calls us and
"We will answer her."
But Asgeir knew much more,
Much more than his crew,
And it was not Norway
Whose siren call he answered.

At this point from nowhere
A band of seabirds appeared
And shadowed the warships,
Grey, ragged, stiff-winged,
Nomads of the deep,
Skimming the spray,
Riding the rollers and
Ploughing low troughs.
For a while, from the stern,
Mary watched the wanderers,
Her hair banner-billowing
In the onrushing wind.

When Asgeir joined her
She just stared at the sea
As it grew greener and greener.
Without glancing at her lover,
She said: "They are the souls
"Of lost seafarers, sea-nomads for ever.
"Not one of them is a stranger.
"They know us, and we know them.
"That one there is Skidi Njalson,
"That one banking is Vog Cnutson,
"And there, following, is Einar Hrolfson.
"They want to make amends
"For their sentry failure on the shingle.
"They are our guardian angels.
"Their lead we should follow."

As she spoke the western sky
Went steadily from blue to slate,
From slate to jet and
Lightning crackled while
The wind strengthened.
The sea waifs stopped following
And effortlessly started leading.
The slightest wing tilt,
Was all it took
To overtake the ships
And swing sharply southwards
To more welcoming skies.
Asgeir did not delay.
Mary's magic had never failed
And so, the lost souls
Commanded the helmsman.

The storm came in a fury
So powerful it felt
As if Loki had unleashed

All the devils, giants and trolls
In a foretaste of feared Ragnarok.
But the souls of the fallen
Had saved the souls of the living,
Steering the sea-lost to the gale's fringe,
So Stormmaster and Waverider
Could put their names to the test,
Merit-winning, but only just
In a wind-fuelled whistling
Of whines, wails and groans and
Ghostly screams in the rigging.
Storm-tossed and sea-green were they
For five days and five nights.
So dark was the midsummer sky
That Asgeir's miracle light stone,
His all-seeing ocean shepherd,
Was as blind as in bleak midwinter.
But then, as suddenly as it brewed,
The tempest faded to a flat calm.
A golden dawn greeted
The salt-caked survivors.
Sun kissed their flayed faces
As the lost souls of their comrades
Skimmed the silver surface
And the bloated corpses of sea beasts
Floated slowly past, clear testimony
To the hammer anger of the gods.
What sort of storm kills whales?
But even the long dead give life
And so, a whale fed the forlorn
Whose snorting sea-steeds had
Somehow stayed together.
As the crews regained strength,
Like thirsty dogs given water,
A gentle, warming breeze arose
And the sea skimmers as one

Turned northwards where
The ocean's shimmering haze
Framed the outlines of trees
Rising from golden sands.

So, the sea-battered
Followed the seabirds' lead
Only for the long-winged shearers
To vanish in the horizon haze,
Their mercy mission over.
Once again, the Vikings
Were alone on a foreign sea
But solitude never lasts long.
As they circled the oasis
The seductive songs of women,
Soothing after so long,
Snaked across the sea
Like a temptress's scent
At spring's festival of renewal.
Fierce spearmen who had fought
Furies beyond fearsome
Were entranced, seduced,
Softened, disarmed, charmed,
Led by the loin into the lion's den.
In a bay of unsurpassable beauty
They saw the chorus on the sand
And careers of roving and violence
Evaporated like mist in summer sun.
Swimming in the bath-warm sea,
Or padding silkily on the wide sand,
Or plaiting a friend's long tresses,
Were nature's angels,
Not just two or three,
But three-score, raven-locks flowing,
Smiling, welcoming, warming,
Sun-brown, bow-lipped,

Ripe for soft kissing,
Ripe for plucking,
And nude, all nude,
All wholly unashamed,
All at ease, so alluring,
Irresistible, utterly irresistible.
And there the sirens smiled
And left light dainty footprints
In a sand so white it dazzled
Like virgin snow in spring sun,
So fine it hovered, floating,
Like a bride's veil in the breeze,
And so soft it caressed toes
Like first sheared lambswool.
Asgeir longed to swim to them.
Mary, his muse, was by his side,
But his spellbound blue eyes
Were wide open, dreaming,
His mouth and lips lust-dry
And the spell all-powerful.
No helmsman was working
The bewitched dragonships.
The wooden steeds were lust-struck.
Stormmaster and Waverider
Needed no further bidding
And began to edge ashore,
Snorting, wind-whinnying,
Drawn ever inwards, ever landwards,
By the mystical power of women.

Seafarers cast off
Salt-stiff leather,
Months of misery
Melting in dazzle-light.
Skarde Arneson dived over,
Into the sun-soaked sea,

Painting a white path
To the pouting sand sirens.
Only three crew escaped
The call of the magical choir.
The Half-man did not care,
Odd Oddson did not care.
Only Mary truly cared,
For her lust-led lover
And for her fragile life.

So as Vikings stripped
To swim with Skarde
Towards the soft kisses
Of shore vixens and sure sex,
Mary's appeal shattered the spell.
"Stop, stop, stop,"
She shouted, pointing,
"Archers, archers, there,
"Up there, up in the trees."
As soldiers sobered up
Hel's hangover began.
Skarde was on the sand now
Loin-led, lust so long unfed,
But a single singing arrow
Left his boiling lust to wilt
For a blood-filled ever more.
Asgeir at last came to,
A commander once more,
But much too late to save
Groin-guided Ingi Thorsson.
Deft with a dagger
But daft with the women,
He was stormed on the sand
By strong-armed tribesmen
Right out of range
Of boat-borne arrows.

As if waking from a nightmare
Stormmaster and Waverider
Watched as he was hauled
Around the headland,
His feet leaving ski trails
Through the soft sea-snow.
Two sets of twenty oars
Drove tormented dragonships on
Just in time to see Ingi
Be staked down in the sand
Beside two naked natives
As wild savages vied
To scorn the captives.
But death came quickly.
No days of life-lingering
As on the long-left prairies.
A short, sharp speech,
A long, sharp blade,
And a shivering native
Was salmon gutted
From neck to navel.
As he bucked and screamed
The gloating god-feeder
Grabbed through the gore,
Groped inside his chest,
Wrenched out a beating heart
And, with a wolf's snarling bite,
Swallowed the pulsing blood
Like a wassailer downing
Mead from a drinking horn.

Stranded Ingi Thorsson struggled
With the solid sand stakes
As the next groaning neighbour
Fed the flesh-fiend
Whose frenzied thirst

Was far from quenched.
By now axe-armed Vikings
Were racing to the rescue
Only to face native bowmen
Who promised pointed death
As Norse marksmen
Menaced the same.
In this stand-off on the sand
Asgeir and brave Vee Ma Gog
Advanced to the naked heart thief,
His teeth dripping hot blood,
To save Ingi's living heart.
Vee Ma Gog's hands revealed
A terrible choice for his chief:
Ingi could walk and fight again
Only if another white man
Fed the heart hunter.
The sea rovers were far too few
To fight, too few, truly too few,
So Asgeir wisely sacrificed
One for the many.
A warlord sends men
To die so their comrades
Can live to win again.
And so it was in the sun.
Odd Oddson was brought,
Hauled from the hold,
And paid the price
For his cowardice -
Crew-carried with contempt
To the cruelty of man-eaters.
As always now, he was silent,
As always now, his face was still,
No struggling or shouting,
As lithe Ingi was unshackled and
Scrambled, shaken, over the sand.

Cold-hearted warriors watched
As the warships' watchman
Was shoved sandwards,
Staked down with callous glee
And his gizzard was gutted.
But Odd's skin stayed white
And no pain-wail escaped
His motionless, pallid lips,
And nothing was torn
From his newly-opened chest -
No blood, no gore, no heart.
The heart-hungry butcher
Rummaged, rootled and raged,
But a human heart he could not find.
The sirens suddenly stopped singing,
Silencing their heavenly-hell serenade,
Bowmen melted into the jungle
And all the gore-hungry fled.

Chapter 40

Only Mary ran up to Odd
Only Mary cared whether
The dunny digger
Lived or died.
Dodging the blood-soaked sand
Beside the butchered natives
She wove her maid-magic.
Weeks earlier, when dragons
Had salved hellish wounds,
She had saved puddles of piss
In golden gourds dropped by
Wailing prairie women.
She poured a droplet on Odd's
Sliced, bloodless stomach.
A fizz, a hiss, and the skin sealed
Leaving only a black scar
From scrawny neck to navel
To complement the coward's
Blackened fire furnace feet.
"Scum you may be,"
She mouthed, unsmiling,
"But you are our scum."
Not one word of thanks
Did white-faced Odd utter,
Not even the briefest blink
Of weak acknowledgement.
Even a Halfwit knows
When he has no future.

Asgeir growled over the sand,
Death-maker drawn, ready
To undo Mary's medicine.
"Why," he roared, "waste
"Warrior-mending magic
"On such a craven coward?"
But Mary soothed him,
With words, this time.
"This," she said,
"Is killing with kindness.
"Leave him here
"And he will die alone,
"Forgotten for all time,
"One more lost warrior
"Swallowed by the sea.
"Heal him here
"And he'll go home,
"Yellow coward's scars
"On public display and
"His loathsome name shamed
"'Til Ragnarok's clouds enflame
"The fleeting fancies of men.
"Death offers honour;
"Life feeds dishonour
"Which is worse than death."

Asgeir frowned and faced
Odd Oddson before
A flicker of cruelty
Crossed his brooding brow.
"You are right, my Mary.
"Shame means living death.
"Let him return so Norway knows
"And Norway always sees
"The miserable shame of

"Bjerk the Brainless and
"Sour Odd the Heartless."

Is mercy a sin in a leader?
Was mercy Asgeir's weakness?
Or was his life-giving less mercy
And more a cruel life sentence?
Views among the Vikings
Were evenly split, letting the Halfwit
Chip slowly away at Asgeir's power.
But one shipmate was impressed.
For weeks the Half Man-Half Woman
Had spurned the silent sniveller.
But magic is mortal man's seducer.
And so, the Half Man and the Halfwit
Haunted the stern's putrid hold,
Turning their prison into a viper's nest.

Asgeir had more pressing problems
Than this hissing pit of poison.
His precious lightstone told him
His fleet was further south
Than any Norse he had known before.
Worse, they needed fresh food
And water to find the fjords again.
This island was flush with woods
And lush with life,
A larder for the lost.
But food never lies free.
If you seek something
So will others
And if you seek something
Your foes will seek it more.
So, when you want something
You will always face a fight.
And even the sun-kissed

Must expect to kill to live.
But Viking axemen were few
And frenzied man-eaters were many.
Fletched arrows dripping poison
Lurked in the gloomy jungle,
Bows braced by knowing natives
Hunting blundering strangers.
A warlord fights to win.
A warlord picks his battles.
A warlord weighs the odds
And dodges wipe-outs.
So Asgeir ordered his men
Back to their boat sanctuaries.
But Mary, praying sand-prone,
Rose and promised salvation.
"Salvage the native heads," she said,
"And I will find food for everyone."

Asgeir complied with her command
And an axe swiftly hacked off
The lifeless heads of the mutilated.
"Sail north," she said, "until I say,
"And then you'll all see why."

Another day dawned
Under another azure sky,
And on a sparkling empty sea
Mary gave the signal
For drifting dragonships
To drop swollen sails
And ready dried-out oars.
"Here," she said, "is where
"You will find food and water."
Stormmaster's old hands trusted her
But Waverider's captive crewmen
Heard merely a mad woman's ravings.

"Water, here?" shouted one.
"We'll all be as mad as you
"If we swallow this saltwater."
But Asgeir Dragontamer scowled
And all dissent was cowed
While Mary, head held high,
Shrugged off the grumblers.
"Hand me the heads,"
She said, and stared
At their unseeing eyes
And rough, frizzled locks.
She turned, grim face fixed,
To the two strongest sailors.
"Take one skull each
"And as soon as I howl,
"Hurl them hard
"Towards the sun.
"And you," she yelled
To the lazing oar-pullers,
"You will haul north
"As if harried by the hot breath
"Of Loki's Hel-hounds."

As hard hands grabbed
Weather-beaten ship wings,
Her buckskin-clad knees
Kissed the seasoned deck
And she sank into
A blank-eyed trance.
Her back bucked,
Her body pulsed,
And a wolf's howl
Flew from sea to sky
Cutting the calm air,
And Thorald Thick-Knee
And Finnvid Five-Chins

Grasped the gore-natives'
Matted hair and span the heads
Round and round before
Flinging them like slingshots
Far out into the flat calm.
"And now," commanded Mary,
Mind-recovered, eyes reborn,
"Bind the sails and pull those oars
"Like your lives depend on it."
Any hesitation, any hostility
To being bossed by a woman
Melted as lightning forked
And wind whipped the millpond
And the roar of a million lions
Outpaced the foaming mares' tails.
Stormmaster and Waverider raced,
Sails fed by the storm fury,
Oars fuelled by devil dread,
Until the spirit-maid whispered
Words of calm, words of control.
"Pull about," she said, "wait and watch."

Sails lowered, oars rested,
Dragonships slowed and panting crews
Watched awe-struck while the distant sea
Boiled and foamed and fumed,
Before the deep flung skywards
Two mountains North Cape tall,
Coned like Saracens' helmets,
Covered in verdant forest
And flanked by flatlands
Of lush humid jungle,
Bannered by a pall
Of wispy white smoke
Whose sulphur smells
Wafted over the water.

As swiftly as the island
Was born, peace returned
Until only a slight swell
Rocked the dragonships
Like a baby in its cradle.

"Here," said Mary, "is your haven.
"Here you'll find food and water,
"And birds beyond beauty.
"Go there now, sail on."
She glared at the grumblers,
"And never doubt me again."

Valhalla may be heaven
For wine-loving warriors
But it will have to be magical
To trump these twin peaks.
Powdery white sands,
Honey-sweet fresh water,
Net-friendly fattened fish,
Even fish flying on wing fins,
Nesting turtles, meat for months,
Ripe, juicy, plump fruit,
And no natives, not one,
No poison arrows, not one,
No man-eaters, not one,
Just food, water and safety.
As the sea-strivers stocked up,
Birds as big as buzzards,
But dazzling where they're dull,
Flew alongside, showing the fruit
That was safe to eat, flaying
Skins with huge yellow bills
Or hooked blood-red beaks.
One bird adopted Vee Ma Gog,
Another made for Harbar the Hairy,

Rainbows on beating wings.
Vikings marvelled at the beauty before them:
Wide-winged, magpie-long tails,
Our drab black and white
Banished by lustrous plumage,
Painted by the life-loving gods,
Scarlet and green, yellow and blue,
Purple and indigo, chestnut and violet,
And soon their crow-like squawks
Were swapped for snatches of Norse.
Curses, of course, the cruder the better,
Caught their child-like fancy.
But not all the locals were friendly.
Other flying jewels soon spotted
The worthless, the useless, the shameless,
And took turns to shit on Odd,
A white hail haunting him
And the Half man, his soulmate,
Showing that even in heaven
Some men can always find Hel.

On the beach were riches
For storm-battered boats:
Bleached wind-dried bones
As tall as pine trees but
Stronger and much lighter.
The Stormrider commanded
That the fleet's worm-eaten masts
Be removed and replaced
By the ancient dragon bones
To breathe new life into
These long-lost beasts
And his sea-bruised boats.
Paradise provides all.
Paradise reaches beyond
Its own secret perfection.

Chapter 41

Tempting though it was
The time came to quit
This port of plenty,
This land of colour,
For the bleaker, colder
Northlands of Norway,
To swap blue and gold days
For black and white nights,
Warmth for winter's
Frozen white-outs.
Warriors woo pleasure
Wherever they wander,
But a warrior without war
Is worse than a weakling.
And no warrior was keener
Than the fleet's father
To fly back to fjord frost.

Overnight itching wanderlust
And growing, festering war lust
Worried away at their hearts.
Men happy to swim and sup
Became restless like swallows
The moment amber and brown
First stain summer's leaves.

No voyage was ever easier:
Veer north and let the westerlies

Waft the wanderer's home.
Food-rich, water-wealthy,
The well-fed crews rowed out.
A last longing glance
At sea's sparkling paradise,
And the Blood-Eagle
And the sun-faded Ice Bear
Swelled with wind power,
And long-leisured Vikings
Were reborn and revived
By the sea's cooling breeze.

And so, they set sail
Trophy-full,
Booty-brave,
Dragonships decorated
With skulls and scalp-sticks,
Painted shields and eagle-guilded hatchets,
Crew clad in buckskins,
Harbar the Hairy
Prince of the prow,
Resting by his master,
Unsmiling Vee Ma Gog,
His mind forest flown,
The last of his tribe,
Stained glass on wings,
Feather-light on his shoulder,
Just as Harbar's jewel
Sun-basked on his.

The journey north was
As wind-woven easy
As the wild cruise south
Was a wind-wrecked ordeal.
So, the oar-muscled downed tools
And amused themselves

As seamen will always do
When wind-freed and battle-safe.
Warriors let their arms laze
And exercised their minds.
Ketil Killfast was muddle king
So he launched the first riddle.
As dragonships devoured
Mares' tails and dismissed
The rolling swell's might,
He chanted his challenge:
"I hover everywhere,"
He said, viper-eyed,
"Whenever Vikings raid.
"But my big brother
"Is much, much rarer
"Whenever Vikings raid.
"I float unseen in the air,
"Wafting over, ghostly,
"Sour and sickly sweet,
"Sweat-soaked,
"Shieldwall-shaking,
"White-eyes wide,
"Spittle-flecked,
"Tongue-drying,
"Leg trembling,
"Bowel-loosening,
"Making a man's bass
"Higher than a woman's screams.
"You can smell me,
"You can see me,
"You can hear me,
"You can taste me.
"But my big brother
"Is nowhere to be smelled,
"Nowhere to be seen,
"Nowhere to be heard,

"Nowhere to be tasted,
"But desired by all
"Praised by all
"Prized by all.
"I bring name shame.
"My big brother
"Brings only honour.
"But sometimes
"We two are one.
"And the real battle
"Is who will win."

"Being bladdered and
"Staying sober",
Bellowed one bruiser,
To be knocked back
By Ketil's slow headshake.
"Having the runs and
"An iron stomach,"
Breathed another
Only to spray-splinter
Like a winter wave
On Ketil's word rock.
The Halfwit fidgeted
For he knew the answer
But knew to stay silent.
He ranked no more
A crew member
Than the crawling crabs
Abandoned on the beach.
To blurt out
The riddle-solver
Would merely garland
His gutless shame,
Highlight his dishonour.
So the scumbag scowled,

Dead-eyed and sullen
As other dolts fumbled
To unmask Ketil's mystery.
Mary knew the answer too,
But mastered her tongue,
A woman in a man's
Guileful word games.
It was left to
Broddi the Bloody
To lance the word boil.
"It is fear and valour,"
He called, cheerily,
"Cowardice and courage."
And so Ketil yielded the deck
And Broddi posed his puzzle.

"I come from nowhere
"And return to nowhere
"But while I live
"I can care or kill.
"Light will I bring,
"Winter warmth too,
"A cooking cauldron,
"Kisses me even as
"My fierce embrace
"Fans life into heather-ling.
"But from me there is
"No favour, no class, no loyalty.
"I find friend or foe
"However well hidden.
"Boats large or small,
"I sea-maul with ease,
"King's great halls, too,
"And slaves' mean hovels.
"Green I turn black
"Blue, I turn black,

"Beauty I turn black.
"From my barbed tongue
Man has no escape."

Replies rang out
Proclaiming plague
Or a woman's fickle love,
Weathered kindling wood or
The sea-road's weather moods,
Until Mary, wise eyes rolling,
Broke the deadlock
And rolled male eyes
All around. "It's surely obvious,"
She fumed, "it's fire."
Vikings smiled half smiles,
Without warmth or humour,
Wary of the witch-wise,
But worthy Broddi handed her
The ship riddler's ring.

Stunned crewmen
Watched the mystic maid
Don the skald's mantle
As she launched her challenge:
"Women live in my thrall
"Men die in my clutches.
"Mirrors, a glassy lake,
"Sagas and heroes' legends,
"All fuel my force.
"Wars are declared
"And men die in pain
"To feed my greed.
"Yet I am false, fake.
"I only live, fleetingly,
"In men's fevered minds.
"I am nothing more than

"Their burning creation and
"Eternal, blinding curse."

First to guess was
A whine on the wind,
A warrior who was
A world leader in his answer.
"Tis greed," grimaced
Grim the Greedy,
The guardian of the dragon's arse,
His malice as active as ever.
Mary shook her red mane
And looked across the crew
As Grim's groans rolled over.
"Booze," gave Asgeir,
But Mary's eyes gave him
No triumph this time.
"Gold," growled another,
"No, silver," ventured Vee Ma Gog.
But valiant Hrolf Hardheart
Vanquished the word-veil.
"Vanity," he imparted and,
With a maidenly curtsey,
Mary reclaimed her oar bench,
And let the warrior spin his web.

"First to land," he said,
"Last to leave,
"Finely worked,
"Wood born,
"Teeth bared,
"Fire and fear,
"Beast and beauty,
"The dead given life,
"The living given death,
"Carved delicacy."

"Easy," growled one gold seeker,
"Tis Asgeir, tis the skipper."
But Hrolf Hardheart's eyes
Roved over the sea-rovers.
"A sword," said an oarsman,
"A flaming torch," chimed
Rudder-ruling Kollbein Sigvidson
But no man cracked the code.
And then the crudest crewman,
Gizor Flokison, king of cursing,
Flaunted the answer in his florid style:
"It's the fighting fucking dragonhead,
"You fucking cunts, you woolly wankers,
"I mean, its fucking bollocking obvious,
"You bunch of Thor's cocksuckers."

And so, he took the deck
And for the first time
In his oath-filled life
He spoke freely without a curse.
But as always, he showed
Just how to lower the tone.
It was his gift from the gods.
Some men are good at fighting,
Some men are good at wordplay.
But this man was good for the gutter.
But as he prepares to plumb
The lower skald-depths,
Let us look to the stern
Where, nestled in the rear, were
The Halfwit and the Halfman,
Hiding from their bird-blight,
The flying jewels that
Treated them as toilets
Every time they wanted
To release their white rain.

Bile also still flowed
To gold-hungry grumblers
From Grim the Greedy,
Still gabbling and brooding above
The dragon's great arse,
Still grieving for revenge.
Also sat with the outcasts now
Was a discontented Waverider
Who felt his battle-valour was due
Better rings than Asgeir gave him.
Ozur Skuldson was his name,
A Swede who had strayed
Into the wild western wars
After several spear summers'
Raiding along the East Road.
Warlords, he said, had to win,
So Asgeir was worthy.
But warlords also had to reward
And here Asgeir had failed him miserably.
Hacksilver could not feed his loot-lust
And so it fuelled his jealousy.
For sure, Grim the Greedy was
A worse leader, always running,
Always hoarding, always flogging,
But never, ever giving.
But there are gifts and gifts.
And the value of a gift is ever
In the hopeful eyes of the beholder.
So, learn from this: For the vengeful
Vengeance justifies all.
So Ozur and Grim became allies,
Along with the Halfwit and Halfman,
All driven by a seething, writhing,
Rising bile of resentment.
"Bide your time, my boys,"
Leered Grim, "Bide your time."

In the hall, Sven supped
And smiled slyly at Wersil
Whose eyes were granite-still.
Most of the winter warriors were
Transfixed by wine and beer, fable and food,
And the warming prospect of a skald-dance
Devised by the hemp-spinner.
But five spearmen escaped the skald-spell
And they alone could read
The unreadable. A glance,
A glint, and these warriors, too,
Were merely biding their time.

Out at sea, as Grim and his misfits
Steamed and fumed in the stern
Gizor Flokison took centre stage,
Legs braced against the sea swell.
And, for the first and only time
Since his coarse, foul, voice broke,
He spoke without a single curse.
"Nobody can own me,
"But all may share me,
"A long lingering
"Reminder of meals past
"And mead-merry nights.
"No rank respecter, I,
"Kings and queens,
"Warriors and workers,
"Slaves and livestock,
"I'm common to all,
"A great, natural, leveller.
"No body owns me,
"But all may share me."
But riddle ended, he wobbled,
And could not control himself:
"And that's fucking it,"

He scowled to the laughter
Of his relieved crew-cousins.

All knew no answer lay
In lofty concepts for Gizor,
So they mined the midden
To win his word challenge.
A burp, a belch, a beer-brain
Were all brought forth before
A lone voice from the front
Floated back on the sea breeze.
"It's a fart, you fools," came the cry.
And all peered at the prow where
Aethelfrith's weather-beaten skull
Had suddenly woken to wordy life.
But this skull spoke Norse,
Where Aethelfrith had struggled.
And so Grim meddled again.
"You're not Aethelfrith," he growled.
"Who the hell are you?"
And so, the skulls squabbled,
Back to back, both fed
By their own blind anger.
The for'ard skull glared forward,
Condemned to scan the seas for ever,
And all learned of his lament:
"The monks treasured me
"As a marvellous relic of their Lord,
"The skull of a long-lost disciple,
"Odin only knows which one.
"But I am no more a holy man
"Than I am a whole man.
"Fifty winters have waxed and waned
"Since a sword severed my neck,
"In a long-forgotten fight
"In a long-forgotten blood feud,

"Not even my bloody blood feud,
"But my blood fell, for sure.
"I slipped away swordless.
"And now every day is December.
"No Valkyries for me, No Valhalla,
"Warriors only in Odin's beer halls.
"I was sold to the monks in fraud
"By a trader who frosted fools
"To forge a holy fortune.
"One fact was fair,
"I once was a carpenter,
"A monk-loved craft,
"But from icy, cloudy Reykjavik,
"As far from their hot Holy Land
"As a monk's miracle saint can get.
"In death my skull was cosseted
"And revered by the cross-wearers
"As in cruel life I was buffeted
"And whipped by stress and war.
"And now I am once more back to
"Being buffeted by the fates.
"My life and death have formed
"A full miserable circle."

Chapter 42

As night fell, sails were lowered,
And Kollbein Sigvidson released
The rudder and trailed his net,
Hoping the full moon would lure
A fresh haul of the sea's silver bounty
Splashing to the surface and his belly.
The ever-vigilant gods were smiling and
As Vikings snored, the cod came.
At the rising of the sun his net served
As a steel anchor stopping Stormmaster
From speeding back to the friendly fjords.
The dragonships were far from alone on the saltway.
Circling like sharks were the black fins
Of a school of whales, snorting and spraying,
Sporting necklaces of white barnacles,
Each keen on a share of Kollbein's catch.
"Haul what we need," said Asgeir,
"And release the rest. What we don't take,
"The whales can swallow." And so
A silver snow bounced and flapped
Upon the oaken deck, a quivering,
Gulping promise of a feast.
A flick of a rope and the rest
Broke free, bubbling and boiling
The blue into a food frenzy of white.
But they flew from the dragonship
And slipped into the jaws of the giants.
The leviathans closed in and one,

Larger than the rest, flipped over, upended,
And slapped the fish into submission
With his double-headed piebald tail.
As the Blood-Eagle and the Ice Bear
Embraced the breeze, Vikings watched
The sea monsters move in for the kill
Amid eerie wails, clicks and whistles.
Mary massaged her magic bone,
Breathed deeply, eyes closed,
And said: "I can hear them talking,
"Telling their brothers across the seas
"How the surging dragonships shared
"Their silver harvest on the high seas."
Asgeir shoulder-shrugged,
His mind focussed on fresh fish
And finding the fastest way home.
But Mary, ever the wise-woman,
Watched with eyes that see worlds beyond.

Chapter 43

As days passed the nights lengthened,
The sky's life-giver paled to yellow,
The sea road steadily darkened
From blue to green to grey
And a familiar fishy tang
Flavoured the wind-salt.
The vaunted Viking sea ploughs
Were dwarfed by tall black cliffs
And green fields rising well-watered
From the restless, bountiful deep.
Seabirds from home gave their welcome.
Gannets and puffins, guillemots and shags,
Black-backed gulls and stiff-winged fulmars,
Located the ships better than a lightstone.
Gulls' black heads and red bills had given way
To delicate black ears and drab beaks
While the puffins' multi-coloured masks
Had tumbled, leaving greyer, smaller bills.
Knots of little waders twisted,
Piping their calls over salt marshes
While summer's swallows sped south,
Forked tails like streamers in the wind.
Spirits rose: run this Saxon gauntlet and soon
The fjords would hail the raiders' return.
"Two weeks to Norway," shouted a spearman,
"Two weeks to Kristen and the bairns."
But Asgeir the bushy bearded
Cut all the crews' cheering short.

"Three weeks," he said, "three weeks left.
"We have scores to settle, raids to run.
"Don't lower your shields, not yet."
And in the stern, the malevolent
Sniffed more than the salt air
As smiles and laughter turned to
Scowls and rising resentment.

But nothing binds the rift-torn better
Than a death threat from outside.
Seething crewmen, driven to distraction
By dagger-ready, quest-crazy shipmates
Will smother weeks of squabbling at sea
And rapidly rejoin their band of brothers
The minute enemy spears glisten nearby.
And so, as the westerlies blew them
Between the Angles and the piratical Franks,
Fear reforged this fighting band – for now.

Four Saxon ships, each bigger and faster
Than the dragonbone-masted dragonships,
Glided relentlessly over a glaucous sea,
Sail stripes of red and white, green and yellow
Swollen into bows every bit as powerful
As those of the death-rainers braced aboard.
So near to home, but too far to run,
So the seafarers had to fight or die,
With a spluttering death in the deep panting
It's cold, clinging breath on their necks.
But Asgeir was determined not to die
With Norway's wind newly in his face.
A shout, a shaking of hand signals,
And Waverider pulled beside her sibling.
Long wet ropes were cast and caught,
Leather and hemp were lashed
To masts, prows and sterns

So two dragonships
Turned into one:
One fighting platform,
One fighting force,
One war weapon,
And nakedly dared the
Saxon marauders
To make murder.

But any Valkyries hovering over
The looming sea slaughter
Would have been licking their lips
At the prospect of welcoming Norsemen,
Not Saxons, to their eternal embrace.
With superb seamanship
The striped sails surrounded
The Ice Bear and Blood-Eagle
And began to rain death
Of finely feathered ash
Into the raiders' sea shelter.
But rune-written shields
And Black Hair bison shields
Combined with rusting chainmail
And Norse-steel helmets
To keep the Valkyries waiting.
Asgeir wanted to force the fyrd to board,
To fight a land battle on the salt lake,
But the Saxons held back, safe at sea,
Starving their swords and spears,
Trying instead to sate their arrows,
And Asgeir knew helmets could hold off
Slaughter for only so long
Before chainmailed bodies
Plunged into the black depths
And Stormmaster and Waverider
Became the Saxons' newest prizes.

Hope there was none,
Help there was none
But Hel was alive
In the chill gloating of
Fletch-rich Saxon archers.

Asgeir moved to Mary
Herself wisely helmeted,
But her wide, white eyes
Meant her witch magic
Was impotent today.
Floating over the battle,
Above the singing arrows,
Over the crashing waves,
Outshouting the creaking ships
Came a gleeful, malicious taunt:
"You're all going to die,
"You're all going to die,
"He's taking you to your doom,"
Was Grim's delighted dirge,
"And little Asgeir's to blame.
"You were much better with Grim."
All Asgeir could possibly do
Was command and cajole
And crave, plead, for a miracle.
When flaming feather-flighted arrows
Fizzed and steamed over mare's tails,
Mary scanned the wind-waves
And then she smiled deliverance.
Closer came the spouts
Spraying here, spraying there,
Encircling the encirclers.
Rising up from the unseen deep
Of their secret salt empire,
First one, two, three, then four,
Five and, finally, six

Surged skywards, sea-dripping,
Six huge black whales,
Leaping and landing
Like axe-felled ancient logs
On the Saxon sailors' fragile ships,
Shattering shields, wood and bone,
Shredding proudly striped sails
Into a pauper's flapping rags.
Seconds earlier Saxon swords
Had scented an easy victory.
Now they grovelled and pleaded.
Hands that seconds earlier
Would have killed carelessly
Now struggled, stretched out, entreating mercy,
Seeking pity from their unpitying victims.
Such are the twists of battle.
Men are always joyful
When they alone are killing
But howl like babies for mercy
When blades break open
Valhalla's heavy doors for them.
How swiftly can the hunter
Become the white-eyed hunted.
Lucky were the ones without chainmail.
The richer Saxons sank like stones
Leaving paupers gulping on the surface.
But mercy was not in Stormmaster's power.
One whale, more brutal than the rest,
Rose up and pounded the flounderers
With his vast two-finned tail and
Where he led the other whales followed
Until Saxon oarsmen, swordsmen and spearmen,
The armoured and bare chested
Had sunk, broken, below the waves,
To feed the fish that would nourish their killers.
Carnage completed, the forest of fins

Was swallowed by the sea
As swallows skimmed the surface,
Chased south by cackling thrushes
Fleeing Norway's fir forests.
As reborn Norsemen savoured survival
A sour groan rose from the dragon's arse:
"Shit, shit, shit, shit, shit, shit, shit."

Chapter 44

Stunned were the sea strong
At fresh proof of Asgeir's greatness.
Stunned too was Asgeir
At the rage of the whale warriors.
But as flotsam slid past
He slashed the ties that bound the boats
And set ragged sail for the east.
Behind him, he could hear
Ketil Killfast quiz Hrolf Hardheart.
"Was that the ninth ordeal
"Or do others, possibly worse, lie in wait?"
"Perhaps," said his battle soulmate
"We'll know ninety bloody ordeals.
"Maybe they'll never end.
"Maybe that's Odin's idea of an ordeal."

Through the sea the Saxons
Call the Channel they sailed
To a point where white cliffs
Glistened on either side
To form a seafarer's funnel.
And then, two spots on the surf,
Stormmaster and Waverider
Headed north, raising hopes,
Lifting hearth-seeking hearts.
At Asgeir's command they kept
Just out of sight of land
And out of sight of sentries

But near enough to see
The sea's light land-darken
Over the Vikings' killing shore.
And then, on a weak east wind,
Asgeir ordered a westward turn.
Most obeyed willingly but some,
All from Grim's old Waverider crew,
Growled their resentment.
Above the dragon's arse
Grim dripped his poison.
"Now is your chance,"
He hissed to the Halfwit,
Who nodded to Ozur Skuldson.
"They want to set sail homewards,
"Not risk death on his private raid.
"Lead them and become their warlord.
"Lead them and grab my loot."
Ozur knew all the discontented,
And mutiny took just a moment.
Swords scraped from scabbards,
A battle cry rose above the deck.
Dragontamer was at their mercy.
"We're going home,
"You glory-hunting git.
"You can come with us
"Or we'll dump you in the deep,
"And we'll see if your whales
"Will help you anew," roared
The Geat ship-grabber.

Asgeir, his sword still sleeping,
Stared Ozur straight in the eye.
"We're going where I say.
"Then, and only then, we go home."
Then he bellowed so all could hear:
"One more raid, two more days

"And then we will be Norway-bound."
But as Grim happily shouted "Mutiny"
And the Halfwit, the Halfman
And the blood-sated war-weary
Hailed their new hero
Ozur snarled a cruel laugh.
He too bellowed: "I am your warlord.
"You will go where I say – and I say
"We swing North for Norway.
"And you Dragontamer, Stormrider
"Whale warrior, whatever you're called,
"You die now and no Valhalla for you."
The turncoat raised his sword and
Swung it at swordless Asgeir's head.
Asgeir danced sideways and
Drew his belt dagger, certainly
A poor defence against a sword
And scarcely better than nothing.
But before the Swede could strike
Death flew silently across the sea.
An arrow lanced Ozur through the cheeks,
Then another through his chest.
Braced against the sea-rollers
Was Ozur's old commander,
Ring-rich, battle-hardened Kjartan,
Bow in hand, disgust on his brow.
As Ozur slumped in his pulsing blood,
And leathery hands seized the rebels,
Kjartan's resolve reunited the crews.
"You heard Asgeir," he shouted, doggedly.
"Westwards we go. Where Asgeir goes
"We all go. Would you trade
"A proven warlord, a lucky leader,
"For a trio of Halfwits, puppets all,
"Their greasy strings pulled by Grim?"

So, the dragonships snorted westwards
And at dusk slid into a great broad river,
Mouth buckskin brown with bank-mud, and,
Better still, clear of men. The back door
Was wide open and the Vikings stole in.
Moonless was the night,
Sightless were the Saxons
And silently the oars
Muffle-steered the ships to
The skipper's private prey.
As skulking marsh fowl shrieked
The longships tied up
Alongside a willow copse
And here Broddi and Hrolf
Commanded the rearguard
While Kjartan and Ketil
And six other sword-skilled
Melted, spectral, into the night.
None asked their destination
None sought their foe's name.
There was no earthly need.
Asgeir led and they followed.

Dawn rose bleak and chill,
Breath-fogging, finger numbing,
A marsh mist slow to clear.
A heron cronked, a wader whistled,
Ducks squabbled in a ditch
And the Vikings waited and watched.
The world-rovers lay in wet grass
As Asgeir told them their mission.
"No gold this day, lads," he said,
"No killing either. I want one man,
"One man only, and he must live.
"He is nothing worth looking at
"But he is worth much more than gold,

"And soon you will all see why.
"He is tall, with long grey hair,
"And a scar across his long face,
"A sword gift from the Norse
"For he is a worthy foe.
"We wait and watch and
"When I rise you will know
"What to do. But live he must."

Slowly the wan sun
Chased the mist away
And revealed small fields
Whose fruit-rich hedgerows
Held a red and black harvest,
A lure to hungry villagers
Now looting with nimble fingers,
Fingers that spin fleece
Now seeking a safety net
Against winter's dark dearth.
Walking with them, paces apart,
Were their men, their defenders,
Who did not deign
To stain their fighters' fingers.
A gentle nudge from Asgeir
Announced the unsuspecting,
The sword-scarred greyhair,
As tall as great Vee Ma Gog
And almost as brawny as Harbar.
Slowly, he wandered ahead,
Perhaps for pleasure,
Perhaps to protect,
But he was a poor patroller,
Not looking, lost in thought,
Muttering to himself,
Zigging and zagging,
Leisurely going over the fields,

Now fumbling towards the trap,
Then weaving and turning away,
Then back towards his waiting foes
Then unwittingly walking off,
Once more, dreamlike,
Chaotic, meandering, mindless.
"Are you certain it's him?"
Whispered Ketil, perplexed.
"He's like a lost sheep.
"Are you absolutely sure
"He glitters more than gold?"
Asgeir's eyes glowered
And all knew to leave
Any questions 'til later.
And then the lone greyhair
Slowly zigged their way
Never to zag again.
Out of sight, out of hearing
Of his hamlet's heroes,
He was in a heavenly reverie
When the Dragontamer rose
Battle sword in hand,
And before he could call
His thick neck was kissed
By Deathbringer's cold teeth.
And before he could flee
The other loot-claimers rose,
From their waterlogged lair,
Swords drawn; daggers ready.
The Saxon knew hope
Had flown far away.

Most men, ambushed by Vikings,
Would be bald-eyed and gasping,
Holding hands up and life-pleading,
But not this hard-faced greyhair.

He looked at Asgeir man to man
And said in his slow, calm Saxon:
"You've come. I always knew you would."
Asgeir's loyalists, belly slicers ready,
Listened in complete bafflement.
"Like it or not, you are coming with us,"
Said their leader and lord.
"Your blade you can keep.
"You are our winter guest.
"Do as we say
"And next spring
"You can return and
"Keep kin and neighbours
"In awe with your sea-saga."
The scarred battle-oak nodded.
"One thing only I ask,"
He said, his voice even,
"Is to leave a sign
"So my family all know
"Death has not claimed me."
Asgeir agreed grimly.
"You are our honoured guest.
"Leave the life sign."
And so the strapping Saxon
Strode to the hedges
And harvested a handful
Of plump, ripe blackberries
And arranged them in a ring
Around his everyday knife,
Stabbed into the soft turf.
"I take you at your word.
"You could have killed me
"But you swear I am your guest.
"Know this, and know it well.
"If I am still your guest
"When spring's first swallows nest

"I will find a new dagger
"And you will all be death's guest."
A last glance over the green,
A curt nod, a cursory prayer,
And the Saxon stepped out
To a fearful, uncertain future
With his heavily armed hosts.

Chapter 45

Across the sea,
Beside a frozen fjord,
Alone against Sven's slaverers,
Snorri knew the time had come
To make his final skald stand.

But a word of warning,
Lest you were still unsure.
Wersil was a vile man,
Charmless, merciless,
In battle, ruthless,
But his warlord's strength
Was also his weakness.
He owed his fame
To his family name.
He was Wersil Svensson
And Sven's blood breeding
Brought him high standing.
True, he had made his name
On that ill-fated early raid where
His elder brother of yellow mien
Had showered shame on Sven,
His name never more to be breathed
Before his brooding former father.
But Wersil felt entitled
To deference and honours,
To women and wine,
To blind obedience

And to loot-wealth.
His father had fought
For all that he had -
Wealth, women, warriors,
Fame that fanned out
From Iceland to the Don
From Jerusalem to Jutland.
No father had helped him;
Every ordeal he had endured
Alone or leading his men.
Sven knew his sly surviving son
Craved to replace and crush him
And daily cursed time's slow pace.
But Sven also knew that
Time would soon test
This would-be warlord,
And then, Thor help them both.

Wersil, alone among the men,
As Snorri had clearly heard,
Had long lost respect
For his grizzled, fading father.
"Fuck the old fool,"
He'd told his shieldmen,
All young valiants like him,
Not Sven's Eastroad veterans.
But as Snorri's saga unfolded,
A flicker crossed Wersil's face.
Just a flicker, but a flicker
On the inscrutable is
Like a tremor on a mountain.

Snorri, meanwhile, supped some beer,
Wiped froth from his beard,
Put down the oaken tankard and
Smiled at the leering meadmen:

"And there we leave them,"
He said, "Sailing north
"Like Norsemen always do,
"After endless raiding,
"After endless ordeals,
"Glittering riches in the hold,
"Hostage in hand, sorry,
"Honoured guest in hand,
"Windborne who knows where?"
He smiled once more,
As the spellbound woke
From his word-witchery.
"Now my skalding is done,
"My tale is told.
"I have taken you travelling
"From fjord to forest,
"From bison grasslands
"To blood-licking cannibals,
"From an island of plenty
"To the Saxon wetlands.
"And I ask you once again:
"When is man not a man
"But still a man?
"When is a man a man
"But not a man?"

Wersil erupted, rising sharply,
And grabbed Snorri's neck breaker.
"This is no saga," he shouted,
It's a pile of steaming shite.
"He's no skald, he's a scumbag.
"He's crept in here seeking shelter,
"Promised us a sea saga and just
"Supped our ale and spun some lies.
"Flying dragons and fighting whales,
"A fantasy land of Black Hair savages

"And warriors riding whirlwinds, my arse.
"As for battling a fire-breathing dragon
"Far out on the high seas, it's all bollocks.
"You've all been out viking and sea sailing.
"Not one of you has ever seen a dragon.
"They don't exist, it's crook's dogcrap.
"And then there's these coloured birds
"With feathers that glitter like jewels
"And a white bear for a friend. Fuck off!
"There's not even a fucking punch-line,
"There's no ending, just no-hopers
"Sailing on endlessly.
"Let's end it now.
"String the little turd up.
"Let's see this twat dance,
"Let's see him entertain us at last."

As the rope tightened round his neck
Snorri remained unperturbed.
"Oh," he smiled, "but a punchline
"There most definitely is, my friends.
"Do you want to listen and learn it or
"Will you do as weak Wersil demands?"

Wersil tugged hard, trying to drag
Snorri out to the skeleton tree and shouted:
"Now, with me. Take Sven, now, now!"
The beer bewildered sobered swiftly
As ten raw wassailers rose
Weapons drawn, shields mounted,
Before Sven's loyal men could move.
Sven reached for his dagger
But a sword sliced off his hand.
"I am leader now," roared Wersil,
"And this skald fraud will dance
"And you will bow before your warlord."

But as Sven silently cradled his bleeding arm,
And his old shieldwall glowered hatred
At the war-whelps, the drumming began.
A hypnotic pulse, as powerful as a drug,
Filled the hall, louder, by the second.
Then spines chilled to an unworldly chanting,
Like ghosts wailing; one line high,
One-line low, next line high,
Like a Lapp shaman's winter spell.
To Norse ears it sounded as if
The haunted in Hel were singing:
"Hey who are you?
"Hey who are you?"
But all in the hall knew
This was no friendly inquiry.
Wersil's men could not move
For fear of letting Sven's men rise;
His veterans could not unleash blades
Before being cut down by the pretenders.
So Wersil's pups stood their ground,
Swords drawn against old shipmates
In a suicidal stalemate in the firelight.

And then the door burst open
Blowing in snow and blowing out the fug.
Snorri, neck chafing, purred pleasure.
"Bollocks, was it? A load of dogcrap?
"A large pile of steaming shite?
"Well, meet Vee Ma Gog.
"He may deign to differ."

Borne on an icy wind, he came,
Brown head newly shaved,
Save for a long, black, plaited
Top knot, a scalp tempter.
His face was warpainted,

Striped red and black,
From crown to nape,
Eyes lost in the soot tint.
On his shoulder squawked
A bird of dazzling brilliance,
Vivid even in the hall gloom.
Strung round his bull neck
Was Grim's greasy scalp;
Gripped firmly in his right fist
Was an Azarapo scalping sword,
And from his buckskin belt
Hung his hungry tomahawk,
Eagle feathers on the thong.

Sven's men could not move;
Wersil's mutineers could not move.
Vee Ma Gog strode safely to the centre
Of Sven's vast bone-strewn feast hall
And spoke in the Norse he knew,
Learned slowly on the long voyage,
In a dreamlike voice unknown
To strangers to his homeland.
"I am Vee Ma Gog.
"Hear my name, all you.
"I am Bear that Kills.
"I am last of Azarapo.
"Fight me and you are fucked.
"Your scalp will hang here
"With Grim's to feed my fame.
"I come from bear forests.
"I come from far away.
"I come over big lake in big canoe.
"I was saved from Sushone fires
"And now I fight as Viking.
"Azarapo gone. Vikings live.
"Vee Ma Gog live.

"Vee Ma Gog kills.
"Vee Ma Gog:
"Bear that kills.
"Hear my name."
He threw his head back
And howled his war cry,
A wolf's howl to wake the dead
And freeze the lifeblood of the living.

Wersil was in shock. His test had come.
"Kill him," he shouted, "Kill him, you dogs."
Scowls greeted his command.
Warriors might battle like dogs,
Warriors might live like dogs,
But warriors are wolves not curs
To a true ring-giving warlord.
But one sapling stepped forward
To challenge the giant stranger.
"I am Saxi, son of Hrothgar,"
He growled, his battle speech
Well and long rehearsed, "I fear no…"
And the fighter got no further,
Gutted by an Azarapo dagger.
Vee Ma Gog had learned Norse
But never did quite learn
The niceties of Norse warfare.
And as Saxi, son of Hrothgar,
Writhed in a spreading red wreath,
Vee Ma Gog sliced off his scalp
Like a spring sheep's fleece,
Held it dripping above his head,
Licked the warm, metallic, red wine,
And howled his latest triumph,
So loud Radnald could hear.
"Come closer war babies,"
Leered brutal Vee Ma Gog.

"I have room on my belt
"For all your soft scalps."

Amid the hall horror, Sven's life
Was slipping away and Wersil
Could feel power slipping his way.
But the door burst open once again,
And the dragonship's shame-cargo
Was shoved in by unseen hands.
"And here," heralded Snorri with pride,
"Are the Halfwit and the Halfman."
There stood the Halfwit, eyes white,
The coward's scars across his rat's face,
And the elegant Halfman, tall, thin,
Frail and otherworldly, more exotic
Than any Slav or Saracen prisoner
Ever sold into slavery by Sven.

But one of Sven's men,
A northerner, an iceman,
Focussed on the coward.
"I know him, yes, him, the Halfwit.
"That's not Odd Oddson.
"He's Sigi bloody Kunzson,
"From my village.
"Always whinging
"Always whining,
"Left my sister with a child.
"See his fuckwit family
"And you'd soon understand.
"These scum lived like pigs
"And made a mast-pole
"Look skald-clever."
The Halfwit looked away,
Resigned to a lifetime of taunts.
But Snorri never liked

To leave his audience
Floundering in the lurch.
"The other Halfwit," he beamed,
"Is being buggered by a bear."
And even as Sven bled
This revelation raised a laugh.
But Wersil was not smiling.
He pulled tight on Snorri's rope.
"Silence, you dogs," he yelped.
"This fable-maker must die."
Vee Ma Gog ignored him.
"Good Snorri speaks false," he said.
"The fat fool was found
"By a painted war party.
"Word travels with trade
"And reached the Sushone
"Just as we saved Seenaho.
"The hideous old Halfwit
"Has found fame
"From the flat plains
"To the fish-full sea.
"The scalp-cravers
"Took in the bear-bummed
"And named him as
"They had found him:
"Bald Fool who is Bearbait.
"But soon they knew his worth.
"Now they keep him and feed him
"And seek his view whenever
"They find a fork in the river.
"And if the oaf says right,
"They all pull to the left.
"And if he says left,
"They all pull to the right.
"One day the warriors
"Will tire of the tosser,

"As we tired of him, too,
"And then he will return
"To the bear's brutal embrace.
"Bearbait he is,
"Bearbait he will be."
He broke, paused, grinned,
And goaded the stunned.
"And now," he taunted,
"We will all learn
"Which of you are bearbait."

With a roar the door
Was flung wide open and
Fierce snow flurries
Cleansed the sweat-fug.
But no-one cared
About the brief Hel blast.
All eyes were firmly fixed
On what swiftly followed:
A brown-white bear,
Whose big ears brushed
The hall's broad beams,
Rolled into the longhouse,
A huge forest bear of cream fur
And frothing, dripping fangs,
And death-dagger claws,
And wide, wide awake
In deep, dark midwinter,
And driven to distraction
By sleep deprivation.
On his shoulder squawked
Another bird of dazzling brilliance,
Glowing in the hall gloom,
Only for it to spot the traitors,
Take wing and swoop
And shit on the Halfwit.

"So Wersil," said Snorri,
"Lord Bollocks-Finder,
"Steaming shite sniffer.
"What fantasy stands before you?"
Wersil began to babble
While veterans of blood raids
Cowered before the ghost bear.
Even Sven's wolfhound
Whined and whimpered,
Bony tail limp between its legs.
"Harbar the Hairy," said Snorri,
"Has a great hunger and
"Needs feeding fast or else
"You will all face his fury.
"So Wersil, who will you feed to Harbar?
"You choose. You're the chief."

Wersil's rope grip wavered.
He dithered and havered,
Brow sweat-dripping, eyes widening,
Before deciding and squeaking:
"Sven… or Saxi…Yes, them.
"They're both dead. Or as good as.
"Feed them to the fucking bear."
Snorri tutted like a disappointed mentor
As Sven's men, his wolfpack, growled.
"So you'd feed your own father,
"You'd feed your own warrior,
"A man who died defending you,
"To a ravening, bloodlusting bear,
"Just to save your worthless skin?
"What, Wersil, are slaves for?"
Snorted Snorri,
Who could clearly see
The strength sapping
From Wersil's young bloods.

Again, the door crashed open,
Again, winter's white reminder,
Again, the drumming and singing,
Blew menace into the firelight
And Wersil's lonely nightmare
Relentlessly led him ever further,
From Valhalla's welcoming feasts.
Lit by the waning glow
Of the hall's untended hearth
Was yet another troll fiend,
Another newly arrived giant.
This visitor from night's terrors
Had a huge horned head,
A head of lush, curling fur,
Half man, half beast, all demon.
His broad arms were ring-banded,
His face red, blue and white warpainted,
A golden torque garlanded his neck,
Black scalps hung from his belt,
His battered buckskin clothes
Were beaded with rampant bears.
And, gripped in his right hand,
A gut-greedy sword
Crowned his coming
Into Sven's sacred den.
He stood in the door
And Hel's inrushing chill
And the relentless drumming
Shared this warlord's words to
The hall's leaderless souls.

Chapter 46

"I am Asgeir," he snarled,
"Son of no man,
"Grandson of none.
"What you now see is what I am.
"All I have, I have earned.
"All I have, I have won
"By my wits, by my weapons,
"And by the war-grit of my men.
"I am not Asgeir, son of Hrothgar,
"I am Asgeir, Dragontamer,
"I am Asgeir, Stormrider,
"I am Asgeir, Mountain-Maker.
"I am Asgeir. Meet your new warlord."

As Harbar the Hairy
Harvested the hall's scraps,
But spurned Wersil's sacrifices,
Asgeir spat out his warlord's law:
"If you want another lord,
"Leave now and never return.
"But if you dispute my title,"
Now the bison stepped forward
Backed by warpainted warriors,
Scalpsticks speared and quivering
In the winter-sour straw floor,
"You will die
"At a speed
"Of your choice.

"I am a kind man.
"You can die quickly
"Or you can die slowly.
"I'll let you decide.
"But whichever, one of you devils
"Will undergo the agony
"Of the blood-eagle."

When Snorri had floated
This sordid torture,
The tankard throng had thrilled,
Cheered, chanted, loudly, with glee.
But no gloating now, no glee,
Just a stunned silence.
Blood-eagle is only wondrous
When you are watching.
It always loses its appeal
When it's your precious lungs
That may be taking wing.

The beastman strode
Past the hall's flickering heart
And up to the high table
Where Sven's violent life
Was trickling slowly away
As he struggled, glassy-eyed
On the beer-sodden straw.
His wolfhound's licks
Could never revive him
But he breathed still
And his lopped sword hand
Still twitched in the filth.
Asgeir's eyes were lost
Under the bison's helm
So none could see

If he savoured the scene
Or held his gaze with horror.

His voice was masterful:
"Mary, we need your magic.
"We need your magic now."
And at this soft command
Snorri slipped easily
From Wersil's loosened grasp.
The tight noose melted,
Mary's long red mane
Replaced Snorri's snow-white.
The skald had escaped
And the sorceress stood,
Smaller, in his place,
But buckskin clad,
Beaded wild beasts
Lining her leathers
Just like Snorri's.
But where worldly Snorri
Had woven bewitching spells
With well-chosen words,
The unworldly white bone
Kissing Mary's pretty neck
Provided all her power,
That, and the spirits' lore
Learned at her mother's knee.
Without even a glance at
Vapid-eyed Wersil
She trod lightly towards
The writhing, waning warlord
Before kneeling gently
By his bloodied head.
A rub of the bone
And Sven was corpse-still,
His bloodied stump relaxed,

Flopping, limp, floorwards.
A low moan swept the hall.
One of Sven's loyalists
A strapping, bearded brute,
Half-rose but before
He could draw sword,
A double-axe brandished by
One of Wersil's sweating mutineers
Made him see sense.
Mary was beyond oblivious,
Trance-borne
To her heaven
By her Irish chants
Before blinking,
And untying the
Small yellow gourd
Hanging heavily
From her beaded belt.
Eyes half-open, she poured
A droplet onto Sven's
Severed, festering stump.
An overpowering stench
Of stale, salty fish
Filled the hall,
Piercing the fear-fug,
Stinging nostrils and
Turning eyes to tears.
But friend and foe saw
The sword stump bubble,
Blister and blacken and
Sven slowly awaken
As his lost hand withered
In the bed of winter debris.
Seconds from death
Before Mary stepped up,
He now stood up himself,

Slowly but steadily,
Cursing and moaning,
Mourning his missing
Battle-mate, his death-meter,
His sword hand, his old friend,
That had slaughtered
Its last in this life.

Staggered by Wersil's treason,
Stunned by the sword's bite
And stupefied by Mary's magic,
He slumped into his warlord's seat
And sat, beaten, in silence,
As if he were watching a battle
From a mist-distant hill.
But the bison-man
Paid him no heed.
He grabbed the gourd,
Black Hair plains plunder,
And growled up to Wersil,
Holding the cure-all under his
Hawk-like hunter's nose.
Not one man moved
To defend the kin rebel.
The rival bands of killers
Were too finely balanced
For either to lower their guard.
So they watched, one eye
On the other, one eye on the drama.
"Breathe deep, traitor,"
Spat Asgeir, bison horns
Held high, shaggy fur
Hiding his bearded face
And heightening, fuelling,
His seething, faceless menace.
"Smell this, you slimy cur.

"This isn't dogcrap.
"This isn't a pile
"Of steaming shite.
"It's stale dragon's piss.
"It saved Hrolf's scars,
"Saved the snivelling Halfwit
"And has now saved your father.
"It even gave Grim's head
"The gift of afterlife.
"All that Snorri told you,
"Every painted word, is true,
"Apart from one little oversight,
"Just one tiny detail."

He cast back his
Curly bison cloak
And lifted the horn head
Like a battle trophy
To reveal his scarred face
Above two years of beard.
Wersil's eyes visibly whitened,
His knees buckled, floorwards,
As the beast-man's eyes
Narrowed into battle slits.
"Snorri lied," he shouted,
His declaration filling the hall.
"I am not Asgeir, Dragontamer,
"I am not Asgeir, Stormrider,
"I am not Asgeir, Mountain-Maker.
"I am Wulf Svensson,
"Wulf the scorned,
"Wulf the coward,
"Wulf the dead,
"Wulf the unmourned,
"Wulf the unmanned.
"But you will scorn me

"No more.
"Wulf the coward
"Does not exist,
"Wulf the coward
"Never existed.
"Wulf is not dead,
"Wulf the man lives
"And long, long before
"This bleak day disappears
"It will be a true coward
"Who will be rightly unmourned."

A glimmer raced across
Sven's vacant face
But Wersil, normally
So inscrutable, let rip.
"Seize him, seize him,
"Seize the raid-coward,
"I saw this snot-sniveller flee
"When I fought on, fearlessly,
"All alone against the Saxon fyrd.
"Why else did Sven sell
"This non-son to slavers?
"He is a worse coward
"Than the whining Halfwit.
"Look hard at my face scar,
"A bravery-borne battle scar.
"Look hard at his scar,
"The whip-slur of a slaver.
"Seize this shame-shifter,
"Kill the ship slave.
"He has no manly right
"To breathe the same air
"As Odin's chosen men.
"Silver, gold, for the man
"Who kills the hall haunter."

But no one moved against
The war-painted warlord
And catcalls filled the hall.
"Silver, gold," jeered a Svenhound.
"Silver, gold my arse.
"You've never even given copper rings."
Another roared in the fire flickers:
"If you're so brave, kill him yourself."
Wersil's eyes darted but
His dream was dying
On greed and valour lies.
And then a ball bumped
And bounced onto the floor reeds
And Grim's ugly flaking face
Rolled into the hall
And lashed the horned pretender
With his only weapon, words:
"Asgeir is no friend of mine.
"Wolves flensed my bones
"After his ungrateful rebellion.
"Now my view is a dragon's arse,
"On my old dragonship, mine, mind.
"But heed me well, war-horde,
"This Asgeir is no more
"A shieldwall shame-bringer
"Than gold lacks lustre."

Asgeir (or was it Wulf?)
Replied with a cold grin,
Like a wildcat playing
With a squeaking mouse.
"So, Wersil, you say you fought?"
Wulf asked, "while I, vile Wulf,
"Fled like a lemming?
"Is that really true, Wersil?
"Are you absolutely sure?

"Do you stand by that lie
"Or would you like, at last,
"To let us all know
"What really befell you?"

But Wersil was beyond reason,
Looking far beyond his brother,
Blurting "coward", and "traitor",
Saliva staining his stubble.
But his father's fame could not
Save him now, that same father
He had just vied to overthrow.
"Well, Wersil," said his brother
In loud, clear, tones,
"That was your last chance
"To undo your years of cheating.
"You have made your cheat's choice.
"So, may I help you remember?"

He clapped his hands
And once more an icy wind
Sobered the spellbound.
The soot-blackened door creaked
And in walked a sail-tall Saxon,
Hair long, lank and grey after
Forty summers of tilling and fighting,
Forehead wearing the white reminder
Of a maiming sword slash,
Forearms bearing many rings,
And his firm steps to the fire
Showing he was a fear defier.
One look was enough for Wersil.
He hurled himself at the intruder
Only to be body blocked
By a clashing steel wall
Sword-built by the warpainted.

Watching Wersil was like
Seeing a tall oak rock
And rapidly drop its leaves
In the first fall of autumn.
But this battle-oak would never
Be reborn when spring's sun
Warmed the thin northern soil.
"So, you recognise him,"
Said Asgeir. "Do you still
"Stand by your death-dealing lies?"
Wersil was grimly silent
But was as wounded as
The father he had wantonly
Tried to topple and kill.
Wersil's men did not relax.
It was too late for that.
All they could do was keep
Sven's men at battle-bay
And entreat Odin to open
His door to the near dead.

Chapter 47

The hall fire was spluttering
But no slave moved to feed it,
Its embers glowing drowsily
On the daggers and swords
Of the desperate and doomed.
Apart from the spitting crackles
And log crumbles of the fire,
The hall was silent as the Saxon
Led the watching warriors back
To a spring morning across
The war road to the West.

"I am Berhtulf, son of Luhtric,"
He began, head held high,
"Viking slayer, shieldwall fighter
"And spear-feeder for the Fenfolk."
Sven's men and Wersil's boys
Strained to feel through the fog
Of the Saxon's strong dialect,
But all growled at "Viking slayer",
And slowly they settled into
His leisurely burr and fenland lilt,
And gleaned enough from his phrases
For the forgotten past to flourish again.
For Vikings and Saxons are two tribes
Split by a common tongue -
Oh, and riven by rival religions.
But a warrior is a warrior

Whichever side of the sea
He wields his blood-sword,
Whether he worships
Christ's cross or Thor's hammer.
"My kin farm and fight," he said,
"In the East Angles' waterlands,
"And have repelled many raids
"By your loot-greedy dragonships.
"Ten long springs ago
"When my war-mane
"Was still all copper-red,
"And a dew-rich mist rose
"Over the night-chilled waters,
"Blazing beacons called out
"The fighters of the fyrd.
"We were all battle ready,
"Shieldwall strong,
"Sharp spears glittering,
"A brutal gore greeting
"Ready for your Ravenfeeders.
"You may remember me,
"But maybe I am just
"One foe among so many.
"I was the axe-flaunter,
"Death-defying out front
"Before the deafening clash
"Of swords and shields."
A rumble of recognition
Swelled in the hall.
"Your lithe young archers
"Chose respect,
"As is only right.
"Courage comes not cheap,
"Weapon-skill comes not cheap.
"Only death demands no price.
"But my display done

"I spotted bushes trembling,
"Outflankers on our left.
"The shieldwall swallowed me
"And with five loyal fighters
"I raced round to find the foe.
"And what did we find?
"The wolf-lord had sent
"Two of his rawest cubs
"To cut their milk teeth.
"The taller had long fair hair,
"And I heard his name called,
"Wulf, this Viking before you.
"The other cub's hair was black,
"His name I heard, too, many times,
"When Wulf risked all
"To try to rescue him."
A low murmur arose…
"Wersil was the lad's name,
"A name," and here he laughed,
"We will never forget.
"They fought sword first,
"Well, fierce Wulf led,
"And Wersil followed,
"A full five paces behind,
"Five festering steps of shame.
"I shouted back: 'The cubs,
"'Their bairns, have been sent,
"'To be battle blooded.
"'Don't disappoint them.'"
"It was I who took them on but,
"Five veterans against two boys
"Where is the war honour there?
"Wulf roared his war cry,
"He slashed and he stabbed,
"I parried and repelled,
"Steel bit steel,

"Steel bit shield,
"And I wear this battle badge" -
He felt his forehead,
"For ever, always, with honour.
"For a sapling he was oak-strong,
"And it was I who was blooded,
"Blooded by a boy fighting in the
"Deadliest of all battles
"For any warrior: his first.
"Head wounds spill life-wine
"Like few others can but
"I fought on, as did this Wulf.
"And Wersil? He held back,
"A boy in a man's battle,
"He thrust his sword just once,
"And I dashed it from his hand.
"Did he reach for his dagger?
"No, he ran, stumbled and scrambled,
"And screamed shrilly for help.
"'Wulf, brother, help me, help,'
"Was his piercing, girlish plea,
"So, Wulf, his brother, broke away,
"Retreating to the trembler,
"Ready to make his kin stand.
"But he received scant reward.
"As he scanned Wersil for wounds
"His brother repaid him cruelly,
"His thanks a knee in the bollocks.
"As Wulf bent double in sick-pain
"Wersil stole his dropped widow-maker,
"And fled, unmarked, unblooded, unbloodied,
"Leaving his saviour to be slaughtered.
"And in the hedge haven of a copse
"We saw the pup get his war scar,
"Self-delivered, a slash to the cheek
"With his own virginal, sheath-warm knife.

"The betrayed brother recovered,
"Battle-rage dispelling the pain,
"And he defied swords with fists.
"Death beckoned but in war
"Bravery wins its own reprieve.
"We overpowered him, spared him,
"Tied him up and only released him
"After your loot-seekers fell at the foot
"Of our Saxon wall of willow and steel.
"We could, should, have killed him.
"Death would have been a kindness,
"But he had won fame before us
"Just as his brother had bought shame.
"So, as you melted back to your boats,
"We let him go – but only after an embrace,
"A warm embrace, between battle brothers.
"Bravery merits respect – even in your enemy.
"Loyalty, too, true kin loyalty,
"Not hacksilver loyalty, is priceless.
"But cowardice," and here he spat,
"Is cursed wherever warriors fight.
"Wersil may not have the 'C' scar
"Carved on his skeletal cheeks
"But I can see it clearly etched
"Into his faker's forehead just
"Like that sulking fool, yes,
"Him, the whining Halfwit."

Sven, his men, Wersil's boys,
All turned to stare at the rebel,
To watch him gulp and flounder
Like a newly-landed haddock
Wriggling on a dragonship deck.
The Saxon continued: "Of course,
"Wersil will have been first back,
"No doubt flaunting his bravery,

"Trumpeting his war-won wound
"And telling how Wulf cast away
"His widow-maker like a coward,
"How his own sword shattered
"On tempered Saxon steel and
"By the time he retrieved Wulf's,
"The wretch had surrendered.
"And when Wulf returned, ragged,
"Unscarred, swordless, taken
"And then freed by the foe,
"The fear lie was writ in runestone.
"Well, I can tell you, Wulf is a warrior,
"A true fighter, fearless, Valhalla-worthy.
"And his men's arms show he is a leader,
"A hall ring-giver, a torque-king.
"I see no rings on Wersil's rabble.
"Does he promise but never pay?
"Treachery in battle breeds
"Deeper treachery in peace.
"Nothing in this brutal life
"Reveals the measure of a man
"Better than the test of battle."

Wersil stopped gulping. "He lies,"
He yelled, but his voice was girlish,
The pitch rising higher and higher.
"He's their prisoner. He'll prate
"Whatever they tell him
"Or his throat will be cut.
"He dances to their tune
"As the skald should to mine."

The greying shieldwall herald laughed,
And woke a well-used dagger,
From its long winter slumber.
"I am no prisoner,"

He grinned, gap-toothed.
"I am Asgeir's guest,
"Wulf's willing witness.
"He came for me, true,
"He took me, no dispute.
"But I always knew he would.
"What I saw that dawn
"Can never be unseen
"So I must testify for him.
"A man can have gold,
"A man can have silver
"A man can have slaves,
"But ruin his good name
"And a man is nothing.
"I knew he would be shamed,
"I knew Wersil would steal
"His hard-won honour.
"I could not in conscience
"Let this blood sin stand.
"Still you may doubt me,
"But I tell you, back home,
"Wulf and Wersil are bywords
"For bravery and treachery.
"On chill winter nights
"We sing of them still,
"And fame and infamy
"Float over the hall fire."
The fyrdman coughed,
Cleared his dry throat,
And sealed Wersil's fate
In acid-dripping verse.

"Let me tell you
"Of the day two
"Vikings raided

"Let me tell you
"Of one of them
"Fearless fighter

"Let me tell you
"Of the other
"Weeping woman

"Let me tell you
"The warrior
"Stabbed like Satan

"Let me tell you
"The wailer fought
"Like a girl

"Let me tell you
"One battled with
"Sword and shield

"Let me tell you
"The other wept and
"Mewled for mercy

"Let me tell you
"One saved the dog
"And defied death

"Let me tell you
"The other stole
"His sword and deserted

"Let me tell you
"One fought with fists
"Flesh against steel

"Let me tell you
"The other faked
"A red war wound

"Let me tell you
"One was a hero
"The other a wretch.

"Oh, when is a Viking
"Not a Viking?
"He's got the hair
"He's got the helmet
"He's got the sword
"He's got the beard,
"He's got the boat
"But what hasn't he got?
"He's got no balls.
"Oh yes,
"He's got no balls,
"He's not no balls
"He's got no balls.

"Oh, when is a Viking
"Not a Viking?
"When he's a Wersil,
"Wersil the weasel,
"Wersil the waistrel,
"Wersil the wailer."

The maligned one whined
And wailed once more:
"Kill him, kill him,
"Kill the miserable liar."
No-one moved,
   Not even Wersil.

But men can be cruel,
Warriors are merciless
When they smell blood.
And so, like sharks,
They circled Wersil
Without ever leaving their benches.
Their laughter lanced him
Like a spear to the loins,
But worse wounds were
To follow swiftly, surely.
Sven's men always loved
A good fireside song
And the Saxon's song was good.
So, they sang the chorus,
Savouring the battle slurs,
"He's got no balls,"
Sang some of the ale-fuelled,
"He fights like a girl,"
Gloated other killers,
Until it degenerated into
An orgy of jeering,
An orgy of laughing,
Humourless, heartless:
"Wersil the weasel,
"Wersil the waistrel,
"Wersil the wailer."

Wersil's face was frantic,
Wide, wet eyes darting,
Left and right, for redemption,
But when his own loyal men
Refrained: "He fights like a girl,"
His shoulders slumped
And Ketil Killfast
And Hrolf Hardheart
Seized their lord's scourge.

With each passing second
Sven's strength returned,
Well, a little crept back,
And the warlord slowly woke
To the tribal power struggle,
That pitched son against son
And son against fading father.

"Wulf," he said, as if
Feeling his way through fog,
"Wulf? Is it you? Can it be you?"
And the spurned son
Seized his chance
To punish his shameless father.
"Fuck off, you old fool," he growled,
"You sold me into slavery,
"When you well knew
"What Wersil was like,
"You knew his weakness,
"His slyness, his neediness,
"His long years of lying,
"His long years of relying
"On me for his sole protection,
"But you alone sanctioned my rejection,
"You alone sold me into shame,
"Into slavery, into death by flogging,
"You alone swallowed his lies whole
"Like a spawning salmon,
"Swallows a fisherman's fly,
"Autumn-blind to reason
"As it swims on and on
To watery destruction."

The one-handed warlord
Was stunned: obedience
Not defiance was his men's duty.

The last man to swear at Sven
Had left his skull on a spike.
"Don't you speak to me like that,"
He barked, but his bile fast faded
When he found Wulf's fist
Thrust firmly into his face.
"If I tell you to fuck off,"
Wulf roared, "You fuck off."
Like a flower past its bloom,
Sven's proud shoulders wilted,
Just as had vainglorious Wersil's.

Even when Sven was winning fame,
Invincible on the plunderers' war road,
Twenty-five slaughter-summers past,
Bloodletting and hacking his way to the top
He had always known
This dread day would come.
Every wise warlord knows,
Even in total victory, that
Survival ensures death,
That eluding enemy steel
And a glorious Valhalla wound,
Only yields the wilting of the years,
And inglorious, bruising humiliation
By a stronger, cockier, younger buck.
As stags' rut to overthrow
The tree-lord of the does,
As a wolf pack topples
Its greying, toothless leader,
So warriors will one day turn
Narrow-eyed on their warlords.
All that was left to stump-sore Sven,
Heart-sore, life-sore Sven, was to plead.

"Why, son," he whined, "why
"Didn't you just tell the truth?
"Why couldn't you speak out and
"Fight your corner with facts
"As you ever fought with fists?
"Words would have saved you,
"And me, from this slave curse.
"And why, why, did you save me
"For the ice-Hel of a living death?"
Asgeir, (or was its Wulf?) laughed,
But no smile, no joy,
Lit his blazing eyes,
No flicker of forgiveness.
"Why?" he growled, "why?
"You would never have believed me.
"Whatever I did you ever favoured
"This witch-wretch, Wersil the weak.
"You would have whipped me yourself
"For whining, for lying, for tale-telling,
"For unmanning Wersil's precious name.
"I needed hard proof so I bowed
"To your power-fuelled blindness,
"I submitted to slavery, bitterly,
"And vowed to get sweet revenge.
"I fought my way to freedom,
"Won sea-wide warrior fame,
"Emerged as a winning warlord,
"Leading two dragonships
"To new lands, new seas, new foes.
"And all the while my anger raged
"And gnawed at my soul like a rat.
"And now the proof is put before you,
"The Black Hairs, the bear, the scalps,
"The dragon's piss, the purple birds,
"The Saxon's freely given testimony.
"I needed proof. Now you have it.

"I let you live so you would know,
"And all would know, of your folly,
"And so you would know all knew.
"I let you live so you could die, daily,
"In an ice-cold Hel of your own creation,
"With the golden gates of Valhalla
"Slammed firmly shut in your arrogant face."
A Saracen spear could not have been deadlier.
Sven's lifeblood seemed to drain away,
His authority, his very name slain by his son.
His men, who minutes earlier, had been
His to command, his to cajole, his to kill,
Watched this wreck with barely concealed pity.
Men who had proudly shouted his name
When Snorri launched his winter's tale
Now shunned him, swiftly forgot him,
Another Viking floundering in time's sea.
Even Wersil's boys lowered their swords
As the tide swept them to Wulf's side.
So it always is with the powerful.
One minute feared, the next forgotten,
Their might at the mercy of the fickle fates,
Held or lost by a slip of the sword,
Raised or razed by one bad mistake.
Kings are only kings while they win;
Crowns were never meant for the weak.

"And now," roared Wulf, dragonship steel
Flashing the menace of his warlord claims,
War-painted warriors snarling support,
"You will get your wish.
"Outside in the snow glade
"We heard your glee at the blood-eagle,
"Heard the forest-floating chants.
"Well, now is your chance.
"So, who wants to fly, face down,

"Feeling sea's salt sting on his lungs?
"Who wants to spread his wings?"
He walked slowly among the killers,
Bison head and curled horns back on,
Eye-balling each sword-beard:
"Do you? Do you? How about you?"
And every one of Sven's bloodletters
Lowered his eyes, read the reeds,
And then one dropped onto his knees,
Crunching on the fetid feast remnants,
Then another, and another until
All pledged loyalty to the death
As their new leader's battle rams.
Better a spear in the guts in spring
Than a blade in the back today.

All but one. One alone held out.
True, Wersil blinked first at
Wulf's death stare, nose to nose,
Glancing away, face fire-red,
But kneel he would not
Even when Ketil Killfast
And Hrolf Hardheart tried
To shove his shoulders down.
But then Wersil knew already
The web woven for him by the Norns.

And so, the old oak door
Creaked wide open once more,
The icy blast a taste
Of this morning's lesson.
Steam rose from the bearded
As their boots crunched the snow,
Crisp and shin deep,
Captor and captive,
Wulf and Wersil,

Leading all the way
To a dazzling shoreline
Frozen like mirror glass.
Kjartan the loyal was waiting,
Stout mallet in hand,
Stakes already stone solid,
Hammered into tide-mud
Ice-set like granite.

When the throng was ready
Wersil looked slowly around,
Bidding farewell to the familiar shore
And then he shed his bearskin,
Lifted his woollen shirt and
Gave them to a slave attendant.
And so began his descent to Hel.
He knelt, lay face down in the frost,
His hands and legs tightly bound
By walrus thongs to wooden stakes,
And he paid the price of his treason
In a spray and pump of blood and steam.
First Kjartan cut open his back,
And broke each rib with an axe
Before the butcher spread
Wersil's blood-red lungs
Across his weeping, wilting back.
And all that was left was to wait
For the tide of floes and saltwater
To wash in, steadily, wave by wave,
Slowly, leisurely, but relentlessly,
Remorselessly, death riding on its ripples,
Promising to flay Wersil with its sting
And smother him in the winter snowlight.
In life Wersil had cheated and lied.
He had cloaked his cowardice well.
But in death he displayed his courage.

No sound, no cry, did he make, not one,
As his back gave birth to the blood-eagle.
No wailing, no whimpering, no whining,
No screaming, no moaning,
Even when ravens feasted
On his still pulsing flesh.
Too late, the boy became a man.
Vee Ma Gog spoke for many
When he declaimed: "The weasel
"Has died a worthy death."
And so, as winter's salt sea
Lapped Wersil's bloody mouth,
And licked his hawk nose,
Asgeir – or was it Wulf?
Gifted his brother his freedom.
He knelt beside Wersil and
Placed his sword in his hand,
And let virtue and valour open
The great golden gates of Valhalla.

Wulf grew to be a great warlord.
Mary became his witch-wife.
He had other women
As all warlords should,
But Mary was his muse,
His soul-mate, his magician.
Sons and daughters soon followed
And raid-wealth built a dynasty.
But the past lies always with us.
If you walk along the blood-shore
You will see, still, to this day, raised up
A runestone, its tribute writ in red,
Its message short, its message sharp:

Here died Wersil Svensson
Flying with the blood-eagle,

Dying in the sand.
In life weak,
In death brave.
He died sword in hand.
This stone was raised
By his brother
Wulf Asgeirson.